THE LANGUAGE OF *Secrets*

THE LANGUAGE OF Secrets

Dianne Dixon

DOUBLEDAY   *   New York London Toronto Sydney Auckland

DOUBLEDAY

Copyright © 2010 by Dianne Dixon

All rights reserved. Published in the United States by Doubleday, a division of Random House, Inc., New York, and in Canada by Random House of Canada Limited, Toronto.

DOUBLEDAY and the DD colophon are registered trademarks of Random House, Inc.

ISBN 978-0-385-53063-7

PRINTED IN THE UNITED STATES OF AMERICA

For Dan

. . . the beast residing at the center of the labyrinth is also an angel.

*

THOMAS MOORE

THE LANGUAGE OF *Secrets*

Justin

822 LIMA STREET, SUMMER 2005

*

As Justin was bringing the car to a stop in front of the house on Lima Street, Amy reached for his hand. He pulled away—making a quick, unnecessary adjustment to his shirt collar. He didn't want her to know he was trembling.

This complicated place in which he'd spent his childhood looked deceptively serene. Like an old-fashioned summer house where wood floors are polished to a warm glow by small bare feet, rooms are filled with cool breezes, and the jigsaw puzzles inevitably have missing pieces. Justin's memory was a lot like one of those puzzles. It, too, had missing pieces—blank spaces where important parts of his past should have been. It was bizarre. It was the truth. And he could no longer ignore it.

"Do you want me to come?" Amy asked. "Or to wait?"

He wanted both. He wanted neither. What he said was, "I want it to be tomorrow. Or an hour from now. I just want for this to be over."

Justin had ceased dealing with this house more than a decade ago, but in all the discarded years, he'd never forgotten its details:

the perfumed sugar smell of his mother's closet, the indentation on the wood frame of his bedroom window that resembled the smiling face of a clown, the fish shapes in the sea green tiles on the bathroom wall.

And he remembered his family: his mother, Caroline—her low, clear voice, and the songs she'd taught him to sing; his sisters, Lissa and Julie, and his feeling of terrified delight when they would push him higher and higher in the swings in the park across the street. And Justin remembered watching his father run, and he remembered how fast he could move—faster than any little boy could ever follow.

What Justin no longer recalled was why he had let so much time pass without ever returning to his home or contacting the people who lived there. In college and in the ten years following, when he'd been rising swiftly through the ranks of hotel management, he had always come up with the same superficial answer when asked about his family—nothing more substantial than that they lived in California and that he was fond of them but not close with them. This is what he'd told Amy in the course of their whirlwind courtship, and it was what had been told to her parents when they had been given the news of Justin and Amy's marriage.

It was a story Justin had repeated countless times. With each recitation, he knew he was deliberately choosing to let go of his past. But he didn't know why.

"Justin, this place is amazing." Amy's voice seemed to be floating toward him from a great distance. "It looks like some old-fashioned, really remote vacation home and yet here it is, less than twenty minutes away from Los Angeles."

At the sound of a small, fussy cough, Amy turned her attention away from the house. She leaned over and quickly reached into the backseat—for Zack. He was waking up from his nap, squirming and eager to be free of his car seat.

There was something in Amy's swift, fluid movement that made Justin think of the first time he'd ever seen her. In London. Crossing the lobby of the hotel in a peach-colored dress. Her legs had been bare, and lightly tanned. Justin had immediately wondered what it would be like to rest his face between those lightly tanned bare legs; how the heat of it might feel, how the color of it might be the same peachy hue as her dress, and how the taste of it might be the taste of honey.

Now, as this odd trembling fear was moving through him, Justin wanted nothing more than to rest his head in Amy's lap, simply for the warmth and comfort of it. But instead, he got out of the car. He walked away from his waiting wife and baby and went toward the strange place in which he had accomplished his growing up.

As he climbed the front steps, he caught sight of his own reflection in one of the wide windows that flanked the door. He glimpsed what appeared to be a shadow of himself, gazing out from inside the house, and he had the sensation that time was shifting into an undulant half speed, slowing and collapsing inward. His crossing of the wide wicker-furnished porch felt surreal.

He hesitated for a minute, thinking about the fast-moving kaleidoscope of events that had unexpectedly led him back to Lima Street: Amy coming to London to attend a wedding in the hotel he was managing; falling in love with her the moment he saw her and getting married in a rush; conceiving Zack on their wedding night; the job offer from a Santa Monica hotel that came on the day Zack turned six months old; and then a few weeks later, only eight days ago, landing at the Los Angeles airport and hearing Amy say: "Justin, the first thing you need to do, now that you're back in California, is get in touch with your parents and your sisters. It's important. For Zack. I want him to know his family."

If it had been left to Justin, it would have taken him much longer, perhaps a lifetime, to return to this place.

When he rested his hand on the bell beside the front door, he heard the lock click almost immediately and the door was swung open by an Asian teenager. The sight of this girl in her skimpy T-shirt, tight jeans and red baseball cap, seemingly so at ease in his parents' doorway, confused him. He cleared his throat to steady his voice before he spoke. "Mr. Fisher or his wife, are either one of them at home?" The blank way the girl was looking at him made him feel off balance, as if he needed to explain himself. "I'm their son," he said.

"Sorry, there's nobody named Fisher here." The girl shrugged and closed the door.

Justin had never conceived of his mother, or the rest of his family, not being in this house. The idea that they were gone left him stunned.

It was several minutes before he turned away from the closed door. He was almost at the sidewalk when the door opened again and the girl called out to him: "Wait! My mom says the people we bought the house from . . . their father, the old man who lived here, he was named Fisher. She says she has the address of the place he went. After he left here."

And with that, the destination for Justin's awkward homecoming was no longer the house on Lima Street.

*

The convalescent hospital was a squat cinder-block building, pungent with the smells of antiseptic and floor wax and decay, bustling with nurses in bright uniforms, repellent with the furtive, indecorous enterprise of courting death.

The moment Justin had walked through the front doors, his

skin had begun to crawl. He was relieved that he'd taken Amy and Zack home before coming here.

He'd been standing at the receptionist's window for several minutes. She was oblivious to him, prattling away on the phone. There was a large snow dome on the counter near her elbow. Justin picked it up and then deliberately let it drop. It landed with a shattering bang.

The receptionist looked up; the surprise in her eyes was immediately replaced by something self-conscious, flirtatious. It was a look Justin often noticed in the eyes of women when they first saw him. He'd been a teenager when he had initially become aware of it, but he hadn't paid much attention. He'd been moving too fast.

He had exploded out of high school. Within twenty-four hours of graduation, he had arrived in Boston, checked in at the university admissions office, signed the papers confirming his scholarship, rented half a room in a sweltering apartment alive with rats and reggae, and begun a part-time job as a bellboy in a boutique hotel.

Justin had dark hair and green eyes; he was six-foot-two, lean, wide-shouldered, with the body of a swimmer and the hint of a dimple when he smiled. Back in Boston, his looks had elicited the same response from the hotel's female guests as the one he was receiving now. The hospital receptionist was blushing as she was saying: "Can I help you?"

"Robert Fisher," Justin told her. "I'm his son. I want to see him."

The receptionist glanced away just long enough to scroll through the information on her computer screen. When she looked back, she was flustered. "You know what . . . I think you're gonna need to talk to the administrator. I'll page her. You can wait in her office." She pointed toward the end of a long corridor. The walls were blank, the color of snow, and running the length of them was a series of open doorways, their edges painted glossy black and bordered in yellow-gold. The passageway resembled an austere art gallery lined with massive gilt-edged picture frames.

Justin moved past the reception desk, into the corridor. On the other side of one of the open doorways was an old woman lying on a high, narrow bed. Stick-thin, blue-white. A comatose remnant ravaged by the passing of her own existence. The sight of her made Justin shudder.

He looked away. Through another of the doorways he glimpsed an old man. Large and powerfully built. An individual who might once have commanded troops or welded the steel of suspension bridges but who was now a relic perched on the edge of a hospital bed. Fast asleep. His legs splaying, his hospital gown opening. The last of his dignity slipping away.

Justin felt as if he were suffocating. The girl in the red baseball cap must have been mistaken. There was no way his father could be in this pile of human wreckage. Justin could remember seeing him with Julie and Lissa, watching him pick them up and swoop them into the air effortlessly. A man so vital and strong couldn't be in a place like this. This was a holding tank for death.

In a few rapid strides, Justin was at the end of the corridor and through the door of the administrator's office. It was small and untidy—and, to Justin's relief, unoccupied. He needed to be alone. He needed, literally, to catch his breath.

He was panicky. He suddenly knew he wasn't ready for this. There were too many missing pieces—too much incomplete information. He had no idea where his mother was, and he couldn't even muster a clear recollection of his father's face.

Within minutes the cramped, stuffy office was closing in on him like a cage.

He stood up and grabbed his keys from his pocket. But just as he was preparing to leave, the hospital administrator walked through the door. She was a featureless woman, dressed in shades of beige. "Sorry to have kept you waiting," she said. "I understand you're Mr. Fisher's son?"

This woman's sudden appearance had ended any hope of escape; Justin was trapped.

"We weren't aware that Mr. Fisher had a son." The administrator was looking down at her hands, studying them with an odd intensity. Then she said: "Your father passed away. Two weeks ago. He had a second, very severe stroke. Your family didn't inform you?"

The room seemed to shift and ride dangerously high to one side, like a boat hit by a rogue wave. There was a long silence. Then Justin heard his own voice and was startled by how calm and matter-of-fact it sounded. "I've been away," he said. "Up until last week, I was living in London. I haven't seen my family in a long time."

"How awful that you had to come home to this kind of news." The administrator was taking something from a shelf near her desk. She gave Justin a look of genuine sympathy as she said: "We've been holding a few of your father's things. I was about to put them in the mail."

She handed Justin a small box. Taped to the front of it was a carefully lettered shipping label.

*

The nursing home's doors closed behind him and Justin was once again in the parking lot. Two hospital workers, a man and a pretty

girl, were leisurely loading a gurney—with its bagged and zip-
pered occupant—into the back of a mortuary van. They were
smiling and chatting. With a quick move, the girl peeled off one of
her latex gloves and slingshotted it toward a nearby trash can; it
sailed in like weighted silk. She did a little victory dance: "You owe
me a Starbucks." She laughed, and her companion gave her a high
five. Less than an hour had passed since Justin had first arrived in
this parking lot. Time enough for a father to be lost and a cup of
coffee to be won; for a world to be shattered and for the world to
remain untouched.

Instead of going to his car, Justin sat on a bench and watched
the mortuary van drive away. Long after it had gone, he continued
to sit, holding the small, carefully labeled box in his lap. Several
cars came and went, then a delivery truck and a fat man on a
Harley. Two old women in an ancient lurching Cadillac. A gawky
kid with a skateboard and a gaggle of girls eating ice-cream cones
wandered along the sidewalk. A squirrel corkscrewed back and
forth on a power line, emitting frantic chattering screams. And
Justin simply sat.

He was letting it in, again and again: the fact that his father
was dead. He knew he should be inundated with memories, consumed with sorrow. But there was no flood of memory, no sadness.
There was only a sense of dread—a chilling knowledge that the
splintered door to some long-buried chamber was quietly being
forced open.

*

Sierra Madre and Lima Street were about ten miles north of the
address on the box he had been given at the hospital. He should
have been able to find his way easily, but he was driving through a
completely unfamiliar landscape. He was lost in a maze of curving
streets, lush lawns, and stately homes. Then, finally, he saw that he

was passing a city marker, a simple stone plinth topped by a concrete urn cascading with flowers and foliage. At the base of the plinth, in neat bronze letters, were the words SAN MARINO.

Like its marker, the city itself displayed both restraint and abandon. It was a Southern California town with roads named after martyred English saints and mansions reveling in an abundance of Tuscan tile.

The house Justin had been looking for was positioned atop a terraced lawn. A blond woman in a blue work shirt and mud-speckled jeans was at the side of the driveway, energetically digging a flower bed.

When he saw her, Justin's eyes filled with tears. Somewhere within this stranger he could see the little girl who had once been his sister. He lowered the car window and all he could manage to say was: "Did you used to be Lissa Fisher?"

The woman leaned on her shovel and watched as Justin got out of the car. "Do I know you?" Her smile was warm. She was pulling a strand of hair away from her face, leaving a faint tracing of dirt on her cheek. A precarious tilting sensation, a feeling of being in terrifying free fall, swept over Justin. He tried to speak, but no words would come.

He saw that his silence was making the woman uncomfortable. She tugged on the shovel a little, as if preparing to leave.

"I went to Lima Street," he said quickly. "I thought Mom and Dad would still be there, but . . ." Suddenly the words were tumbling out of him, almost incoherently. "At the nursing home they told me about Dad. They had some of his things. They were going to send them to you but I thought that if I brought them it might be a good way for us . . . for me . . . to reconnect and . . ."

The woman was already recoiling, holding the shovel in front of her, backing away. "Who are you?"

"Lissa, I'm your brother. I'm Justin."

Lissa's voice was angry, tinged with fear. "Whoever you are. Whatever your game is. I want you off my property. Now."

She turned and bolted toward the house. The slam of her door reverberated like the sound of a gunshot.

*

His sister's rejection had been so venomous and so complete that it had shaken Justin to his core; it had spun him back toward his old habit of walling off all thoughts about his past.

After returning from San Marino, he had tried to concentrate his attention on his new job. And on Amy and Zack.

But he'd been unable to ignore the nagging questions about his family that had been raised by his return to Lima Street. This morning, the continuing absence of answers to those questions had finally overwhelmed him. He had called the convalescent hospital to request the name of the cemetery in which his father was buried.

Now, Justin was walking through a maze of jumbled headstones—most of them cracked and crooked, none of them rising more than a foot or two above the uneven graveyard grass.

It was September. Santa Ana winds were feeding wildfires on the mountains. The air had the heat of furnaces and the smell of cinders in it.

As Justin approached his father's grave, he was feeling dazed and hollowed out.

It had nothing to do with the heat or the fire. It had everything to do with what was waiting for him at the grave site.

He was not walking toward just one headstone; he was walking toward three.

The newest was his father's: "Robert William Fisher . . . December 14, 1941–June 16, 2005."

The next grave marker read "Caroline Conwyn Fisher . . .

May 1, 1943–October 31, 2004." It belonged to his mother. A flash of pain shot through Justin; it was almost unbearable. A piece of his heart had been ripped away.

As he turned toward the third headstone, Justin's eyes were blurred with tears. The stone was smaller and far more weathered than the other two. It took him a moment before he could clearly see its inscription:

THOMAS JUSTIN FISHER
AUGUST 5, 1972–FEBRUARY 20, 1976
"TO LIVE IN THE HEARTS OF THOSE WE LOVE
IS NEVER TO DIE."

Justin had come in search of his father's grave. And he had found his mother's. And his own.

*

The discovery of a headstone bearing his name had been so ghoulish, so incomprehensible, that Justin hadn't known what to do or to feel. He had, of course, gone home and told Amy. But then, after that, he'd said he didn't want to talk about it anymore.

It was now November. Thanksgiving was only a few weeks away and Justin was at home. Determinedly calm. Sitting at the end of a lounge chair, bathed in sunshine.

Zack was on the patio floor at Justin's feet, captivated by the windblown petals of a white rose that had fallen from its bush. He was carefully picking up petal after petal, solemnly delivering each one into Justin's outstretched palm.

Zack's contemplative, unblinking gaze unsettled Justin. He wondered what it was that his son wanted of him. Was Zack expecting him to magically transform these scattered scraps into a dewy white rose, perfectly reassembled in all its intricacy? Or did Zack simply want to know that when he held out his own hand, his father's would be there waiting for him? Strong and open and ready?

Justin had no idea what Zack expected, or what he thought. Zack was foreign territory. He was a baby, and Justin didn't feel completely at ease in the wordless, unknowable world of babies. But Zack was also his son. The simple act of looking at him— seeing the sleepy brown eyes and honey-blond hair that were so like Amy's, watching the dimple appear in Zack's cheek when he laughed, the dimple that was so like his own—produced a rush of love and protectiveness more powerful than any emotion Justin had ever experienced.

Zack let the last of the rose petals drop from his hand. He rested himself against Justin's leg and yawned. Justin picked him up. He lay back, closed his eyes, and allowed Zack's warm, dense baby weight to settle against his chest; as he did, Justin knew that he would, without question, give his life for this little boy—and that he would, without hesitation, take the life of anyone who dared to harm him.

The tenderness of this moment was the only thing Justin wanted to think about, the only thing that he was allowing himself to think about.

*

"Did you find everything you were looking for?" The remark was addressed to Justin, but the clerk's gaze was fixed on something at the far end of the store. Justin tossed his American Express card onto the counter, letting it land beside two bottles of wine that were already there.

The nap he'd taken with Zack had used up most of the afternoon, and now he was running late. He glanced impatiently in the direction of the clerk's mesmerized stare.

A girl was standing at the magazine rack. Her face was hidden by a fall of auburn hair, but her crop-topped, miniskirted outfit left the rest of her on grand display. She was beautiful, and the sight of a beautiful woman always brought a rush of pleasure to Justin, an instinctive spark of joy similar to the feeling he got from seeing a mint-condition muscle car or a perfectly hit baseball. These were the places where, for Justin, art and grace could be found.

The second or two he spent looking at the girl were seconds in which he briefly forgot the fog that surrounded his life.

The clerk was ringing up the two bottles of wine: "Wow. DuMOL. That's a seriously outstanding chardonnay."

"My in-laws are coming to dinner," Justin said.

"You guys must really be into the good stuff." The clerk handed Justin a receipt and carefully slipped the two bottles into a bag.

"I'm into good, my father-in-law is into expensive. This gives us both what we like." Justin picked up his wine and headed for the door. The clerk went back to gazing at the girl with the auburn hair.

As Justin was leaving the store, he almost collided with a man and woman who were coming in.

The man did a double take. His face lit up with a grin. "Justin Fisher. My God, what are the chances of coming to the States for a holiday and running into you?" He spoke with a crisp British accent. "How are you enjoying being back in your homeland, m'boy?"

Justin had not a clue as to the man's identity, and it frustrated him. For as long as he could remember, he had been plagued by the inability to recognize people's faces. He was often in the awkward position of talking to someone, of having to feign a cheerful famil-iarity, while he was desperately trying to figure out who the person was. The blankness was so complete that Justin could spend hours with people in business meetings and then, when he met those same individuals on the street a few days later, they'd be complete strangers to him.

"Darling, this is the great Justin Fisher." The man smiled at his companion, then looked back at Justin. "This is my wife, Fiona. I'm not certain, did you two ever meet?" In the split second Justin took in deciding how to respond, the woman came to his rescue. "No," she said. "Actually we never did. But Trevor often speaks of you, Justin. He so enjoyed it when you lot would have your after-work get-togethers in Cadogan Square."

Justin laughed. Not with amusement, but with relief. He now knew who the man was. He had been the manager of the hotel across the street from Justin's in London. "Great to see you, Trevor. Next time I'm in the UK, we'll have to get together. Sorry I can't stay and talk, my wife and I have a dinner party tonight and I was supposed to be home helping in the kitchen ten minutes ago." He shook the man's hand, gave the woman a quick kiss on the cheek, and was already sprinting toward his car as he said: "Wonderful to have finally met you, Fiona."

When he was safely inside the car, it took him a few minutes to calm down. The encounter with the Brits had rattled him. In light of the strange events set in motion by his visit to the house on Lima Street, Justin's visual amnesia and the odd blank place it occupied in his mind suddenly felt diabolical—like brushing against the rot of insanity, or evil.

*

"So, Mom, are you raking in the cash?" Amy poured the last of the chardonnay into her mother's glass.

"By the carload, honey. By the carload." Linda's laugh was full and hearty, the product of a voice that had years ago been burred by whiskey and sanded with cigarettes. Justin was sitting across the candlelit table from Linda, thinking about how much she and Amy resembled each other. They had the same expressive brown eyes, the same effortless grace. Looking at Linda, Justin could see how lovely his wife would be in middle age. Amy glanced up and caught Justin studying her. She winked at him before turning her attention back to her mother.

"Judge Atwater," Linda was saying, "you remember him, Amy darling. Always used to come to parties and stay way too late. He had that toothy wife who was supposed to be related to the Kennedys."

Amy's father interrupted the story with a boisterous laugh. "Good thing the old guy's got a checkbook as big as his prostate. Your mother relieved him of a million two this afternoon. To underwrite some community center for ghetto kids."

"Daddy." Amy gave her father a quick frown. "Nobody says *ghetto* anymore."

Her father looked at her over the rim of his wineglass, baiting her a little. "So what am I supposed to call the poor bastards?"

"Underprivileged."

"Baby girl, get up in the morning and call the boil on your backside a beauty mark all you want, but come the end of the day, you're still stuck with the same festering bag of pus you started with."

"Oh Don, for goodness' sake." Linda threw her napkin at him. "Dial it down. We're trying to have a civilized conversation here."

Don lobbed the napkin back at his wife and turned to Amy. "Kiddo, you're never going to solve the problems of the poor, the hungry, and the pissed-off with a dictionary. The only way those kind of problems get solved is with brains, with a core group of the poor and the pissed-off who give a shit, and with cash. That's where your mother comes in." Amy's father sat back, smiling. "This girl of mine is the best thing that ever happened to charity in L.A." Amy's mother gave him a kiss that was as swift and sweet as one passing between a schoolgirl and her first love.

Justin finished the last of his wine and glanced at his watch. He had never been at ease with Amy's parents. They were a daunting combustible mix of big money, high visibility, and vaguely undignified beginnings. Linda had once been a Vegas showgirl. Don had traces of South Philly in his speech and the swaggering body language of a gangster.

Don liked to brag about how he'd gone backstage at the Tropicana and introduced himself to Linda by presenting her with a marriage proposal and the keys to a new Corvette; and Linda liked to tell the story of how she had accepted the keys, then told Don she had a date and that he'd have to wait for an answer to his proposal.

They both reveled in telling the tale of their initial seventy-two hours together. At the end of those seventy-two hours, Linda said she'd learned all she needed to know about Don. That he was a concert promoter. That his last name was Heitmann. That he was funny, generous, a little crass, and a guy who wanted to see the world and succeed in the music business. Don always concluded their story by saying that on the seventy-third hour they got married, drove out of Vegas together, took on the world, and then "goddamned conquered it."

It was Justin's suspicion that Linda, over the years, had carefully refashioned the woman she once was: She had observed refinement and style in the people and places she'd encountered, and then applied them to herself in polished, tissue-thin layers. Now, aside from her lusty sense of humor, there was very little evidence of the showgirl that she had been. Linda was a smooth, seamless, self-made pearl.

Justin moved his attention to Don. Don's transformation had not been as complete as Linda's. The international travel and the staggering amount of money he'd made had improved Don's table manners and given him a more refined wardrobe. But in spite of those surface enhancements, he had never lost the menace—or the feral instincts—of a street punk.

Don turned abruptly and fixed Justin with a quizzical look, as if he had somehow read Justin's thoughts. The intensity of the look made Justin fumble his hold on his wineglass. Don laughed and said: "You're a little jumpy, kid."

Then he got up and went to the alcove bar in the living room and cracked the seal on a bottle of expensive bourbon. His movements were aggressively proprietary: the deliberate opening of the scaled bottle, the careless tossing of ice cubes into a crystal tumbler, the overly generous pouring of the drink.

All of it annoyed Justin, and he sensed that Don knew it and took pleasure in it.

"Come outside, kid. Keep me company." Don strolled out onto the patio without waiting for Justin to reply. Amy gave Justin a little shove as she and Linda began to gather up the dinner plates. "Go visit with Daddy. Please, sweetie. For me?"

Justin shook his head. "Sorry. I'm not up to a one-on-one with your father tonight, Ames."

Amy's wineglass was still on the table. She slid it toward Justin and whispered, "Just five minutes, please." The glass was almost full. After Amy was gone, Justin drained it. Then he went outside and waited for his father-in-law's opening gambit.

Don was stretched out in one of the lounge chairs, sipping his drink. He was gazing at the night ocean, listening to the breaking waves. After a few minutes, he said: "So this weird crap with your family, it's quite a story. Amy tells me you found out both your parents are dead . . . that you went to see one of your sisters and she freaked out . . . and that when you were scoping out your parents' graves, you came across one for yourself. She also mentioned you've been moody and fucking hard to live with."

"I don't know what else I can tell you, Don. That's pretty much it." Justin's reply had a quiet "Don't fuck with me" quality to it.

"Yeah? Well, maybe that's it and maybe it isn't. Smells to me like you're trying to cover something up."

Justin moved across the patio and angrily planted himself in Don's line of sight. "You're way off base."

Don shifted his gaze so that he was again looking toward the sea. He continued as if Justin hadn't spoken. "If you are covering something up, I don't give a crap. I don't give a crap about your family, your past, or anything you did before you married my daughter." His eyes were expressionless. His voice was low. "All I'm saying is there's no need for fairy tales and bullshit. Whatever the truth is, fine, so be it. End of story. You got a good life going for yourself, kid. Don't fuck it up."

"Thanks for the input, Don." Justin started back toward the house. He knew that if he didn't get some distance between himself and this arrogant asshole, he was going to hit him—hard enough to split his face open.

Don sat up and turned toward Justin. "Listen to me, kid," he said. "I'm trying to help you out. What I'm saying is, you're back in L.A. It isn't London or anyplace like it. In this town, who you are is who you are at this moment. Nobody gives a fuck about what anybody did in their past. As long as you're good-looking, or you make movies, or you can throw a basketball, or you have a talk show, or even if you're nothing but an ugly prick who's just plain fucking rich, this town'll roll over for you faster than a fat whore taking a slide on ice."

Justin grabbed the empty bourbon glass from Don's hand and motioned toward the house. "It's cold. Let's go in."

Again, Don went on as if Justin hadn't spoken. "I bought you this place as a wedding present so that when you and my daughter moved back to California you'd be set up with the right address. You both got looks. You both got style. You both got me and my money behind you every step of the way. And in this town, pal, life doesn't get any better than that."

Before Justin could speak, Don waved him off. "I know. You have a good job and you're on it with everything you got. You're a good provider. All I'm saying is . . . as long as I'm around, you're working with a net. No shame in that. The only thing a man has to be ashamed of is not doing what it takes to keep his family safe and happy. Nothing comes before that, nothing. So whatever you're trying to hide with all the smoke and mirrors about sisters who don't know who you are and headstones that say you've been dead for thirty years, forget about it. Shut it down. It's history. And nobody in California gives a shit about history."

Justin knew it was true. He was in a place that didn't care about things that were dead and buried. But he sensed that what had been unearthed by his return to California wasn't dead, and that it wouldn't allow itself to stay buried.

Caroline

822 LIMA STREET, FALL 1971

*

The screen door banged open and Caroline came running out of the house. "That was a married people's kiss!" She was barefoot, dressed in a T-shirt and shorts.

Robert was halfway across the wide porch and heading toward the steps. He wore a three-piece suit and had a garment bag in one hand and his briefcase in the other. "What?" He stopped and turned to look at her.

"It was an eleven years in, romance at room temperature kind of thing. I've had mosquito bites take longer." She went to him, pressed her lips against his, then slowly pulled away. His mouth tasted like coffee and toothpaste. "I hate it that we kiss like married people." The October morning sun was warm on her body and a flutter of desire was making Caroline want to pull Robert back into the house.

"But we are married people. I like being married people." His kiss was quick, companionable. "The kitchen faucet's leaking," he said. "I'll take care of it when I get back."

The flutter of desire faded, and Caroline turned her attention to cleaning up the drifts of sand that Lissa and Julie had brought back from the park across the street. They had used it to make a beach for their Barbie dolls.

Robert was at the curb now, tossing his things into the trunk of the car. He waved to her. "I'll call you from Fresno. Love you!"

She returned a perfunctory wave. Irritation and disappointment were already filling the space desire had so unexpectedly opened and then abandoned. She moved the sole of her foot across the little beach her girls had made. Lissa and Julie were three and four, just a year apart, and when Caroline had been their age, she had loved playing in the sand. She'd gone to the beach every day. To a real ocean beach. A fabulous postcard coastline that glittered like a jewel, its air sharp with the smell of sea salt and warm tar and eucalyptus. The beach in Santa Barbara.

Santa Barbara was where Caroline had met Robert. She'd been just seventeen, excited about her first day at college, and she had run into the path of an oncoming bicycle, Robert and Barton's.

Robert, a blond fraternity boy in surfer trunks and flip-flops, was steering; Barton was perched on the handlebars. Both of them fell as Robert swerved to avoid hitting Caroline. When they got to their feet, Robert was smiling. Barton was serious and self-conscious; blushing to the roots of his coppery hair; seeming too tall as he scrambled to pick up the books Caroline had dropped. When he handed them to her, he gave a quick bow of his head— shy and reverential—the gentle gesture of a gentle soul.

It was Robert and Caroline who had become a couple. But it was Barton who had been the one to hold and console Caroline each time she and Robert swore they were breaking up. And it had been Barton to whom she had gone when she failed chemistry and when one of her roommates had died in a skiing accident and when, after weeks of waiting, Caroline's period had failed to arrive and she'd begun to be sick to her stomach every morning.

It was Barton that Caroline was thinking about now as she was sweeping the last of the sand from the front porch. A station wagon was passing the house; the female driver was dressed as a witch—a reminder that Halloween was tomorrow, and that Barton was leaving for New York on November 1. Caroline's impulse was to go inside and call him, to say one final good-bye. But just then, Lissa and Julie burst out of the house, bristling with indignation.

Julie was trying to wrestle a tiny Smurf doll away from Lissa. "Mommy," she was saying. "We were going to play Smurfs and I choosed Smurfette first! Tell Lissa I get to be Smurfette."

Lissa threw herself at Caroline's legs, clinging tight and insisting: "No. It's my turn!"

Caroline gathered her up and did a little waltz around the porch, tickling her cheeks with butterfly kisses. "I have a good idea . . . There are *dozens* of Smurfs. Why don't you both be a Smurfette?"

Julie shook her head and sighed, clearly exasperated by Caroline's ignorance. "Mommy, that won't work."

Lissa leaned close, her breath damp and warm on Caroline's cheek. "In the Smurfs there's only one girl." She whispered this, as if trying to shield Caroline from embarrassment. Then her chin began to quiver and her eyes filled with tears. "And that's no fair," she said.

Caroline breathed in her child's sweet scent—baby shampoo and crayons and vanilla. "No, honey. It isn't fair. It isn't fair at all."

As she said this, Caroline wondered how it was that young children, unconscious of the workings of politics or theology, had such clear awareness of the concept of fairness. It was a sensitivity so keen, it reduced them to tears when they discovered that absolute justice was unavailable. Caroline wondered if, in the mysterious place from which children had so recently come, there was a realm where the human spirit existed in a perfect balance between right and wrong. "What a sweet thing it must be," Caroline murmured into Lissa's ear, "that place of complete fairness."

Lissa laid her head on Caroline's shoulder and sighed softly, as if in benediction, or resignation.

Caroline remembered how strongly she had once felt about the issue of fairness. She had begun crying out for it when she'd been about the same age as Lissa and Julie were now. But when little Caroline would weep that something was "no fair," her mother would simply shrug and say: "You want fair? Go to Pomona."

And the idea of Pomona had become a talisman for Caroline. For years she had imagined it as an Eden, a place of perfect justice. But the summer she was eleven, she and her mother took a road trip and Caroline discovered the truth. Pomona was nothing more than the site of the Los Angeles County Fair. Her imagined paradise had turned out to be a low-slung, gritty place, more desert than garden, more blight than beauty. Caroline had looked up at her thin, dry, tightly wound mother and had hated her. Her mother had taken away the purity of Pomona and left in its place a brawling carnival soaked in spilled beer and the piss of prizewinning pigs.

"You know what, girls?" Caroline said. "Mommy can't fix it that there's only one Smurfette in the whole world. But Mommy can fix s'mores. Lots and lots of s'mores. Hundreds and millions and gazillions of s'mores!"

During the next hour, her children's delighted laughter was all Caroline heard. Then the phone rang.

For a moment, she wasn't certain that anyone was at the other end of the line; there was only the indistinct background noise of a restaurant, or perhaps a cocktail lounge. She was about to hang up, when she heard his voice.

"Ah. Sweet Caroline" was all he said. And she instantly knew who it was. She had never forgotten the sound of him: rolling velvet, edged with filaments of diamond dust. Seduction traveling with the promise of things both beautiful and cutting.

"Mitch." Simply saying his name created an electricity in Caroline, a sensation that felt like fireworks and brandy.

Caroline didn't notice that Julie was trying to boost Lissa high enough to reach an open jar of caramel sauce on the kitchen counter. Both girls tottered and fell. The jar broke. Caramel sauce splattered across the floor. The dog yelped. Lissa shrieked. And Julie shouted "You dummy-head!" at the top of her lungs. Caroline wedged the receiver between her shoulder and cheek and dropped to her knees, checking to see if either of the girls had been hurt.

"Sweet Caroline, have I called at a bad time?" Mitch sounded faintly amused. His tone embarrassed Caroline. She could picture him, immaculate and cool, phoning from a chic eatery or an elegant bar—some fastidious region where there were no sticky kitchen floors or little girls screaming "dummy-head."

"Mitch, I didn't turn out like the women I'm sure you hang around with now. I'm a mom with two kids and a dog. My life is noisy, okay? I don't spend my time quietly clawing my way up the ladder at some big law firm and then basking in silky silence while I get my nails done and my legs waxed."

"Hmmm. I remember a lot about those legs. But I don't remember much silence." He paused, waiting for Caroline to respond.

She wanted to erase how envious she'd just sounded of the

kind of sleek, accomplished women who were a part of his life. She wanted to come back at him with something light and witty. But she was too distracted—worried about the broken glass and the fact that the girls weren't wearing shoes.

Mitch chuckled. "Ah, but that was a long time ago. When we were all young and beautiful. You, of course, were especially beautiful in the buff. But I digress. The purpose of this call is to ask if you and my old buddy Rob might want to have dinner with me tomorrow night."

"What? You're not in Chicago? You're here?" Caroline took a towel out of the sink and wiped at the mess on the floor. Her face had flushed the moment she'd realized he was in town. All it had taken was the thought of seeing him.

"Yup, for two days. Doing a deposition in a major criminal case. Very high-profile. Big article in this month's *Newsweek*. I'm in L.A., at the Baldwin. You know, we should call Barton, too. Get the whole gang together. The last time the four of us were in the same place at the same time was at your wedding, Sweet C. We're overdue. So what do you say? Eight-thirty tomorrow night? Here at the hotel. My treat. Champagne, caviar, and lots of French crap with truffles on it."

"Tomorrow night? We can't. It's Halloween, the girls need to go trick-or-treating. And besides, Robert's not here. He's in Fresno. He went to an insurance seminar." Caroline immediately wanted to take the words back. They made her feel like the idiot wife of a small-town businessman, carelessly revealing the excruciating blandness of her life.

"Okay. Forget Rob. And Barton." Mitch's voice was low. There was the slightest hesitation before he spoke again. "It's you I want to see."

"I want to see you, too." Caroline was dropping bits of broken glass into the trash—tiny jagged shards slipping in among the remains of a blueberry muffin and a crumpled coloring-book likeness of a fairy princess. "I mean, I'd love to, but . . ."

"So if dinner's out, have lunch with me instead. Come on, Sweet C, who knows when we'll ever see each other again. Bring pictures of the kiddies. And I'll show you snapshots of my overvalued co-op and my dog. A lot of people think there's an uncanny resemblance."

"Between you and the co-op or you and the dog?" she said.

Caroline heard him explode into laughter and she felt effervescent—like someone she used to be.

*

It was late. The girls were finally asleep. There was perfect quiet in the house.

Caroline lifted her foot from the water and traced the tiny fish shapes embossed on the tiles of the bathroom wall. She'd lit candles on the shelf above the tub and had sipped half a glass of wine. She was relaxed and ready to go to sleep.

She lowered her foot and lay, for a moment, savoring the quiet. When she got out of the bathtub, her movements were slow and dreamy and she saw that in the candlelight she looked radiant. She raised her arms above her head and moved in graceful circles around the bathroom, watching her misty image in the mirror and flirting with the momentary belief that what she was seeing—this sensuous angel—was the truth. Breasts perfectly round and lifted, skin that was flawless, a belly that was tight and unmarked. For an instant, she imagined what might happen if Robert could see her like this, confident and shimmering; if he could see every inch of this exquisite nakedness.

She stumbled over a pair of rubber ducks on the floor, and

almost immediately she heard the phone ringing. Not wanting the noise to wake the girls, she opened the door and ran out of the bathroom.

The fog on the mirror was sucked away. The sensuous angel had vanished.

In the bedroom, Caroline lifted the receiver and heard Robert say: "Hi, honey. Sorry to call so late. Did I wake you up?" His voice sounded solicitous.

"No. I was taking a bath. Now I'm standing here nude and dripping." There was a silence, and for a second, Caroline hoped she had set off a spark. Then Robert said, "Everything okay with the girls? You guys all ready for Halloween tomorrow?"

"Yeah. We're all set." Caroline yanked the sheet off the bed and used it to dry herself. "How was the drive up?"

"Long. Uneventful."

"Well there are worse things than uneventful, I guess." She tossed the sheet aside and pulled on an old pair of sweatpants and a wrinkled T-shirt. Then she lay on the bed and stared at the ceiling. She felt heavy and dull.

"So. How was your day, honey? Good?"

"It was fine, Robert. Oh, guess who called?"

"Who?"

"Mitch. He's in L.A. for some kind of meeting. He wanted to take us to dinner tomorrow night. Barton, too."

"Too bad we won't be able to make it." There was a faint edge to Robert's voice. "He should have let us know he was coming."

"Yeah, I guess it was all pretty last-minute. He was disappointed about dinner but he ... uh ... he said maybe that we could ... that I could meet him for lunch instead." Caroline was up now, pacing.

"So you're going to have lunch with him?"

She glanced down at her colorless T-shirt and wrinkled sweat-pants. "I don't know. I don't know if I'm up to it."

"You sound tired. Get some sleep. And don't forget to lock up first, okay?" Robert's tone was gentle, but the comment made Caroline feel combative. "Robert, if there's one thing I'm good at, it's taking care of this house. And my children."

"I know. But I love it when I can take care of all of you. Maybe being away is making me feel disconnected. I love us. I love being a family."

Caroline didn't answer him; she laid the receiver on the bed and went across the hall. Into the bathroom.

She took off the T-shirt and the sweatpants. And then she looked at herself in the mirror. This time, there was no angel in misted candlelight. There was simply Caroline—alone—needing to feel beautiful.

When she returned to the bedroom and picked up the receiver, Robert was saying: "I love you, Caroline. I'll always love you. No matter what. You have to believe that."

She hung up the phone with such gentleness that there was no click as she lowered the receiver; there was only silence, as if there never had been a call at all.

Caroline went downstairs, then out into the backyard. She sat in the moonlight. For a few minutes, tears flowed. After they were gone, she stayed gazing at the night shadows, thinking about a cream-colored dress she had bought a long time ago and never worn, and about how perfect it might look on her now, in the lobby of an elegant hotel.

*

"Sorry you had to wait." The valet opened Caroline's car door and offered her his hand. "Welcome to the Baldwin. Are you check-ing in?"

"No. I'm meeting someone for lunch. Just lunch." Caroline knew she looked flustered, and that the valet was amused.

He grinned as he handed her a claim check. "Well, enjoy yourself."

As Caroline walked away, she saw the valet exchange a glance with the doorman who was standing near the hotel's etched-glass entrance. It was a look that said they'd noticed her and liked what they saw: a woman with good legs and green eyes and hair the color of dark chocolate; a woman in a revealing cream-colored dress and stylishly high heels. It made Caroline feel desirable, and alive.

The air in the hotel lobby was cold and smelled of rose-scented perfume. A string quartet was playing soft, elegant music. And everywhere there were well-dressed men, beautiful women, and extravagant arrangements of expensive flowers.

Being in this opulent setting was stirring excitement, and guilt, in Caroline. She desperately needed to believe that there was no harm in having come here; no harm in wanting Mitch to see her the way she looked today, and wanting him to think it was the way she looked every day. No harm at all—if it was only for the length of a lunch.

When Caroline was approaching the entrance to the hotel restaurant, a man across the lobby was putting his arm around a woman who had just arrived. He kissed the woman's cheek; she gestured toward the restaurant. He whispered something; she hesitated. He whispered again. This time, she smiled and let him lead her into an elevator.

Caroline watched as the elevator doors closed. She knew there was much more than lunch awaiting her here. She understood that it would take very little for her to be the next woman stepping into an elevator, waiting to be carried away.

She was almost running as she came out of the hotel, hoping to catch the valet before he moved her car. She wanted to go home and get away from what she had come so close to doing. But the valet and the car were gone and an airport bus was idling in the driveway. When the bus pulled away, Caroline saw the spires of the church across the street.

It was St. Justin's—Barton's church.

*

The doors of his office slid apart and Barton looked at Caroline with absolute, radiant joy. "Oh, what a lovely surprise!" He opened his arms and gathered her into them as if she were a cherished treasure. "I thought we'd said our final farewells on the phone last week."

"Me, too. But it turned out that I was in the neighborhood, so here I am." Caroline spoke without looking up at Barton. She didn't want to move away from him just yet. His embrace had always been something unique—strong, yet infinitely gentle. And Caroline loved the way he smelled: elegant citrus-scented aftershave and fine cigars. To her, being hugged by Barton was the physical manifestation of the word *delicious*.

He held her at arm's length and studied her. "Wow, you look fantastic."

Caroline saw the same was true of him, and she realized that it had been true for quite a while. Barton had grown into his height and his copper-colored hair had mellowed to reddish brown. His face and body had filled out and made him handsome. "You grew up and got so good-looking," Caroline said.

Barton ducked his head in the fleeting bow he always made when he was embarrassed. And seeing that gesture told Caroline that no matter how much Barton had changed physically, his spirit remained the same. He was as an adult what he'd been as a boy: empathetic and intelligent.

30

He took her hand and twirled her around as if they were dancing. "So," he said. "This incredibly attractive getup you're wearing, is it all just for me?" It was the happy question of a kid opening presents at Christmas—no hint of insinuation or innuendo. But Caroline was embarrassed—suddenly uncomfortable with being in a place filled with such innocence.

A watercolored light was coming through a stained-glass window. There was a modest wooden cross on the wall, and an open Bible on a low table beneath it. On Barton's desktop there was a snapshot of a fresh-faced woman wearing hiking clothes and standing in a snow-covered meadow.

Caroline was surrounded by simplicity and virtue; it was making her feel shoddy.

"No," she told Barton. "I didn't get dressed up for you. It was for something else entirely." She pulled free of his grasp and turned her attention to the photograph on the desk. "This is a wonderful picture of Lily. I wish she could've come out to California more. I think all of us would have been really good friends. You two should be planning to live here, you know, not in New York. You're breaking up the team, Barton. You're going to go away and get married and we'll never see you again. That's not fair."

"Was it fair when you and Robert got married and moved south, leaving the rest of us alone and bereft on the beaches of Santa Barbara?"

"Bereft for how long? A couple of months? Then we were back together. You were in seminary in Pasadena. You lived ten minutes away."

He smiled. "Well, be that as it may. For those few months the rest of us missed you fiercely." He started to take the photo Caroline was holding. She moved it out of his reach.

"What 'rest' of you? It wasn't exactly a cast of thousands." She glanced at the picture again, then put it back on the desk. "You, me, and Robert. That's all there ever was, just the three of us. And Mitch. And it was hardly the same thing. I got married because I had to and we moved because Robert had to. Our wedding was at city hall, on the way out of town, with everything we owned jammed into the back of a U-Haul. That's not exactly 'The Manhattan Nuptials of Ms. Lily Hamilton in the Cathedral of St. John the Divine,' is it?"

Barton took her hand and held it lightly. "I was at your wedding and I remember you wore a white eyelet dress and beach sandals. You carried a single sunflower and you were beautiful." He stopped and looked her over from head to toe. "Which returns us to the subject at hand. Your present sartorial splendor, and the reason for it."

"Is it all that important, really?" Caroline moved away. He was being Barton; being intuitive. He was making her uncomfortable.

"I think perhaps it is . . . Perhaps somewhere in that fabulous outfit there's something that's troubling you, and me. It could be I'm disappointed that you didn't get all dressed up just to come to say good-bye to me."

"The truth is, I wasn't even planning to see you today. I'm here completely by accident. I don't think I knew it when I got dressed this morning, but I probably had some very questionable activities in mind for this outfit." Caroline did a suggestive little shimmy, trying to pass the whole thing off as a joke. "It's Halloween, Barton, this is my Housewife Out for a Day of Slutting costume. Couldn't you tell?"

He sat on the edge of his desk, folded his arms, and calmly waited for her to say whatever it was she was wanting to tell him. His silence rankled her.

"Well don't you have anything to say? I just made a confession to you, Father. It's your last day in L.A. Aren't you going to give me some kind of penance to do on your way out the door? A few Hail Marys or something?"

"Wrong church. You've got us confused with the Catholics. The Episcopal way of dealing with human frailty isn't quite as cut-and-dry."

" 'Human frailty'? That's what they're calling sin these days? What a nice little euphemism." Caroline angrily pushed aside a stack of books and sat in the chair across from Barton's desk.

"I don't see life in black and white, Caro. You always have." Barton's expression was calm. "You've always been harder on yourself than God ever thought of being."

Caroline picked up a magazine and busied herself with it. She didn't want Barton to see how deep her anger went, how envious she was of his elegant wedding and of the things he had always so easily possessed. Things she imagined that he, and people like Lily, took for granted. All the priceless things that gave them dignity and made them whole. Things like parents who adored them for simply having been born. Things like bedtime stories and birthday parties—and addresses that didn't change with the erratic regularity of a broken traffic light.

These were things Caroline had never had. The lack of them had made her sick and rootless. And jealous.

She knew that people like Barton hadn't been churned through a gauntlet of nameless men circling through their mothers' beds in a sloppy parade, leaving nothing in their wake but bruises and broken promises.

People like Barton and Lily hadn't been sent out into the world grasping for sanctuary and perpetually choking on fury.

Caroline was pretending to be busy with a magazine because

she didn't want Barton to know how much her envy of him humiliated her.

"So. Have you indeed sinned?" Barton asked. "Or did you only get as far as the outfit?"

Caroline laughed in spite of herself. "I only got as far as the outfit."

"That's what I suspected." Barton put his arm around her and walked her over to the sofa. "Oh how I'm going to miss you, Caro."

"Barton, I can't believe I'm losing you. You're my best friend. How am I supposed to survive you being in New York?"

"Look on the bright side. Perhaps I'll be bounced into the street within moments of my arrival. Going from an associate rector to having my own church is a big step, but attempting to go from California Boy to Manhattanite is a leap of monumental proportions. It's right up there with attempting to change gender. Or species."

Barton and Caroline settled on the sofa and Caroline leaned against him. It was comfortable and easy, an old familiar pattern. For a moment, they were content not to speak. Then Caroline said: "I'm dressed up because I was going to meet Mitch."

"He's here?" Barton sounded startled.

"Across the street, at the Baldwin."

"Caro, you've been down this road before, and it's always been littered with land mines."

"I know." Her voice was profoundly weary. "I think I just wanted to have lunch and flirt . . . and maybe feel the kind of intensity that I used to have with Mitch . . . like I was the center of the world. Just for a couple of hours, I wanted to feel like everything hasn't changed."

"Some things haven't changed." Barton rested his arm lightly across the top of her shoulders. "You were the center of the world to Robert back then. And you still are. Perhaps he's fallen out of the habit of telling you, but I know he adores being married to you."

"Maybe he adores being married. But I don't think he adores me. Being with me, when we're alone." Caroline wanted to explain that it wasn't the routine daylight things that had failed to flourish between herself and Robert; it was the explosive visceral things of the nighttime.

Caroline shifted away from Barton. Her voice was quiet. "I don't think you can have sex the way Robert and I do and feel like the center of the world."

Several seconds passed before Barton said: "I have opened up a very private hurt, Caro. That wasn't what I intended." There was apology and concern in his voice. "Do you truly want to tell me about this? You don't have to, you know."

"But I've always told you everything. It would throw our balance off if you left not knowing all of it." She pulled at a loose thread in the sofa cushion. It was a long time before she finished her thought. "And besides," she said, "if I don't tell it to you, I may never tell it to anybody."

Caroline hesitated, searching for the right words. "When Robert and I have sex," she said, "it's like we just barely bump into each other and slide away. As if we never really make contact. He's always so cautious, like I might break, or explode." She waited, wanting Barton to have an answer to this unanswerable question: "How can Robert love me but never *want* me in a way that makes him hungry to be inside me?"

"Oh, my poor Caro." Barton gently interlaced his fingers with hers.

Caroline's sigh was full of sadness as she murmured: "I'm

starting to hate it when he touches me. It makes me feel so alone that I want to die." There was a brief silence; then she said, "You always know how to fix everything, Barton. But you can't fix this. Even if I could keep you in California forever, you could never tell me how to fix this, could you?"

Barton turned her so that she was looking into his eyes. "I can tell you that Robert loves you," he said. "And that your little girls love you. And that God loves you."

Caroline dropped her gaze and Barton rested his cheek against the top of her head. When he spoke again, his voice was a whisper. "And I love you. No matter how hard it is, you can't die, Caro. Because we all need you. Because I can't imagine life without you."

A tear had fallen onto Caroline's cheek. As she wiped it away, she realized that it was not her own.

*

The exquisite peace Caroline had found with Barton vanished in the few minutes it had taken to leave the church, cross the street, and see Mitch standing on the steps of the hotel.

The sight of him jolted her. Nothing about him had changed. His eyes were still the clear blue of an Alaskan lake. His hair, like her own, was the color of chocolate. His clothes were impeccable. His body was trim. And he was smiling. It was the smile of man who would forever be a mischief-making boy.

When Caroline walked toward him, she was shivering. "I had changed my mind. I wasn't going to meet you," she said. "I only came back here for my car."

"Uh-uh, you came for me. Because it's quarter to two and I've been standing here since twelve-thirty, willing you to show up." He pulled her into his arms and lifted her off the ground. "God, you feel good." He buried his head in her shoulder and whispered, "Want to get naked?"

"No."

He allowed her to slip out of his embrace. "Okay. Then let's have lunch. I'm starving."

"I can't. I need to get home," Caroline said. But as she said it, Mitch was already leading her toward the hotel. The etched-glass doorway was shimmering in the afternoon sun, like a column of diamonds.

*

By the time Caroline was back in her car, waiting to leave the hotel driveway, rush-hour traffic was braiding itself into gridlock.

Caroline knew that when she got home, she would have to face Mrs. Marston, the grandmotherly old lady who lived next door—she would be curious as to why her baby-sitting assignment had gone on for so long. The girls would be fretting about being late for trick-or-treating. And Mrs. Marston would see that Caroline had returned empty-handed, without a single box or bag to support the story that she had spent the day shopping.

She rested her head on the steering wheel, ashamed, thinking how Mrs. Marston would know the truth the minute she walked into the house. The old lady would see that in the space of an afternoon, Caroline had become a cliché: just another housewife leaving her children alone with a baby-sitter while she ferreted out a release from her own loneliness.

Caroline was suddenly frantic to get home, but she couldn't see a break in the oncoming traffic. She pounded the horn, and there was a shriek of raucous laughter; a group of people in Halloween costumes was moving past her car. A man in a vampire suit lunged toward her, leering from behind a hideous mask. Caroline screamed. Almost immediately, someone was knocking on her window.

It took her a moment to realize that it was the hotel valet, who was smiling at her and saying: "That guy was a jerk. Don't be scared. Everything's cool." He was showing her that a limousine was turning into the hotel driveway, interrupting the traffic and providing her with a means of escape.

Caroline had to go several blocks before she could find her way onto the freeway. When she made the turn, something inside her tightened. She sensed the overwhelming scope of what her single astonishing moment of impulse might have caused—and the staggering price it might ultimately require her to pay.

Justin

*

The sand under Justin's feet was warm. The air was cool and fresh. He was surrounded by sunlight as pale and yellow as hammered gold.

Justin plunged into the surf and began to swim. Slow and steady. Concentrating only on the feel of the water and the lull of the quiet.

It was a moment of peace and beauty.

But in an instant—no more than a heartbeat—the peace and the beauty vanished and Justin was being paced, stroke for stroke, by absolute misery—by the discovery of the death of his parents, by the gunshot slam of his sister's door, and by the image of his own name on a gravestone.

He tried to elude these things by thinking of Amy, by remembering each note of a mellow jazz trumpet playing "When I Fall in Love." It was the music that had surrounded them the first time he kissed her.

The shadows kept flitting closer.

Before he could escape them, their weight hit him with stunning force. The impact was terrifying, and it was seductive: a combination of profound fear and a strange calm.

In the calm, he slowly surrendered to the fear. He let the water close over his head. It was as if he were being pulled down by something sweet and gentle. It was promising that, on the other side, the riddles and terror and pain would disappear and he would find peace.

After a while, his heart slowed to the point where it seemed to quietly stop.

He saw palaces of spinning light and heard the songs of whales vibrating, like church bells, deep in his brain.

The world briefly detonated into silence.

Then suddenly the water was churning with movement and noise. Someone was shouting his name. An arm came around his chest and he was being dragged backward through the waves.

Moments later, two men were staggering onto the beach, carrying him between them, his body loose and without volition, like something already dead.

*

One of the men who had pulled Justin from the surf had been Ari Silver, a new neighbor, whose terrace faced the beach. Justin and Amy had met him briefly on the day they'd moved in. Their town house was next door to his.

At Ari's insistence, Justin underwent an exam at the local hospital and was released an hour later. The only prescription: a good night's sleep. The near drowning, the doctor said, had done no lasting harm.

The incident had happened earlier that afternoon. Amy was still worried, and afraid.

Her uneasiness was making her glance at Justin, and hesitate, as she put each of the objects onto the bed. He had asked her to do this for him, but now she was waiting to see if he wanted her to stop.

When he remained silent, she continued laying out one item after the other, until she had arranged them in a neat semicircle—the things that had belonged to his father, the entire contents of the box Justin had been given at the convalescent hospital. There was a small radio and some cheap earphones, a battered brown wallet, a hairbrush, an old Timex watch, and a plastic-framed photograph of a towering Christmas tree. A family was standing in front of it: a blond man, a dark-haired woman, and two girls who seemed to be about ten years old—all of them sporting red sweaters and uncertain smiles.

Justin was lying on his back, his hands folded and resting on his stomach. He was wearing a pair of pajama bottoms and his hair still had traces of sand in it. He turned his gaze in the direction of the open balcony door and looked out toward the ocean. "That's it?" he said. "That's everything?"

Amy held up the empty box. "That's everything." Then she said, "Are you sorry you asked me to open it?"

Justin shook his head from side to side, very slowly. Amy could see the depth of his pain. It made her feel as if her heart was breaking.

He picked up the plastic-framed photograph as Amy began to repack the box. "Maybe I did die all those years ago," he said. "And I went to hell. And that's why I wasn't available for the family Christmas portrait." He let the photograph drop back onto the bed.

"Justin, I don't understand all this weirdness, but there has to be a logical explanation. We just need to find it." Amy finished repacking the box. Then she leaned over and kissed his forehead. His skin was smooth and cool; it smelled of the sun and the sea. It made Amy wince.

It was the same scent he'd had on him when he'd been dragged unconscious from the ocean a few hours ago—just as Amy was arriving home from a trip to the market with Zack and hearing frightened shouts coming from Rosa, the housekeeper. She was screaming: "Mr. Justin! Madre de Dios! Oh my God, what has happened to Mr. Justin!"

Rosa was in the living room, standing at the open patio doors, pointing toward the beach. In the time it had taken Amy to run out of the house and get to the water's edge, Justin's body had slipped from Ari Silver's grasp and landed on the sand. Amy had struggled to pull Justin upright; his skin was waxy and cold.

In that moment, Amy had felt some essential part of Justin begin to recede. She could feel a strange shadow—the one that had been cast by their visit to the house on Lima Street—moving across the landscape of their lives and bringing a deadening chill.

Amy repositioned the box containing the old watch and wallet, then settled onto the bed close to Justin.

They lay side by side, perfectly still, like figures in a painting— a portrait of a young couple adrift in the master bedroom of their California town house, surrounded by open angular spaces and clean wood floors, wrapped in dazzling sunlight pouring through towering plate-glass windows.

It was Justin who broke the silence. "When you kissed me a few minutes ago," he said, "why did you jump like that?"

"You were cold and I could smell the ocean in your hair." Amy faltered, and then she said, "I guess it scared me . . . I can't stand the thought of you ever going into the water alone again."

"I know I'm messed up right now, but not as messed up as you think. You don't need to worry that every time I go for a swim I'm going to die." There was bitterness in his voice. "Hey. I've got the grave. I've got the headstone. Technically, I'm dead already."

Amy angrily pushed away, glaring at him. "That's not funny. There's nothing about any of this that's funny."

"No. It isn't funny. It's fucking terrifying." He rolled over onto his back and closed his eyes, shutting Amy out.

"Justin, please!" Amy took his hand. "That headstone is nothing more than an old piece of rock. It's been in that cemetery for a long time. It was there when I met you in London. It was there the first time I slept with you and the day we got married and the morning Zack was born and the night we drank that bottle of crazy expensive champagne to celebrate you getting the job here in L.A." Amy's tone was fierce. "However that lump of stone got into that graveyard, we don't need to let it derail our lives. Nothing changed when you found it, except that you found it. Your life is about now, about you, and me, and Zack. And our future. Nothing else matters."

Justin opened his eyes and studied her for a moment. There was sadness in his voice, and something that sounded like embarrassment. "Amy. There are huge chunks of my life that are missing and I have no idea where they are. They're just . . . gone. It's so messed up. I'm me. I'm here now. I know that. But there's a lot of stuff I don't know. Stuff I can't find."

"Like what?" Amy asked.

"All kinds of things. Like I know that at one time I had a teacher who drove this really cool car. An old MG. He kept it in perfect condition, and it was green. British racing green." Justin paused, took a deep breath. "And I have no idea what his name was or what grade I was in or what my school looked like. Or what I looked like."

Amy's response was something between a whisper and a murmur. "What do you mean?"

Justin's voice was full of strain. "I don't know." He reached across Amy and picked up the box. "At times, it almost feels like I never existed," he said.

He upended the box and allowed the contents to fall onto the bed. "These are the things my father had with him when he died. Do you see anything of me in here? Anywhere at all?"

The battered wallet landed in Justin's lap; he picked it up and shook it. Its contents rained down onto the bed: a pair of credit cards, a five-dollar bill, a stained pharmacy receipt for two razors and a can of shaving cream, an expired driver's license. And then, from a side compartment, came a small snapshot.

It was the creased, faded image of a beautiful girl. She was standing on a beach, flanked by two boys. One was tall, with coppery red hair; the other, blond and holding a surfboard. Both were looking toward the camera, smiling. The girl was glancing at the fourth person in the picture: a boy, lying in the sand at her feet, looking up at her and laughing.

Justin turned the photograph over. The back of it was blank except for a line of numbers: 768884. They looked hastily written, jotted down with what seemed to be a child's green crayon.

*

Justin and Ari had been running, steadily increasing their pace, for the last forty-five minutes.

"Do you want to turn back?" Ari's question came out between gasping breaths. "Or do you want to keep going and die?" He glanced over at Justin. And then he grinned.

Justin's lungs were on fire and his legs felt like jelly. "I'm not stopping till you drop."

"Ask and you shall receive." Ari staggered to a halt and sat down. "I'm dropped, man. I am so dropped."

"That's what I was hoping you'd say." Justin jogged to the water's edge and flopped onto the sand. He lay on his back, letting the waves rush in around him and then pull away. The stinging cold of the water against the peppery heat of his body was delivering both pleasure and pain. It was a long time before Justin opened his eyes. When he did, Ari was standing over him, watching him.

"I'm in four inches of water," Justin said. "Can't have much of an accident in that, now can I?" He got up and jogged away. He didn't look back at Ari; his tone made it clear he had no desire to pursue the subject.

Ari caught up to Justin and fell into step beside him. "Since I've already pissed you off, we might as well go ahead and get into it."

"There's nothing to get into. I've told it to Amy; now I'm telling it to you. What happened out here a couple of weeks ago was an accident." Justin sprinted away again. Ari caught up to him and said: "Is it possible that there are no accidents?"

"You're sounding like a shrink."

"I am a shrink." Ari shrugged. "But even if I was nothing more than a new friend and neighbor, which I also happen to be, it wouldn't get past me that you didn't answer my question."

"All that happened was I went for a swim and I got tired. I couldn't make it back in." Justin slowed his running and came to a stop. Ari did the same.

Observed from a distance, they could have been taken for brothers. They were nearly identical in height and coloring. Justin stepped in close to Ari, warning him. "I didn't come out here that day to try to fucking kill myself."

"I saw you go in," Ari replied, "and I saw the look on your face when you started to swim out. You may not have been aware of it at the time, but it's entirely possible that you went into that water wanting to commit suicide. And if I'm right, that's serious. We need to talk about it."

"It's bullshit." Justin started to move away. Ari stepped in and blocked him. "I was there," Ari said. "I helped save your ass. I helped pull you out of the water. And I am, in fact, a goddamned shrink. I know what I saw. Now tell me what the fuck really happened."

Justin shifted his gaze away from Ari's before he spoke. "Maybe you're onto something. I don't know. But I can't get into it right now. It's too complicated, okay?" As Justin turned back to look at Ari, he saw a lifeguard from a private club farther up the beach sprinting in his direction.

The lifeguard shouted, "Yo, TJ!" and Justin replied, "Yeah!"— a response that was automatic and instantaneous. It was the reply of a man instinctively answering to his own name; and as he did it, Justin went pale. But the lifeguard didn't notice; he'd already run past and was exchanging boisterous greetings with a kid carrying a boogie board.

For a moment, Justin and Ari remained silent. Then Ari came closer. He was mapping every nuance of Justin's face as he said: "Who's TJ?"

The question hit Justin like a grenade. His body buckled under the impact. He slowly collapsed onto the sand and began to tremble. He was in a barrel-rolling darkness, and in the darkness there was a black cocker spaniel puppy with a sky blue ribbon around its neck and a grand piano imploding and the sound of music being shattered and the bitter-sharp smell of gun oil and a *click!* and a small perfect circle of cold as the barrel tip of a cocked rifle pressed against his temple and his own voice in an eerie child-like register sang the words "Do I Know My Name Yes I Do Yes I Do" and a flow of blood snaked away, coiled back, and snaked away again.

Ari stood over him and repeated, "Who's TJ?"

Justin was shaking so violently, he could hardly speak. And

when he replied, "He's the other me," he vomited. Puke splattered up from the sand and frothed onto him, foul and chaotic; and he heard Ari ask: "What do you mean, 'He's the other me'?"

"I don't know," Justin whispered. "God help me. I don't know."

Caroline and Robert

*

It was, in a word, fabulous. Its exterior: a mirror-smooth mocha frosting dusted with scatterings of hazelnuts. The interior: four towering layers, each separated by silken bands of cream laced with brandied cherries.

Caroline had placed this majestic creation on a cut-glass cake stand that had belonged to Robert's mother. Now she was putting it on the old oak table in the center of the kitchen. It looked dazzling—and out of place, like an emperor's crown deposited on a workbench.

"Well," Caroline asked. "What do you think?"

"Big," Justin said. He was wide-eyed with delight at the magnitude of Caroline's handiwork. Lissa lifted him up so that he could get a better view of it.

"Isn't that the best cake you ever saw, Justin? Ever?" Lissa asked.

Julie was on the other side of the table, studying the cake. "Mommy, did you really make this all by yourself?"

"Yes, Mommy made it all by herself." Caroline put her hand to her forehead in a gesture of mock exhaustion. Then she winked and said, "And, I made a really big mess doing it, so I'm going to need help cleaning up before Daddy gets home and it's time for his party."

"We'll help. We'll clean the beaters." Julie pulled the frosting-covered beaters from the electric mixer and gave one to Lissa.

"Me, too. Me, too!" Justin held out his hand.

"When you're finished," Caroline told the girls, "you can put the candles on the cake."

Justin immediately tugged on Julie's sleeve. "Candles, please." She shrugged him off. "You can't light candles, Justin. You're too little."

Justin was indignant. "Not too little. I'm three!" Lissa picked him up and hugged him. "Don't worry, Justin. When you're almost eight, like me, you'll be able to do candles, too."

"Justin, for now you can hold the candles," Caroline said. "And it will be your job to give them to Lissa and to Julie when they ask, okay?" She gave him a handful of candles and he happily began dispensing them to his sisters.

It was five-thirty. December. The world outside was already dark. The kitchen was filled with warm butter yellow light, and as Caroline watched her son's happiness, she was in a gentle reverie. She was remembering driving away from a lunch at the Baldwin Hotel and sensing that she might be pregnant. She was remembering that before she had even turned onto the freeway that would bring her back to Lima Street, she had decided that if the child was a boy, she would name him for the beautiful quiet place in which, earlier in the day, she had touched purity. She would name him Justin.

As Caroline turned her attention back to the kitchen, she experienced an inexpressibly sweet feeling of happiness. She saw Julie and Lissa, busy decorating Robert's cake; Justin, trailing after them, holding out additional candles for the taking; and the dog, circling the room, its tail softly thumping against chair legs and cabinet doors. Moments like this proved to her that she'd succeeded in giving her children the exquisite gifts of a home and security—gifts her childhood had never given to her.

In Caroline's growing up, there had only been herself and her mother. When Caroline would ask about her father, her mother's response was always the same: "You don't have one." Then there would be a contemptuous laugh, and she would add: "He's gone."

He had never been there, and so Caroline was free to endow him with mythic importance, to believe with all her heart that there was nothing more powerful than the magic that came from not being a fatherless child.

It was to a father's absence that young Caroline attributed the knockabout life she and her mother lived.

He wasn't there. And they moved from one place to another, often in the dead of night, frequently just steps ahead of a bill collector or lecherous landlord. Never safe. Never settled.

And once, when Caroline had needed school clothes, she stood beside her mother in a department store and watched an application for credit being dropped into a wastebasket. Charge accounts, the saleslady said, were not available to divorced women. To Caroline, the label *divorced* had sounded nasty, like a stain.

A father wasn't there, and Caroline grew up eating alone in dreary kitchens while her mother paced bleak bedrooms, becoming more bitter and distant with each change of address, with each passing year.

Now, as Caroline watched Lissa and Julie putting the last of the candles on Robert's cake, she was thinking about how much safer her children were than she had ever been. She was remembering the earthquake that had occurred, during the time she was pregnant with Justin. It had arrived in the early hours of the morning, breaking windows and raining chimney bricks into the fireplace. Caroline had been terrified.

A few days later, the girls had been playing with a friend in the backyard. Caroline had heard the other little girl ask Lissa and Julie if they'd been afraid. "No," they'd said. "We knew our daddy would save us." And with that, Caroline had felt a wonderful joy. Her girls were not like her: damaged and needy. They were confident. They were whole.

"Daddy's home!" All three children were rushing past Caroline, racing toward the living room.

She was about to follow them, when she noticed the dog. His nose was resting on the edge of the kitchen table; his attention was fixed on Robert's cake. The dog was a large animal with an enthusiasm for food that bordered on obsession. Caroline shooed him away. He retreated to a spot near the back door but never took his eyes off the glorious cake.

Caroline heard the opening notes of the Beach Boys' "California Girls" boom out of the living room, and Lissa shouting: "Mommy! Mommy! Come and dance with us!"

"Hey 'Mommy,' hurry up and get in here!" It was Robert calling to her now. "It's my birthday and I want to dance with my wife!"

"Your wife is on her way!" Caroline shouted. She picked up the cake and went to the door that led to the basement. The door was warped and required Caroline to push against it once or twice before she could get it to open. When it did, a sweep of cold air came up from the darkness of the earthen-walled area below the house.

At the top of the steep basement stairs was a narrow landing, and a wall into which several storage shelves had been fitted. Caroline slipped the cake onto one of the upper shelves.

"If you're not out here by the time I count to three, I'm coming in!" It was Robert again.

Caroline quickly closed the basement door and left the kitchen.

In the living room, Robert was dancing with the children. The song was "Little Surfer Girl." When he saw Caroline, he immediately pulled her toward him. Julie's and Lissa's attention quickly turned to determining which of them could execute a perfect cartwheel.

Justin's attention turned toward the far end of the hallway.

The dog was there, leaning his considerable weight against the basement door and working to push it open.

What happened next took only seconds.

Justin stepped between the dog and the door just as the door gave way. It banged open and cold air rushed out, bringing the scent of cake with it.

The dog lunged forward.

And in that split second, there was the sound of a small body hitting against the stairs. Plummeting toward a cement floor.

*

"Mr. Fisher?"

Robert looked up and saw a very young nurse standing in the doorway of the hospital waiting room. She was holding a clipboard. "I'm sorry," she said, "but I need to go over some of the information your wife gave us."

Justin had been brought into the emergency room less than an hour ago. Caroline rode in the ambulance. Robert followed, almost immediately, in the car, after he'd called Mrs. Marston to come and stay with the girls. But it had been Caroline who had taken care of all the paperwork. Then she had gone into the examining room to be with Justin, where she still was.

The nurse sat down across from Robert. Her movements were tentative and awkward. "Mr. Fisher, I need to ask you some—"

"Whatever it is, can't it wait?" Robert couldn't clear his head of the image of Justin lying on his back, motionless, his gaze seemingly fixed on the landing above him—and on the dog, frantically circling and barking.

Robert hadn't noticed when Justin left the living room. He hadn't heard the scream Justin must have screamed when he began his fall toward the cement floor. Now all Robert could think about was *why* he had been so blind and deaf. He was sickened by the thought that his lack of connection to his own son had somehow contributed to the awful thing that had happened.

He had tried to rectify his problem with Justin countless times. But he had never found a way to do it. At some point, he had decided to establish a connection with Justin by taking him on a special father-son outing. Each time Robert discussed this idea, he saw the joy it gave Caroline—and each time his lack of feeling for Justin prevented him from making it a reality, he saw how much it wounded her.

Robert swore to her time and again that things would change. He needed, desperately, to make Caroline happy. She was the map by which Robert navigated his life.

From the first moment he had held her in his arms, he had been amazed, obsessed, and afraid. And he'd stayed that way for the entirety of his marriage. He was still amazed that a woman so beautiful and sexual would have him; he was obsessed with keeping her, and afraid that her love for him was something that could be easily erased by someone with the sort of style and confidence that he could never muster.

It was Justin who had slammed onto the concrete floor, but it was Caroline who had Robert's attention at the moment. He was thinking about a Thanksgiving dinner four years ago, remembering how radiant she had been.

He had no way of knowing—during that routine family gathering—that less than a month later Caroline would bring a monumental change to his life, something that would leave him stunned, and feeling furiously cheated.

As they were all gathered around, watching Robert's father carve the turkey, Caroline was laughing and joking with Robert's brother, Tom. An ambergold light was pouring through the windows at the far end of the room, making everyone look resplendent and virtuous.

It was a beautiful scene, but Robert was too restless to remain part of it. He quietly pushed back his chair and left the table. He wanted to be somewhere else. He was tired of life in the house on Lima Street. He had literally been born in the place—squirming into the world as his mother sprawled on the kitchen floor, comforted by a young neighbor named Mary Marston.

And on the day of his birth, it seemed to Robert, the house had claimed him and marked him as its prisoner. He tried his best to escape it, but he had failed.

He spent his teenage years constantly traveling away from Lima Street—to the beaches of Southern California, to Huntington, Trancas, and the Rincon. He had dreamed of a life in which he would craft custom-made surfboards—an existence that would never require him to wear a tie, or carry a briefcase, or possess a neatly printed business card.

But in his early twenties, the house had abruptly reasserted its claim on him and Robert had returned to Lima Street with Caroline at his side. He had put on a tie, and picked up a briefcase—and he had felt in his pocket the weight of the newly printed business cards that bore his name.

As Robert walked into the kitchen, Caroline was calling to him from the dining room: "I just told everyone about how you doubled the size of the agency this year."

He reached for the bottle of scotch that was in the cabinet above the refrigerator and heard his brother shout: "Hey, congrats, man!"

"Yeah," Robert shouted back. "Born to sell insurance. That's me." He poured himself a drink, and within seconds his mother was in the room, giving him a delicately constrained smile.

Her voice was shivery with self-effacement as she said, "If only I could find a way not to be so terribly upset when I see a man I love with liquor in his hand." She smiled again, this time with a coquettish sparkle. "I should try to be a braver girl, shouldn't I? Less sensitive, more like Caroline. But I can't help myself." She picked up Robert's glass and poured the scotch into the sink.

Robert knew what was coming. He'd been hearing it for thirty years.

"When I was a little a girl," his mother was saying, "it was so awful to walk in here and see that my father was drinking. It was only when he drank, you know, that he was mean to my mother and me. Only then."

She paused and smiled another one of her pretty-girl smiles. "When he wasn't drinking he was very kind. I see the same kindness in you, Robert. Although now, most of it goes to Caroline, of course. But I saw it in you the moment you were born. It's how I knew you would always be my precious gift from God."

She held her arms out to him, and he understood he was once more being taken captive by her delicate despotism. And he deeply resented it.

His resentment had begun with the arrival of the acceptance letter from his first-choice college, the college his brother, Tom, was attending, the University of Hawaii. His mother had been at the kitchen table. "Oh," she had said. "Hawaii. You'll be so far away. And I'll feel so alone." Then she had looked off into some sad middle distance and sighed: "But that's what men who are loved the best seem to do, isn't it? They abandon you and go away."

Later, Robert realized that his mother had never forbidden him to go to Hawaii; she had simply prevented it by making it seem like an act of brutality.

And after all these years, he was still in this same kitchen, with his mother slipping her arm through his and saying: "You must never tell Tom, but you've always been my favorite." Her hand was cool on his skin, familiar and slightly repellent. Robert wished he could get away from her, and stay away.

The only woman's caress he had wanted was Caroline's.

It was what he was wanting now as he sat in the hospital waiting room with this fidgety young nurse. He was in need of Caroline's touch, her presence, her assurance that she didn't in any way blame him—or his lack of fatherly involvement—for Justin's accident.

Before the nurse could launch into her questions again, a burly doctor appeared in the waiting room doorway. "Mr. Fisher, your son's been taken to X Ray," he said.

Robert held on to the arm of the chair as he stood; his knees were shaking. "How badly is he hurt?"

"It'll still be a while before we know." The doctor was already headed back through the doorway. "I'll come out again as soon as there's any news."

As the doctor left, the young nurse was searching through the forms on her clipboard, mumbling: "Oh, gosh. I didn't bring the right one." She jumped up and rushed off, narrowly avoiding a collision with a shabbily dressed man who had edged his way into the waiting room. He was making a stealthy, efficient search of each trash can along the wall before moving toward the exit door. As the man walked past, Robert saw—at the bottom of his thread-bare shirt pocket—the outline of a thin hand-rolled cigarette.

Again, Robert's thoughts went to that Thanksgiving weekend, when a joint—and then his brother, and, finally, Caroline—had led him to heartache and to violence.

It was in the evening, after Thanksgiving dinner was over. A crisp autumn wind was scattering leaves onto the path between the house and the garden shed, and the air had the aroma of wood smoke and fireplaces in it.

Tom was saying: "Holy crap, Robert. Does Caroline know you store your stash in Dad's old toolbox and keep it out here where Mom grew all her little seedlings? Damn. That is priceless!"

"Hey, it's not just any stash." Robert held up a plastic bag containing half a dozen joints. "What we have here, my brother, is Thai stick." Robert removed a joint, then returned the bag to the battered toolbox. Tom leaned over and inspected the contents: a jumble of bulbless flashlights, corroded pliers, and hardened duct tape. "The old man and tools. What a joke," Tom said.

Robert put the toolbox back on its shelf above the shed door, and he and Tom walked toward the house. As Tom took the joint from Robert, he lit it and said: "You've done a great job with the old palace, Rob." They stood, passing the joint between them, studying the house: the place Tom had escaped and Robert had resurrected.

Eventually, Robert and Tom drifted around the side of the house and onto the front porch. They sank into a pair of wicker chairs, putting their feet up on the table that was between them. There was a slight movement at the other end of the porch, and Robert realized Caroline was there.

She was almost lost in shadow, lying in the wide wooden swing, her head pillowed against its arm and her legs tucked under a light blanket. She looked as if she'd slipped off to sleep.

It pleased Robert to see that Caroline was nearby; he gave himself over to the lazy haze of a sweet high. He was mellow and, for the moment, content to be with his brother. "How's Hawaii?" he asked.

"Good," Tom said. "The university pays me to read and talk about the same great books I would read for free. I'm adored by my female grad students. I get laid on a regular basis and I can see the Pacific Ocean from the back door of my apartment."

"Sounds like you've got a lot to be thankful for."

"No more than you. You have the big house. Beautiful wife. Great kids. The premier insurance agency in dear old Sierra Madre. You've grown up to be the son Dad always wanted, man."

"Yeah," Robert said. "Happy Thanksgiving to us all." There was a quick, creaking sound, as if Caroline had moved ever so slightly in the swing. Robert was immediately uneasy, wondering if she was awake, worried that she might have heard the undercurrent of sarcasm in his voice.

Tom held the joint up as if he was saluting Robert with it. "To the Fisher boys and all that they have become!" He chuckled. "Man, back in the day, who would've thought you and I would ever be sitting out here smoking dope, with Mom and the old man upstairs, and us not giving a shit if they come down."

Robert laughed. "Oh, we'd give a shit. We'd be back being thirteen again in a blink. Because we're high and it's half-dark and the old man would be in the doorway, backlit from inside the house. And he'd look like a ham-handed linebacker waiting to kick our butts."

"He ever kick your butt, Rob?"

"Nah. He talked about it a lot though."

"He used to pound me like sand." It was only Tom's voice that was available to Robert; his face was obscured by the gathering darkness.

"I don't remember him ever hitting you," Robert said.

"Not that kind of pounding. The 'in the name of making you a man, my son' kind. Every football practice, every game, he'd be there standing on the other side of that chain-link fence—for hours. And then later he'd tell me how I needed to be more of a hustler here, less of a hotshot there. You remember how it was, every night at dinner."

"He couldn't help it," Robert said. "Sports and insurance. That's all he had. It's all he knew."

"So I got the sports and you ended up with the insurance." Tom stayed quiet for a moment; then he said, "And thus the two-bit legacy of the father is passed on to his sons." Tom took a hit and tilted back in his chair. "He ever tell you he loved you?"

"No."

"Me either."

"He did, though. He loved you."

"I know." There was uneasiness in Tom's voice. "He loved me plenty." Another silence, and then he said, "How high are you, Rob?"

"High enough."

Tom moved across the porch and leaned against the railing. "I almost ended up with both bits," Tom said.

"What are you talking about?" Robert looked in the direction of the swing. He could no longer see Caroline. She was wrapped in shadow. He wondered if she was awake; if she was about to find out something he wouldn't want her to know.

"I'm talking about the old man's two-bit legacy," Tom said. "I almost ended up with all of it. When he had the heart attack. Remember? It was a couple of weeks before Mother's Day. And on Mother's Day when I called to talk to Mom, he told me about not being able to go back to work for a while. He said he didn't have enough savings and he needed to keep the agency going. He asked me to come home from Hawaii and take over for him."

Tom had nicked the sleepy gauze of Robert's high. Robert sat up straighter in his chair. "And you said no? You told him you wouldn't come?"

"I told him it would take me a while, you know, to wrap things up at school. I said I was right in the middle of writing my thesis."

"And . . ."

"And I lied. The thesis was done. I was just buying time, hoping maybe he'd be able to handle things on his own. Shit, Robert. I didn't want to come home and take the chance of getting stuck being a goddamned insurance agent. I didn't tell him, but I'd made a deal with myself that if he hadn't figured something else out by Father's Day, I'd suck it up. I'd come home."

"Father's Day." Robert glanced toward Caroline, then lowered his voice and said: "That's when he asked me. That morning. When I called to wish him a happy Father's Day."

"I know. I called him that night to say I was coming. I'd put it off all day. Then when I called, he told me he'd talked to you about you coming back to help him out, so I didn't say anything. When I hung up, it was like I'd been pulled off death row."

It took Robert a moment before he was able to respond. "How did you know I'd end up saying yes?" he asked.

"Because I knew you. I knew you'd never run out on somebody who needed you."

There was a soft rustling at the far end of the porch, then the sound of the front door closing. His brother's words had stung him like cuts from a freshly sharpened ax. And Caroline had gone inside. She had left Robert alone.

All he had seen of her in that twilight was a graceful shadow as she slipped away. And now, in the harsh fluorescence of the waiting room, he hardly recognized Caroline as she was coming down the hospital corridor toward him. Her elegant features looked as if they had been coated in candle wax: blurred, and ghostly pale. She looked broken. And there was such strain and fear in her eyes that Robert was afraid to hear whatever it was she was about to tell him.

"Caroline, what's happened?" It came out in a whisper. "What's happening with Justin?"

"They're still running tests," she said. She leaned against him and then collapsed into his arms. She was shaking like a leaf in a windstorm and saying: "Don't let him die. Oh please, God. Don't let him die."

Robert was burning with guilt—believing that if only he had been more attentive to Justin, he might have seen him going into the kitchen, and this terrible night would never have happened. "It'll be all right. He'll be okay," he told Caroline as he held her close. "And after this, everything is going to be better. I promise."

The smells of the cooking and baking she had done for his birthday were still in her hair, and they took Robert back to that Thanksgiving. To the next morning, after the initial pain had been inflicted, when the violence had begun.

It had been early, and the house was cold. There were still faint traces of yesterday's holiday dinner in the air—the smell of roasted turkey and homemade pumpkin pie.

Robert saw that Caroline had made breakfast. When he took his coffee mug to the kitchen table, there was an open bottle of blood-pressure medication there. He jammed its cap into place and slammed the bottle down.

"I've been looking for this goddamn thing for a half hour!" It was Robert's father, striding into the room, clutching the morning paper. "Why can't Caroline use her head? Your mother always left the paper at the bottom of the stairs where a person could see it."

"So what? It isn't your house. Or your newspaper." Each word Robert spoke was edged with hostility. "You turned this place over to me a long time ago, remember?"

His father grabbed the bottle and wrestled the cap. "Goddamn it, I left this open for a reason, Robert. Why did you have to go playing with it?"

"Don't leave your damn pills lying around where my children can get at them." Robert snatched the bottle away from his father.

"How dare you talk to me like that, boy?" His father's voice was a rumbling roar. Once, when Robert was a child, it had cowed him to the point of public incontinence.

But this morning, his roar was outdistancing his father's. "When you asked me to come back here, you said a year. Two at most, and I could go back to my life. But then you stuck me with yours, and took off!"

"Cut the crap. You got the house. You got the agency."

"Want to know something, old man? It was like ripping my own guts out to come back here and help you sell fucking goddamn insurance. But there was one little part of it that almost made the rest of it okay, the idea that when the chips were down *I* was the son you reached out to."

His father's fist banged onto the table. "You had a knocked-up girlfriend and a pile of student loans. How would you have taken care of all that? . . . Caroline and her little 'bun in the oven'? They were about to flatten you. And all you had was some boneheaded notion about surfing for a living. I saved your sorry butt."

"You lied to me. As soon as you were well enough, you left me here and took off to Arizona and never came back!"

"Aw, somebody get me a violin." Robert's father went to the kitchen counter and opened a box of cereal. "You've got the world by the tail, boy. Stop whining."

In one swift, furious move, Robert grabbed his coffee mug and hurled it at the old man. It smashed into the wall just above his father's head and he came at Robert with a violent lunge, ready to strangle him. Robert stood up and his chair toppled backward onto the floor. As he was about to drive his fist full tilt into his father's gut, there was a shout of "Jesus God, what the hell's going on?" and Tom was suddenly in the kitchen, and Robert's fist was slamming into his face, tearing into the skin, going deep, opening a vicious cut.

Tom slowly raised his hand to his cheek. He looked stunned. For a moment, there was an explosive calm: the silence separating the aftershocks of an earthquake.

Then Robert picked up the chair and set it upright again, his hand slick with his brother's blood.

The old man plunged some paper towels into water that was in the sink, clumsily dabbed at Tom's face, and said, "Call Doc Johannsen down the street. See if he's home. You're gonna need stitches." Then he slowly sat at the table, still holding the bloody wadded-up toweling in his hand. "You'll be fine. I got plenty worse than that when I was playing college ball."

"You played for one lousy season," Robert said.

"And then I went into a foxhole in France," the old man snarled. "I played football. I fought for my country. You splashed around in the ocean like a seal, and then, when Vietnam came along, you hid behind the wife and kids and stayed home. The first thing you did when you got your draft notice was to grab a deferment. Don't shoot your mouth off about things you didn't have the balls to qualify for."

Before Robert could reply, Tom stepped between him and the old man. "Let's be honest, Dad. I didn't go, either."

"Your number wasn't called. If you'd've been drafted, you would've gone, Tom. You wouldn't have let anything stop you. You're not a sissy mama's boy, you understand the line."

"What are you talking about?" Robert screamed.

"Being on the line. A real man hunkers down and holds it no matter what comes at him. And you don't bitch about it. That's what a man does. It's what's expected. Wherever life puts you, you hold that line and defend it."

"Well I hate every inch of the fucking line I'm on," Robert said. "I'm sick of it!"

"What's wrong with you, Robert?" It was his mother. She was standing in the doorway. Caroline was behind her, flanked by Julie and Lissa, the three of them wearing flannel nightgowns patterned in star shapes. "Your life may not be the one you planned," his mother said, "but look at all you have, Caroline, and your girls."

"And this house," Caroline said. "We have this wonderful place that belongs to us."

Robert could see that Caroline was bewildered by what he'd said about having a life he didn't want. The look in her eyes was pleading with him to desire the things she desired—to need to be on Lima Street as much as she did.

But Robert was furious. He was too angry to stop himself from shouting: "For Christ's sake, Caroline. I could've had a god-damned house and still have been where I wanted to be!"

Caroline started toward him, then stopped. Her expression told him that things he had kept carefully locked away from her had gotten loose and stung her. And he didn't know how to take them back.

"What's wrong with Daddy?" Julie asked.

The reply from Robert's father was flat and cold. "Your daddy's sad because he can't skip out on his life and go live at the beach like some hippie."

Robert ignored his father; he was focused on Caroline. He needed to make her understand the pain he was feeling. It was as if his heart were beating against a tourniquet of barbed wire.

And the bite of that barbed wire had never gone away. It was still with him as he stood in the waiting room of the hospital holding Caroline close, feeling her tremble, listening to her whispered prayer: "Please, God. Let Justin be all right."

Robert was echoing that prayer. He wanted his son to be safe. And beyond that, he wanted him, someday, to have a life that truly belonged to him—one that matched the shape of his soul.

He wished for Justin the kind of life that he had been dreaming of for himself, in the weeks that followed that terrible Thanksgiving, when he had done such damage to Tom's face.

The truth was, he had enjoyed doing it.

In opening that gaping gash in his brother's flesh, Robert had liberated something in himself—something surprisingly reckless. It had prompted him to make a decision that would change his life. And, of course, the first and only person he wanted to tell was Caroline.

He was in the living room, at the rolltop desk that had stood against the front wall since his grandfather's day. It held the musk of old gum erasers and india ink and dust. In one of its wide, deep cubbyholes, he found what he was looking for: a manila envelope filled with a thick sheaf of papers—the business plan he had drawn up in his senior year of college, the strategy for his surfboard company.

The feel of the envelope in his hand was electric.

He went upstairs to find Caroline, reveling in the thought that this was the perfect time: The girls were still young, easy to move. They hadn't even started school, and Robert knew he could, without much effort, sell the agency and give himself a modest nest egg.

He and Caroline could have a little house at the beach, a location where he could build his business. Even if they had to rough it for a while, it would be fun—an adventure. He was only in his thirties, Robert told himself. A bit of a late start, but not too late.

As he arrived at the top of the stairs, he saw a light coming from under the door of his old bedroom. He put the manila envelope on the flat crown of the newel post, crossed to the door, and opened it.

Caroline was there, standing near the window, in a pretty nightgown that ended just below her knees. Her face was clean—without any makeup. She looked like a teenager. Like the girl she was when she'd first come to Lima Street. Seeing her made Robert feel as if the things he'd been imagining were not only possible but already in the process of happening.

He held out his hand to Caroline. "I have something I want to tell you."

She smiled but didn't move from the window.

He held out his hand again. "Come on. Let's get in bed. I need to talk to you."

There was something hesitant in Caroline's voice as she said: "Can't you tell me here? I want to stay for a minute."

"It's cold in here. Let's go."

"The heat's on. It's fine." Caroline led him across the room. Nothing in it had been changed since he'd occupied it as a teenager. She was taking him toward the twin bed near the window—where the sill had a small circular indentation. Robert diverted her. They sat on the bed that was near the door.

Caroline said: "I have something to tell you, too." There were faint bluish circles under her eyes, suggesting that she was in need of rest. She put her mouth close to Robert's ear and whispered: "You're about to have another house project. For this one, you're going to need white enamel, and lots of yellow paint, and some Winnie-the-Pooh wallpaper."

"Why?"

"Because we're going to have a baby. And I want this to be the nursery."

Robert felt as if Caroline had lifted him up and dropped him from a gut-wrenching height. She might as well have impaled him on a spike. For a moment, he was so shocked that he couldn't think.

When he could hear her again, she was in mid-sentence: ". . . if it's a boy, I know we'll have to follow your family tradition about firstborn sons, and his first name will be Thomas. But I want his middle name to be Justin. And I want us to call him Justin. So—"

Robert interrupted her. "Are you sure? Are you positive you're pregnant?" He felt as if he were seeking information about his own death sentence.

Caroline's smile evaporated. She sounded weary and overwhelmed. "Yes, I saw the doctor this afternoon. I'm going to have a baby."

"But it could be a false alarm." Robert got up, moved away from her. "Like the first time. It could be like that, couldn't it?"

Caroline looked at him as if he had said something horrifying. "What? You mean when we got married? For God's sake, Robert. That wasn't a 'false alarm.' I had a miscarriage. I lost a baby. I didn't invent one."

Robert came back to the bed and sat on the end of it. "I know. I just meant that it didn't work out. The baby didn't make it. I guess all I was trying to say was that it could happen again, couldn't it?"

There was something close to hatred in Caroline's voice as she replied: "Is that what you're hoping for? For me to lose this child?"

Robert rested his arms on his knees and looked down at his feet. They were pale against the dark wood of the floor. The contact calluses on his knees that came from kneeling on a surfboard, the ones that had been there when he was younger, had all but vanished.

He didn't look up when he said: "It doesn't matter what I was hoping for."

There was no way he could make Caroline see that his love for her, and for his two little girls, was as far as he wanted his heart to stretch—that the thought of having another child was devastating him. The only thing Robert had wanted to begin tonight was his flight from Lima Street. But he was already feeling the clench of this new shackle; it was one that was going to force him to remain for a long time, perhaps forever, imprisoned in the place he'd spent his life trying to escape.

"Are you happy?" He asked the question quietly and without emotion. "Are you glad we're having another baby?"

Caroline rose and walked toward the door. "Yes," she said. "I want this child very much."

A moment later, Robert followed her out into the hall. As they were passing the top of the stairs, he hesitated. He was about to come to a stop. But he could sense Caroline looking up at him, so he turned away from the newel post—and from the manila envelope that was resting on it.

He turned, instead, toward his wife. He kissed the glossy crown of her head. And inhaled her perfumed sugar scent. And kept walking.

After that night, Robert and Caroline had gone on with their lives on Lima Street and Justin had been born.

From the minute she first saw him, Caroline was besotted with him. Robert's love had been, at best, uncertain. On some inescapable level, he had experienced his son's birth as the arrival of a jailer. Because of that, Robert had never participated in all the little rituals and games of fatherhood. He'd never played submarines or draped Justin in mountains of bubbles while he gave him a bath. He'd never read him a bedtime story. He hadn't ever taken him to get his hair cut, or taught him how to throw a ball.

No matter how much he had tried, Robert had never been able to love Justin deeply.

And the guilt of that was what was making Robert hold on to Caroline with such intensity as she was pulling away from him, saying: "I need to go back in there. I need to be with Justin."

She gave Robert a look that was, for a moment, filled with the purest love he had ever seen. Then she disappeared through the waiting room doors.

He started to follow Caroline, but the young nurse pulled him to a stop. "I'm sorry," she said. "Only one visitor at a time in pediatrics." She had returned a few minutes ago with her nervous energy and her clipboard.

As she was ushering Robert to a chair, she was saying, "The questions I need to ask you won't take long. But they might take a few more minutes than normal. It's my first week doing things on my own. This is my first job out of nursing school and . . ." She stopped to retrieve the pen that had slipped from her clipboard. "I'm a little nervous. I'm sorry."

"Check back with me later. Please." Robert wanted to be rid of this fumbling girl.

"Actually, all I need is a signature. Permission for your son to receive a transfusion in the event he might need one."

The nurse held the clipboard out to him and Robert scrawled

his name at the bottom of the form. He was buzzing with a sudden fear that Justin might be dying. "Does he need blood?" Robert asked. "I can donate right away. Where do I go to do that?"

"No, he doesn't need it right now. But it's great if you give blood anyway. That way you've made a contribution we can bank. All I'll need is to make a note of your blood type." She was holding her pen poised above the clipboard.

"It's O. Type O," Robert said.

The nurse seemed confused by his answer. "Are you sure?"

"You want proof? I've got it here on my emergency information card." Robert pulled his wallet from his back pocket.

"No. I mean it's probably my mistake. Or maybe your wife wrote down her information wrong." The nurse looked at the clipboard again. "Because I have her as type A. And we know your son is type AB. So there's no way if you're an O that you could possibly be his—" The nurse stopped short.

When her gaze met Robert's, there was panic in her eyes. Neither one of them spoke.

She had told him the truth about Justin, and about Caroline. There was nothing more to be said.

"I was lying in bed. At home. Then I looked toward the window and there was a man in a red fleece jacket. All I could see of him was from the neck to the waist. His torso was filling the window. I could tell that he wasn't anybody I knew, but I understood he was there to kill me. Then he was in the room, standing across from the bed. He had a rifle aimed at me. And I thought, Shit, I don't need this. Then I saw the bullet coming down the barrel of the gun, straight at me. And I turned away, rolled over, so my back was to him. I knew he was shooting me and it was going to hurt . . . the bullet going in. I kind of reached back with my hand. I guess I was trying to deflect the bullet, like it would slow it down, make it hurt less. Then the bullet hit my palm. And it stung like a son of a bitch." Justin hesitated, then added, "That's all."

"That's all?" There was a flicker of surprise in Ari's eyes.

"Yeah. The bullet stinging my hand, that's what woke me up."

"The dream," Ari said. "It was vivid. It seemed real while you were in it?"

"Yes," Justin replied. "I mean the room, me, everything, it was exactly like it is in real life."

"And then what?" Ari had opened his small office refrigerator and was reaching into it, taking out a bottle of mineral water.

"And I woke up and I thought, Great, finally I remembered a dream. And then I wrote it down so I wouldn't forget."

"Want one?" Ari asked, indicating the mineral water.

"No. I'm good." Justin sat back and waited. He was becoming familiar with the rhythms of these sessions. Justin knew when Ari was taking time to contemplate his next move.

They had been meeting twice a week, here in Ari's office, for almost a month. During his first few appointments, Justin had been uncomfortable sitting across from a neighbor in this impersonal yet oddly intimate room with its sleek leather chairs and strategically placed boxes of tissues. He hadn't been certain he wanted to risk exposing whatever dark secrets there were about himself to someone he knew. At the same time, he hadn't been certain he wanted to open himself up to a stranger, either. What he had known, without a doubt, was that he was in desperate need of help.

"How did you feel after you woke up?" Ari settled into the chair across from Justin.

"Glad I'd finally remembered a dream."

"Nothing else?" There was no edge to Ari's voice. But in the way he held the bottle of water and tapped it against the arm of his chair, there was tension. Justin saw it and was surprised. Keeping a record of his dreams had been something Ari had asked him to do. Justin had assumed that remembering this dream, remembering any dream at all, would have elicited a positive response from Ari.

"And in the dream, when you realized the man was there to kill you, how did you feel? Were you afraid?"

"No, I didn't have any emotion on it . . . except, like I said, a kind of 'Shit, I don't need this' feeling. Like it was one more thing coming at me."

"And you clearly understood you were about to be murdered?"

"Yeah. Absolutely."

"And that didn't frighten you?"

"No."

Ari took a sip of water. "Were you frightened when you woke up?"

"No. Why all the questions?"

"Because the dream you just described is a nightmare, you're in the process of being murdered. Yet you feel no fear. And when you wake up and recall the dream . . . again, no fear. No emotion."

"So, what are you getting at?"

"I'm saying that the normal reaction to a nightmare, and to the prospect of being murdered, is fear. You didn't have any."

"And that means what?"

"It suggests that you control your emotions and your mental processes to such a degree that the control is almost complete. It's not only governing your behavior when you're awake and conscious but it's reaching into the subconscious, into your dreams, and clamping down on the flow of normal emotion, of normal processing."

"I still don't understand. What does it mean?" There was concern in Justin's voice.

"It suggests you've locked yourself in, and you've fortressed yourself against something," Ari said. "And that it's big. And that we'll need to be very careful about how we go looking for it."

*

The Pacific Regent Hotel was resplendent with holiday decorations. In every public room, there was a massive Christmas tree hung with jewel-toned ornaments, crowned with a golden angel, and ringed with swirls of emerald-colored moss. The effect was one of magnificent excess.

Justin had come down from his office and was now walking across the lobby. The sight of the extravagant Christmas displays, and of his staff efficiently going about the hotel's business, gradually took his mind off the disturbing session he'd had with Ari earlier in the day.

From the moment he had first begun working in them, Justin was captivated by elegant hotels. To him, they were places of sanctuary. They glowed with warmth and safety, with serenity and beauty. To Justin, coming into a fine hotel felt like coming home should feel.

As he entered the jewelry store in the hotel's shopping area, the girl behind the counter grinned and said: "Mr. Fisher, good news. I found the exact one you were asking about." She took a suede jewelry case from a drawer, and Justin saw that it contained the Christmas gift he wanted for Amy: a perfectly cut diamond solitaire suspended from a length of platinum as thin as a strand of a spider's web.

Justin leaned over the counter to look at the necklace. He was facing the mirrored rear wall of the store. As he straightened up, he caught sight of his own reflection, and then he saw the image of a woman. Her image had moved so swiftly that, for an instant, it gave Justin the impression the woman had gone *through* him. But he realized she had gone *past* him. Out in the corridor, on the other side of the store's glass front wall.

The woman had fiery red hair, pale skin, and sloping shoulders. The combination hit Justin with a wave of recognition that rocked him and left him feeling almost stunned.

He rushed toward the door, leaving Amy's necklace forgotten on the counter.

As he ran out of the jewelry store, he was scanning the length of the corridor, trying to catch sight of the woman with the red hair.

There were people moving around him in all directions, but she was nowhere to be found. Justin sprinted toward the exit doors at the far end of the shopping arcade. As he pushed them open, he saw her. But before he could get to the sidewalk, she was already in a taxi, and it quickly pulled away.

For several weeks, a splinter of memory had been pricking at the edges of Justin's consciousness. The sessions with Ari had been nudging it closer to the surface, and the sight of this red-haired woman had hit like a final, sharp tap. It was out in the open now.

And all Justin could feel was bone-shaking fear. He fumbled for his phone. When he pressed the speed-dial button, he heard "You have reached the private line of Dr. Ari Silver. Please leave your name and telephone number."

"Ari, I need to see you," Justin said. "I know who TJ's mother is."

Caroline and Robert

*

Caroline laid her cheek against Justin's hand, and when her skin touched his, he stirred and made a sound that was something between a sigh and a dreamy giggle. He was not fully conscious, but he knew she was there.

"Your son's a very lucky little boy." The doctor was standing at the foot of Justin's bed. "All he managed to get out of that stair dive was a pretty good concussion, a fracture of the left forearm, and a few cuts and bruises."

"And that's the extent of it?" Caroline said. "He's going to be fine?"

"Sometimes kids his age can bounce like they're made of rubber. We'll keep an eye on him for a while, but yes, it looks as if he's going to be perfectly fine."

The wave of relief that swept over Caroline left her weak. All she could do was smile.

"It's important to keep him as alert as possible for the next few hours," the doctor said.

Still smiling, Caroline nodded. The doctor left the room. Caroline held Justin close. He lifted his hand and it fell, warm and small, into her open palm. She rested her head near his and began to sing.

The song was one she had invented and taught to him as soon as he'd been old enough to speak. She had made up similar songs for both her girls. It was Caroline's way of ensuring her children could never be completely lost from her. In these simple rhymes, she was giving them a compass that would guide them home.

"Do I know my name?" Caroline sang to Justin. "Yes, I do. Yes, I do. My name is Justin. And my name is Fisher, too." Justin's eyelids drooped. Caroline tickled his palm and said: "No, baby, don't drift away. Don't get lost. Stay with me. Come on, Justin. Sing your song."

"My name is Justin . . . and my name is Fisher, too . . ." The words were lisped and indistinct, but Justin was singing. He was awake. He was connected to her.

"Do I know my home?" Caroline sang. "Yes, I do. Yes, I do. I live on Lima Street. Right at 822. Do I know my town? Yes, I do. Yes, I do. My town's Sierra Madre, and California, too. Do I know my parents? Yes, I do. Yes, I do. One's named Caroline. And one's named Robert, too. Do I know my sisters? Yes, I do. Yes, I do. I have a sister Julie. And a sister Lissa, too."

Justin gave Caroline a sleepy, wavering smile and said: "Tell me again, Mommy. Sing me my story."

And all through the night, Justin heard his mother's low, clear voice singing to him: "Do I know my name? Yes, I do. Yes, I do. Do I know my home? Yes, I do. I live on Lima Street. Right at 822."

*

It was after midnight, and Robert's arrival in the house startled Mrs. Marston. She had been dozing on the sofa. She was still groggy as she mumbled: "Robert, why are you back so soon? I didn't expect you for hours."

He was already moving past her. She followed him as quickly as she could, explaining that she'd taken Julie and Lissa to her house and that her husband was with them.

When she caught up to him in the kitchen, Robert was pouring himself a drink.

"Why haven't you brought Caroline and Justin back with you from the hospital? Oh Lord, the child's not dead, is he?"

"No." It was all Robert could manage to say.

The information he'd been given at the hospital—that Caroline had not only betrayed him but had brought him another man's son—was tearing away at Robert.

He was paying little attention as Mrs. Marston said: "The girls were so upset, seeing their baby brother hauled off in an ambulance. Such an awful thing." As she prattled on, Robert moved from one area of the kitchen to another, swallowing his drink in open mouthfuls, trying to recall where he had stored the tax records four years ago.

"Robert!" Mrs. Marston's tone was peevish. "You're not hearing a word I'm saying, are you?"

As he upended his glass to drain the last of the scotch from it, he saw the open basement door, and the birthday cake Caroline had carefully wedged onto a shelf just inside it. He calmly reached in and wrapped his fist around the pedestal of the cake stand. Then with an angry flick of his wrist, he sent Caroline's elegant creation flying toward the open trash can near the back door, but the cake slapped against the wall and splattered across the floor.

"Don't clean that up," he told Mrs. Marston. "Leave it there."

He dropped the cake stand and abruptly walked out of the kitchen. He had just remembered where he'd put the tax records.

They were in a storage container at the back of a closet in the upstairs hallway. Along with the tax forms was a year's worth of canceled checks—and Robert's desk calendar for 1971. He flipped through it, looking for the months of October and November, the time when Caroline would have conceived. Within seconds, he'd found the answer to his question. He saw the notation for the insurance seminar he had attended in Fresno on October 30 and 31.

And he remembered everything.

He remembered the beery smell and hazy light in the cocktail lounge and how tempted he'd been by the woman who was sitting beside him. She had first sidled up to him at the afternoon lecture and then, later, joined him at dinner. A vaguely pretty, slightly plump female with unremarkable legs and an ingenue's excitement about the insurance business. The kind of achingly ordinary woman that in his youth Robert had always assumed he would end up with; the only type of woman (because of his own ordinariness) he believed he deserved.

He remembered the rush: the twisting surge of desire shooting through him when, at the end of the evening, she had kissed him with an open, upraised mouth that was clean and cool and soft. He had wondered what it would be like to revel in such willingness and uncomplicated predictability. He wondered if not being humbled would bring him an erotic freedom that sex with Caroline had never allowed. She was too complicated, too fragile.

He remembered leaving the woman standing, disappointed, at the door of her hotel room. He'd gone back to his own room and called Caroline to tell her he loved her and would always love her. He had wanted to make her believe it—because it was the truth.

It was during that phone call that Caroline had told him about Mitch being in town. The news had filled Robert with jealousy. He knew that Caroline, in their college years, had desired Mitch. And Robert believed, on some level, she had never stopped desiring him.

"Robert, is everything all right?" It was Mrs. Marston calling out from the kitchen. He didn't answer. He moved across the hall into Justin's room. Moonlight was streaming through the window, brightly illuminating the indentation on its sill—the mark that his children called "the clown face." To Robert, it was, and would always be, a mocking condemnation: tangible evidence that his kind of manhood was second-rate.

The mark had been made when Robert was sixteen, during spring break. He had been working in the garage all day, shaping a new surfboard. He had come upstairs to take a shower, assuming the house was empty, but as he was walking toward his bedroom, he realized his brother, Tom, was there.

Tom, stripped to the waist and with his jeans opened and pushed down on his hips, was with Robert's girlfriend, a girl named Claire. Tom was slipping his hand between her legs, asking if she wanted him to stop, and Claire was saying no. Robert, watching from the doorway, was miserable and sick. Tom positioned himself behind Claire and she turned toward the window, and he entered her.

In their excitement, Tom and Claire cried out in unison, and it had sounded like music. Claire spread her arms to steady herself and whispered: "Oh God, I've been going out with the wrong brother!"

As she gripped the uprights at the sides of the window frame, her body being pushed against the crosspiece at its base, one of the round copper buttons on her denim jacket was leaving an imprint in the wood—a mark that vaguely resembled the smiling face of a clown.

By the time that Tom and Claire had finished, Robert was gone. He'd heard his mother's car pulling into the driveway and had run out of the house to intercept her and cajole her. He had needed to keep her from discovering the humiliating truth about his brother, and about his girlfriend, and about himself.

"Robert, what is going on with you? I want you to tell me. Now." It was Mrs. Marston again. She had come into the room and was standing just behind Robert—so close that he could feel her breath on his neck.

Mrs. Marston had helped usher him into the world and had been his mother's closest friend. Robert wanted to deal with her honestly and gently, but he was out of control. His rage at Caroline was what he threw at her.

"You want to know what's going on with me?" he said. "I've spent my life eating everybody else's shit. And I'm sick of it."

Mrs. Marston's gaze was as tranquil as her tone. "I don't appreciate the language, Robert. But I understand the sentiment." She touched his arm and turned him toward her. "At one time or another, we've all had that feeling, but has it occurred to you that over the years other people may have eaten their share of your shit?"

Her words and the calmness of them infuriated Robert. "Mrs. Marston, you've been here from the beginning. You know I got stuck with a life I never asked for. I got screwed over. By my parents. And by my brother. Don't try to convince me to lie down like a good little boy while my wife takes her turn at it!"

Robert had screamed at her, loudly enough to make Mrs. Marston take a few steps back. Her voice was low as she said: "I don't know what has happened between you and Caroline. But I can tell you that it was your choice to come back here after your father's heart attack. You could've said no. We don't just land on the squares where we take up residence. We play our part in choosing them. Haven't you figured that out, Robert?"

He'd wanted tenderness from her. Instead, she'd bitten him. "Shove the platitudes, Mrs. Marston."

"I'm ashamed of you, Robert," she said. "I thought you would turn out better than this."

Mrs. Marston walked out and closed the door behind her. Robert listened as she went down the stairs and out of the house. He could feel the soft thing at his core—the thing that had been bred into him in this place—being cauterized and already in the process of hardening. He could feel it turning to stone.

*

Early the next morning, Caroline came home. When she entered the house, Robert was on the stairs—his expression cold and unreadable.

"Where have you been?" she said. "Why did you leave the hospital and not come back? You didn't even tell me where you were going."

"I came home to be with my children."

The statement fell between them like a sheet of ice.

There was a brief, deathly hush: the silence before the lowering of the executioner's blade.

Robert said: "He's not mine, is he?"

The question paralyzed Caroline.

"It happened that Halloween when Mitch was in town, didn't it?" Robert delivered this as a statement, nonnegotiable.

"Yes, but . . ."

Before she could continue, Robert shouted: "Stop! I've swallowed my last piece of crap, Caroline. It's over."

She scrambled up the stairs, reaching for him. "Robert,

please." He pushed her away with savage force, slamming her against the stair rail. Her words came out thin and choked: "Robert, I'll spend the rest of my life making it up to you."

She was clutching at him now, begging, feeling the house tearing itself open around her—preparing to hurl her children into the broken place from which she had been running all her life. "I'll do anything." She was crying and desperate. "Just please stay. For our children. Don't go. Don't leave them."

Robert's response was unnervingly cool. "I'm not the one who's going."

Caroline couldn't make sense of what she'd just heard. "What are you talking about?"

"I'm talking about Justin," Robert said. "I'm telling you that you're going to pay for what you've done, Caroline."

*

Justin was in the midst of chaos.

In the garage, subterranean pumps were straining against a rising flood. Above the house, a cannonade of rain was rushing out of the night sky, hammering down onto the roof. And in the living room, the five o'clock news was flowing with a litany of crisis.

Justin was sitting in semidarkness; his only light was the glow of the television and the flickering of the fireplace. As he listened to the roar of the rain and the drone of the newscast, he was aware the phone was ringing, but he made no move to answer it.

He remained on the sofa, mesmerized: South of Santa Barbara, a mountainside was giving way and burying most of a small town; in the Hollywood Hills, a monumental mud flow was flattening a house while neighbors desperately tried to reach a family trapped inside; to the east of Los Angeles, a woman, pregnant with her first child, was being swept to her death by a flash flood; to the north, a four-year-old boy was drowning in the foaming waters of a rain-swollen river while a rescue helicopter fluttered helplessly above him.

Somewhere in the course of the newscast, Justin felt Amy slide onto the sofa and nestle beside him. She was wearing a satin robe, and her hair was pinned up and damp. He could smell the scent of fragrant bath oil on her skin. Under normal circumstances, Justin would have gone to the spot where her robe closed across her breasts and he would've kissed that spot and gently pulled the robe open. They would have made love with a leisurely elegance, then wandered into the kitchen and done what they often did after Sunday-night sex—treat themselves to something sweet and delicious. Since it was now winter, the treat would have been hot cider. In the summer, it would be a cold frothy egg cream made from a recipe Amy had gotten from a New York deli owner a long time ago.

But these were not normal circumstances. Towns were being crushed by mountains. Children were drowning in rivers. And Justin was being tormented by the image of a woman with red hair, pale skin, and sloping shoulders.

He watched as Amy took the remote and muted the sound on the television, leaving only the picture available. "That was Daddy on the phone," she said. "He needs to know if we want him to fly Rosa to Hawaii with us to help with Zack." She waited for Justin to acknowledge what she'd just said. When he didn't, she told him: "I'm thinking that we don't really need a nanny. I mean, Daddy's rented this incredible villa, so it won't be like Zack will be cooped up in a hotel room. He'll have a whole house to roam around in. And you know how my mother loves to be with him. I'm sure if you and I go do something on our own, she'll want to watch him anyway, so—"

Justin cut her off in mid-sentence with a cynical laugh. "For Christ's sake, Ames, when do we ever get time to ourselves on one of your father's forced marches?"

"A villa in Maui is hardly a forced march, Justin."

"Look. I don't want to fight about this. I already told you, I've got too many things on my plate right now. This isn't the time for a trip."

"How can anybody not be up for a free week in Hawaii?"

Justin took the remote from Amy and idly flicked through the channels. "I have a lot on my mind. Leave it at that."

Amy went to the television, shut it off, and then stood in front of it, blocking Justin's view. "This is my father's birthday we're talking about. If we don't go, do you have any idea how disappointed he's going to be?"

Each of Justin's words was laced with sarcasm. "You know what your father should do to commemorate all the command performances . . . the birthday trips, the rafting trips, the Let's Go to Europe for No Good Goddamn Reason trips? He should get roadie jackets made up. They could all say the same thing. Another Don Heitmann Punishment Tour." Justin got up and walked out of the dimness of the living room into the brightly lit kitchen.

He opened the refrigerator and took out a bottle of soda. With an angry twist, he removed the cap and let it drop onto the floor.

Amy was already coming through the doorway. It was clear she was ready to fight. "You're telling me lounging around in the lap of luxury is 'punishment,' Justin? Why are you being such a shit about this?"

Amy and Justin had been arguing about this trip for a week, and he knew that if she kept pushing him about it, he would explode. He was struggling to keep calm as he said: "Amy, did your father ask you if it was convenient for you to go to fucking Maui next week? Did he ask me? No. That's because it isn't an invitation. It's a demand. We're being ordered to sit in his villa, eat his food, see places he wants to see, and listen to him rap about his monster cash flow and how it gives him the big fat swinging dick the rest of us should get down on our knees and pray to."

Amy's voice was rasping with outrage. "You're being a monumental asshole, Justin. All my father is trying to do is give us family time together in a place where we can make some great memories. This trip is as much for us, and for Zack, as it is for him." She seemed to be fighting tears as she said: "He's just trying to give us a present."

Her impending tears, genuine or not, irritated Justin—he had no interest in buying what she was attempting to sell. He'd allowed himself to be sold too many times before. Without looking at her, he went back into the living room—back to the numbing comfort of the semidarkness, and the television.

As he was reaching for the remote, Amy appeared in the doorway, looking contrite. She took a deliberate, expectant breath, as if she was about to plunge into the deep end of a swimming pool. "When I was upstairs in the shower," she said, "I had a thought . . . about all this craziness."

Justin kept his gaze fixed on the television. "The craziness that's going on in the rest of the world, or the stuff going on in my head?"

"Both, I think." Amy moved out of the doorway and came to sit beside him. "But as far as you're concerned, I was thinking that you don't have to be any crazier than you want to be . . . that whoever, whatever the red-haired woman reminded you of, it doesn't make any difference. It's in the past, her and that person TJ. Maybe they had something to do with you once, but they're gone now." She moved closer to him. Her lips were brushing his shoulder as she said: "Can't you just decide to put them away, put them back wherever they've been all these years? Can't you just go back to being my Justin? A guy who's willing to spend a week on Maui making his wife really happy?"

Justin wanted nothing more than to make Amy happy. But on the day he had returned to the house on Lima Street, something changed in him, and it was making him increasingly intolerant of the silver spoon that Don Heitmann had jammed down his throat.

"I'm sorry, Ames," he said. "I'm not going. No Maui."

"Why?" Amy looked genuinely puzzled. "Why is my father's generosity such a problem for you?"

Justin realized that if someone sitting next to him at a ball game or an airport had asked him that question, he would have no problem saying: "I have a rich father-in-law who treats me and my wife and child like we're a wholly owned subsidiary. I went along with it because I wanted my wife to be happy. But now for some reason, I can't do it anymore. I need to find my own place in the world. And I'll never be able to do that if I'm always letting another man buy me out of it."

It was a simple truth he could have told to any stranger. But he couldn't tell it to Amy, because he knew every inch of her, every curve, every smooth plane, every secret place from which silky blond hairs sprang. Because they shared a child, and a home, and a bed. Because she was his woman. Because she was the love of his life.

To tell Amy the truth would be to risk losing her, and Justin knew he couldn't survive that. So he pulled her closer and said: "We got off the subject. Tell me about being in the shower and the connection you made between World Craziness and what's going on with your crazy husband."

Amy didn't cuddle against him as she usually did; she stayed sitting upright, leaving a little distance between them. "I was just thinking," she said. "You know, about the bad things in life. And I realized that from the very beginning there's been a map. Starting with the Bible, the Old Testament. There was the flood, then Noah and the rainbow. And the whole story of Christ, the Crucifixion and then the Resurrection. Then all through history, the same thing. The Dark Ages and the Renaissance. Hitler and the Holocaust, then D-day. Communism, then the Berlin Wall comes down. Segregation, then Martin Luther King and the first black person ever to be secretary of state. It's always been there, the map to the way life works out. There's always evil but it never actually wins. It has its moment, but it always gets pushed back by something good." Amy stopped and looked at Justin. "I wanted to tell you about that. I thought maybe it would help."

Justin was watching flickering shadows from the firelight play across the ceiling. "Amy. Before the rainbow, the flood wiped out everything and there are still a hell of a lot more black guys in the slammer than in the White House."

"Well, you know what?" Amy got up from the sofa and angrily hit the wall switch, blasting the room with light. "You're not a black guy and you're not in the slammer and you haven't been wiped out by a flood. You're a guy with a great life and a few odd memories, and there's no reason we can't go to Hawaii and make my father happy. What good is it doing for you to sit around here being tormented? I've got news for you, Justin . . . you're wallowing. And it's getting old. I'm tired of it."

To Justin, Amy's statement sounded petulant and spoiled, as if she was refusing to have compassion for what he was going through. He was hurt, and the hurt flamed into anger. "Well I've got a suggestion for you," he said. "The next time you're standing around in the shower, revving up to think some deep thoughts, you might want to run a quick Google search . . . Try 'Self-Centered Daddy's Girl.' It'll be a real eye-opener."

Justin grabbed the remote to turn up the volume on the TV and block out the noise and the chaos—the sounds of Amy storming up the stairs and the rain pounding on the roof and a child's voice endlessly repeating, "Do I know my name? Yes, I do. Yes, I do. My name is Justin. And my name is Fisher, too . . ."

*

The storms were over. The rain was gone. Southern California was itself again. Pretty women in shorts and jogging gear had emerged from under raincoats and umbrellas to resume their parade on Santa Monica Pier. Just below them, Justin and Ari were descending a flight of concrete steps that led from the boardwalk to the sand. It was a Monday morning and the beach was almost deserted.

Ari had a deep tan and was wearing loose-fitting slacks and a golf shirt. "Bermuda was fantastic," he was saying; "L.A., not so good. Got back last night and found our whole downstairs full of mud. My wife's going to have to take the baby and stay with my mother. How about you? Everything hold together okay?"

"Yeah," Justin said. "More or less."

Ari glanced at Justin. "Okay. I'm thinking maybe that's enough chitchat. Talk to me about what's been going on."

Justin followed as Ari walked over to a shuttered lifeguard tower. They sat at its base, both of them looking out at the ocean. "When we talked the last time," Ari said, "you'd seen a red-haired woman. At your hotel. And you had the feeling she was, or perhaps represented, TJ's mother." Ari waited. It was obvious that he was trying to gauge Justin's reaction. "You told me it rattled you, because you could recognize his mother, but you couldn't remember who TJ was."

"That's not exactly true," Justin said.

"What part of it don't I have right?" Ari asked.

"You have it all straight. That's what I told you. But I don't think it's true that I don't know who TJ is." Justin was enveloped in cold, but he knew it had nothing to do with the temperature on the beach. It was emanating from some internal place, somewhere lifeless and bereft.

"Tell me what you mean," Ari said. "Why isn't it true that you don't know who TJ is?"

"Because when I saw the woman in the hotel, it wasn't the same as remembering someone I had known from the outside, the way I would remember a friend or a neighbor or something like that," Justin said. "It was a feeling of knowing her from the inside, from a place that was intimate. I knew her as if I had been a part of her. I knew how she smelled . . . fresh, like lilacs. And how her hands felt . . . that they were soft and cushy and the palms were this pale pink color. The tops of her hands were smooth and rounded, like pillows. And I could feel how warm the place was at the base of her neck where it went down to her shoulder. I could feel the warmth of it on my cheek. And I know the vibration of her voice."

"The vibration of her voice?" Ari spoke softly, the way he would have spoken if Justin had been asleep and he hadn't wanted to wake him.

"I could feel it on my ear. The vibration." Justin leaned back against the wood of the lifeguard tower. It was cool, slightly damp, and veined with sand. He closed his eyes and listened for the vibration of that soft murmuring voice. He couldn't make out what it was saying, but he could feel himself being caressed by a gentle hand. He was nestled in a place of perfect safety. Slowly, he began to hear the words hiding in the whispers—simple and comforting, like the feel of a string of wooden beads worn smooth by touch and time. "Oh how I love my TJ. Oh how I love my baby."

Justin lingered for a moment in this strange place—the place where he was so lovingly held in the arms of a red-haired mother. After a while, the sensation slipped away. But the knowledge it left was inescapable. "I don't know who I really saw at the hotel," he told Ari. "But I know who I *thought* I saw."

"Who?" Ari's voice was almost inaudible above the breaking of the waves.

"I thought I saw my mother. A mother I didn't know I had. Until now."

"And how do you know it now?"

"I just do. I know it. I know her. I know how it felt to be held in her lap." Justin turned to look at Ari. "I know that I loved her."

"Justin, when you called me from the hotel, in your message you said that when you saw the red-haired woman you knew who TJ's mother was."

"Right."

"So what are you telling me now?"

Another chill passed over Justin. "I'm telling you I was TJ and that the woman was my mother."

"But if you began as Justin Fisher," Ari said, "the Justin Fisher who grew up on Lima Street, whose parents were Caroline and Robert, and you're here now and you're Justin Fisher, then where's TJ?"

"I'm not sure where he is," Justin said. "But I know he's looking for me."

*

After his meeting with Ari, Justin had decided not to go to work. He'd headed up the coast and turned inland. He'd spent hours driving in the hills above the little town of Ojai, trying to piece together the mystery of TJ and the red-haired woman.

And now he was coming into a house that seemed unnervingly quiet. It was almost six, around the time when Amy and Zack should be in the kitchen—Zack in his high chair, Amy feeding him his dinner while silly kid songs were blaring from the sound system. Instead, there was silence.

Last night, Justin had slept on the sofa, and he'd left the house before Amy had come downstairs this morning. He'd wanted to avoid the ongoing fight about the Hawaii trip.

It was only now, as he was walking into an empty kitchen, that he came to an odd realization. He'd had not a single thought of Amy or Zack for the entire day. He had forgotten them, and now it was as if they'd disappeared.

Justin was suddenly desperate to find Amy. Her name came out of him in a hoarse shout. As he ran into the living room, she was coming in from the patio, holding a teddy bear and a tiny pair of sneakers. Seeing her filled him with an incredible sense of relief. "Amy," he said. "You're here."

"Not for long. Daddy's having a car pick him and my mother up and then they're coming for us. They'll be here any minute, and I still don't have all of Zack's things packed." Amy's tone was careful and controlled.

"What? Why are you packing?"

"Hawaii. It's my father's birthday, remember? The plane leaves in two hours. Do you want me to throw some things in a bag for you?" Amy quickly went up the stairs.

Justin followed her and pulled her to a stop just outside their bedroom door. "But I told you. I can't do it. I can't go. Not until we get things worked out, until I can talk to you and explain."

Amy stared him down. "It's my father's birthday. Nothing you can say will make me believe we have to spoil it for him. You're being a prick, Justin." She wrenched free of his grasp. "My first choice is for you to come with us. But either way, Zack and I are going."

She moved toward the bedroom. Justin blocked her path. "We

need to work this out, Amy. This thing with your father, it's got to change."

"Justin, either get packed or get out of my way." She shoved past him. In the same instant, the doorbell rang.

As he stood in the bedroom doorway, Justin watched Amy go out onto the balcony and lean over it. Then he saw her blow a kiss. And he heard her call down to the waiting limousine: "I'll be right there, Daddy!"

Caroline and Robert

*

It was just after ten-thirty in the morning and already it was over.
Caroline was back in the house on Lima Street.

They had left less than an hour and a half ago, the six of them,
in Robert's Toyota, rolling out of the driveway under a blue sky
ribboned with snow-white clouds. Robert was at the wheel, Caroline beside him, and Julie and Lissa in the backseat, wedged
between Robert's parents. To anyone giving them a quick glance,
they would have looked like a family beginning a casual morning
outing—heading, perhaps, to a late breakfast or to a shopping
mall. But upon closer inspection, the Fishers presented a strange
tableau.

Lissa and Julie were pressed tightly together—unnaturally
still, with the look of spellbound children caught in a dark fairy
tale. Their matching navy blue coats were immaculate. Their hair
was perfectly smooth. Their eyes were downcast, unfallen tears
suspended on their lashes.

Robert's mother had an air of disarray, as if she had dressed in
a panic, or a fury. Her face was parchment white against the

somber dark of her clothes. Her eyes were only half-open, swollen and red-rimmed. Every few moments, she would glance at Robert's father and he would look up and hold her gaze, as if he'd been waiting for her to turn in his direction, as if he was on the verge of saying something. But then he would seem to lose his nerve and look down at his hands. They were resting on his knees, roving the fabric of his trouser legs in tight, trembling circles.

After a while, he would look up again, toward the front seat, where Robert and Caroline were.

Robert was gripping the steering wheel with a peculiar ferocity. His expression was closed and marble-hard. Caroline's expression, on the other hand, was as undefended as an open wound. She had the look of someone who was seeing indescribable horror.

When Robert had stopped the car at their destination, he came around to the passenger door and opened it. Caroline sat motionless. She left him no option but to lift her out of her seat.

Robert was forced to move her across the gravel parking lot in the same way he might have moved a lifeless mannequin—by holding her around the waist and raising her slightly off the ground.

Robert's parents and the girls followed as Robert maneuvered Caroline through a haphazard arrangement of low headstones and modest grave markers. Their progress was slow. The ground was an uneven mottle of frostbitten grass and cold, hard-packed earth.

As Robert and Caroline finally came to the far edge of the cemetery and Caroline saw the tiny casket waiting to be lowered into the ground, a wail came out of her so guttural and raw that it sounded as if it had been uttered by a wild animal. At the sound of Caroline's scream, Robert's mother shrieked and collapsed against his father.

"What's wrong with Mommy and Grandma?" Lissa whispered.

Julie looked toward Justin's coffin. It was silver-colored and little, blanketed with a spray of red carnations. "It's because Justin is dead," she said. "And now he has to be in that box and stay in the ground forever and never come home with us again."

Lissa grabbed Julie's hand, squeezing hard enough to make it hurt. "That's a lie," Lissa shouted. "Justin is an angel now and angels don't stay in the ground. They go to heaven and they live there forever." Lissa glared at Julie. "Say it. Justin isn't dead. He's an alive angel. Say it!"

"Justin's an angel," Julie said.

"Angels are just like people." Lissa was crying now. "They need their families to love them. So we're never going to forget Justin. We're going to love him always."

"We're going to love him always," Julie whispered. "I promise."

And then the blank-faced minister standing on the other side of the open grave said the Lord's Prayer and made the sign of the cross and commended Justin's soul to God.

Robert lifted Caroline into his arms and carried her back toward the car. His mother followed them. His father retrieved a carnation that had fallen from Justin's coffin. None of the adults noticed Julie trailing after Lissa. Lissa was walking toward the minister.

"I brought this for my brother, so he could have a friend." Lissa took a small frog from her pocket. "When Justin gets to heaven, could you ask God to give it to him, please?"

The girls then turned and ran past the coffin, fixing their gazes high, not wanting to see the darkness at the bottom of their brother's open grave. Justin's funeral was over.

Now Caroline, Robert, the girls, and Robert's parents were back on Lima Street.

Upstairs in the bathroom, Caroline was still in her coat, standing at the sink, holding a glass under the open faucet. Water was cascading over the sides of the glass. The cuff of her coat sleeve was soaked, the wool sagging, heavy and cold against her wrist.

The bathroom held the scent of Robert's shaving cream and of the oatmeal soap that Lissa and Julie had used when they had taken their baths earlier in the morning. On a row of yellow porcelain hooks there were damp towels, dangling and crooked. Caroline lifted her free hand, meaning to straighten them. But her gesture evaporated and there was a loud shattering bang. She had let the overflowing glass drop from her other hand and smash into the sink. The sound echoed for an instant. Then everything went quiet again, and Caroline took a bottle of Valium from the medicine cabinet and left the bathroom.

In the bedroom, the air was overheated and stale, but Caroline couldn't seem to think of how to open the window. She fell onto the unmade bed and settled facedown.

Several of Robert's hairs were caught in the stitching at the edge of the blanket. The sight of them made her dizzy and sick to her stomach. She rolled away, shook several pills from the Valium bottle, and swallowed them dry. She was looking toward the open door of the closet.

A rounded shape was huddled in the shadows on the floor, against the back wall. Before she got up from the bed, long before she reached into the closet and closed her hand around it, she knew what it was. It was Bunny, Justin's favorite stuffed animal.

On the morning Robert had taken him away, Justin had been playing hide-and-seek with the girls. The closet was his favorite hiding place, and it had been from there that Robert had gathered him up and carried him out of the house for what was to be their first father-son adventure.

Robert's anger over Caroline's infidelity had run wild in the days immediately after Justin's fall. But then abruptly—by what seemed to be a supreme act of will—Robert had become calm, and solicitous of Caroline. He told her he didn't want their marriage to end and he announced that he was, at last, going to spend time with Justin. He was taking him camping. Caroline's happiness had been indescribable.

She had spent days packing supplies and camping gear while she explained to Justin about all the fun he and Daddy were about to have.

Robert, too, had been eager to make the trip a success; he had been so concerned with the details that the night before he and Justin were to leave, he woke Caroline out of a sound sleep to sign emergency medical forms. She had groggily, and happily, scrawled her name below Robert's on the signature line; then they had made love.

Caroline picked Bunny up from the floor of the closet and held him close to her face. She inhaled Justin's scent, and the guttural wail that had come out of her in the cemetery came out of her again.

In the backyard, Julie and Lissa were poised at the top of the slide that was attached to their swing set. They heard Caroline's wail, looked up toward the bedroom window, and exchanged nervous glances.

Julie scrambled down the slide. "I don't want to play here anymore. Let's go to the park."

Lissa looked toward the house, hesitating. "We're not supposed to go to the park alone."

Julie had already run out of the yard. Another keening wail was coming from the upstairs bedroom. Lissa leapt from the slide and dashed toward the open gate, running full tilt past the back door of the house. On the other side of the door, in the kitchen, Robert and his father were at the table.

Robert was methodically peeling the label from an empty beer bottle, arranging the shreds in a tidy pyramid on the tabletop. Caroline's muffled cries could clearly be heard coming from the bedroom above.

Robert's father was holding the fallen carnation he'd retrieved from Justin's graveside, slowly turning it between his thumb and forefinger. "Go see to your wife, Robert."

Robert put the beer bottle down but didn't get up from his chair. "I will. In a minute."

His mother was at the stove. She was stirring a pot of soup with an old wooden spoon; its once-sturdy handle had been worn thin in the preparation of hundreds of meals, all of them now consumed and long forgotten. Another wailing scream came from the upstairs bedroom. The spoon clattered to the floor and snapped in two.

There was an edge of hysteria in Robert's mother's voice as she said: "Everything is breaking apart. Everything's dying, and I can't bear it."

Robert's father rounded his fingers over the wilted carnation and crushed it. "What the hell were you thinking, boy? What kind of idiot father takes a three-year-old on a goddamned camping trip?"

Robert's answer was furiously quick. "You used to take Tom and me camping all the time!"

"Not when you were barely out of diapers," the old man roared. "And not to goddamned Nevada. Not to the goddamned desert!"

"Why did you go so far away, Robert?" All of his mother's artifice was gone. Her confusion was genuine. "I don't understand. If you wanted to take him camping, all you had to do was drive up to Angeles Crest. The forest is right there. What would it have taken? Forty minutes, maybe less?"

These were questions Robert had been careful to answer already. He had explained every detail of the story, first in the telephone message he left for his brother, Tom, and then in the one he'd left for his parents. Tom had called back, making a point of speaking only to Caroline, sobbing as he conveyed his condolences, but asking very few questions. Robert's parents had been a different matter. Their questions had been endless.

Now he could see that the questions would keep coming, that he would have to answer them again and again. He took his time collecting the beer bottle and its shredded label from the tabletop. After he had finished, he said: "Mom, I told you why I went to Nevada. An old fraternity brother of mine lives there now. He was taking his son camping. He and I hadn't seen each other in years. We thought it would be fun for us and our kids to get together. You know, a nice father-son thing. I didn't take Justin out there for him to get bitten by a snake, it just happened."

"How does something like that 'just happen'?" Flecks of the ruined carnation flew from his father's fist as it hit the tabletop. "Why weren't you keeping an eye on him? And why didn't you get him to a hospital, for Christ's sake?"

"I've *told* you. Don't you fucking listen?" Robert said. "We were out in the middle of nowhere. By the time we found a hospital, it was too late."

His mother wrapped her arms around him and whispered: "Oh, my poor Robert." Her cloying closeness was smothering him.

"What are you talking about, woman? 'Poor Robert'?" The old man was bellowing. "If 'Poor Robert' hadn't bungled things from beginning to end, your grandson would be alive right now."

"That's right," Robert shot back. "I'm the reason he's gone. Me. All my doing."

"Robert, no. It's not your fault. It was an accident." His mother was groping for him again. He pushed her into a chair, then leaned in close. His voice was a furious whisper. "Shut up," he said. "You don't know what the hell you're talking about."

Robert walked away, then came back and briefly touched his mother's shoulder in an awkward caress.

There was nothing more he could explain.

Justin had been the embodiment of Caroline's infidelity and the living proof of Robert's inability to keep her from it.

Robert believed he'd had no choice in what he'd done. He could not have imagined staying in this house with Justin in it; nor could he conceive of going away from Lima Street and losing his daughters. But, above all, he could never—ever—think of leaving Caroline.

*

Rum and Cokes in slender glasses. A champagne flute filled with
fresh lemonade. A polished wooden bowl full of macadamia nuts.
An assortment of French cheeses served on a length of cobalt blue
tile. This had become their habit over the last four weeks—a
ritual—as Amy and her parents gathered each evening to watch
the sunset.

Amy was carrying the tray out onto the balcony; her father was
already reaching for his rum and Coke. "The islands agree with
you, kiddo. You look relaxed."

"It's Maui, Daddy. How could I not be?" Amy carried her
lemonade to the balcony rail. The evening breeze was warm, and
sweet with the smell of ginger and frangipani. To Amy, it had a
visceral sensuality. It made her want to run free on the beach, and
want to be touched. It made her want Justin.

She had come to Hawaii intending to leave in a week and had
stayed for a month. At first she'd been too angry even to speak to
Justin, angry enough to entertain the idea of never speaking to him
again. Now she was missing him. She wanted to go back to their

life. But she'd been away so long that she was separated from Justin in every sense of the word.

"Hey, pumpkin," her father was saying. "I got an idea I need to talk to you about."

Amy took a swallow of lemonade. "An idea, Daddy? Or a done deal?" She was cranky, eager for this trip to end and give her the excuse she needed to call Justin and tell him she was coming home.

"I want to talk about this before your mother gets out here. Be a good girl. Sit." Her father pulled an empty chair close to his. When Amy didn't move, he narrowed his eyes and shaded them with his hand. "You're being a brat, making me stare into the sun for no good reason." The sun's fading rays were as mild as a milk bath. She knew her father wasn't suffering. But she understood what he expected—for her to do as she'd been told.

After an irritated silence, her father said: "I bought your mother a house here. It's a surprise and I want you to help with the decorating and the furniture and all that other froufrou crap women need when they get a new place."

"You bought a house on Maui? Why?"

"The other day we saw this 'Open House' sign and we went in, and I could tell right away she was crazy about it. So I figured, What the hell? This way, the whole family's got a place we can come anytime we want. A great spot for Zack in the summer."

"But why do we have to do this now?" Amy was stunned. She needed to get home. She had been gone too long. Justin was slipping away; she could feel it. "I . . . I thought we decided we were going home next week."

"Little girl, I don't know of any pressing reason you have to be back in L.A. Do you?" This wasn't a question. It was an ultimatum. Her father didn't wait for an answer. He simply took her hand, kissed it, and went into the house.

Amy sat for a minute, then glanced at the back of her hand, as if she expected to see a mark there. She could see nothing. The sun was going down. It was already getting dark.

*

In Hawaii, Amy and her parents usually frequented restaurants with elegant menus and staggering prices. But today, Amy and her mother and Zack were in a waterfront fish house in a spot they rarely visited, the village of Lahaina; it was far too egalitarian for Linda's tastes. It was the sort of place where discount coupons were honored, where Hawaii was silk-screened onto peel-off tattoos and pineapple-shaped coffee mugs and "one size fits all" T-shirts. Linda had begun as a member of the tourist class, but she'd come into blossom as the wife of a jet-setter, and had adjusted her tastes accordingly.

She laughed as Zack banged on the tray of his high chair and howled with frustration. The floor beneath his perch was a litter of fallen Cheerios and soggy crackers. "Zack darling, you are expressing my sentiments exactly. That's why you and I are getting out of here right now." As she was saying this, Linda was reading a text message on her phone. "It seems the lovely Willow Chase is running late and won't be here for another twenty minutes."

Amy gathered up her purse and Zack's diaper bag. "No. No way, Mother. She's already kept us waiting almost an hour." Amy, like Zack, was feeling tired and frayed.

Linda was still looking at the text. "She apologizes for asking us to meet her in this dump, but apparently it's halfway between her office and her next appointment." Linda glanced up and laughed. "Willow Chase. What a great name for a decorator. Want to bet she made it up?"

"Mother, Zack needs a nap. So please, just get your purse and your blueprints and all the other stuff that's spread all over this table, and let's get out of here, okay?"

"Darling, I'm taking Zack out of here right now." Linda took the diaper bag from Amy. "I'm late for the contractor. But I really do need those fabric swatches from Willow today. So be an angel and wait for her. Zack can come with me and nap at the house while I chat with Bob the Builder. Do you need money, Amykins? For a cab or whatever?" Linda scooped Zack out of the high chair, then dropped a sheaf of twenty-dollar bills on the table.

Amy shoved the money away, scattering it across the tabletop. "I'm not 'Amykins.' I was Amykins when I was six."

"Darling, are we fighting? If we are, you're going to have to give me some help getting up to speed, because I don't know what we're fighting about."

"We're fighting about the fact that you're waltzing out of here and telling me to wait around for your decorator and take a cab home. You didn't even bother to ask whether or not that works for me. All you wanted to know was how much cash it would take to get it done."

Linda collected the money and quietly put it into Amy's purse. "You still haven't called Justin, have you?"

"No, Mother, I haven't." Amy was annoyed. Her reply had been loud—loud enough to make several people in the restaurant turn to look in her direction. "I thought we were going home this week. I was waiting till we got back, so I could talk to Justin in person. Then all this stuff with the new house came up. And boom, just like that, we're staying. And we don't even know for how long."

"It's not your house, pumpkin. There's no reason you have to stay."

"That's a load of crap." Amy had lowered her voice to a whisper, but the intensity in it was fierce.

"Amy, you're misbehaving." Linda settled Zack on her hip and gestured toward the roll of blueprints on the table. "Please get those and carry them to the car for me. I really need to get going."

Her mother's exit was subdued, elegant, accomplished with a graceful nod and a quick smile. Amy's reaction was complicated: a blind intersection of emotion—a collision of frustration and envy. Linda had the capacity to stand back while others flailed and raged; she responded to outpourings of raw emotion with cool, distanced composure. Amy resented this. It made it seem as if her mother never cared enough about anything to fight over it. And Amy's stay on Maui had left her spoiling for a fight.

As she moved her chair away from the table, preparing to follow her mother out of the restaurant, Amy saw a man at the far end of the bar watching her. He was of medium height, slim, with a golden-brown tan. He had sleepy almond-shaped eyes and what Amy had always though of as "poet hair"—dark, wavy, and of a length that brushed the base of his shirt collar. For an instant, she thought she knew him but then realized that what she knew was the look of him; he resembled someone she had once been in love with, a boy she'd almost married.

The man at the bar gave her a slow, teasing grin. She looked away. When she looked back, he was in laughing conversation with the bartender.

Amy grabbed up the blueprints and the money and the scattered baby toys—the warring totems of her life—and quickly walked toward the door.

The sidewalk outside the restaurant was filled with a river of slow-moving pedestrians—sauntering honeymoon couples, groups of giggling college girls admiring their own reflections in store windows, and old people standing stock-still and taking tentative licks at cups of sweet Hawaiian shave ice. At every turn,

Amy was being forced to weave past, and sidle by, and push her way through. And with each frustrated step, the intensity of the irritation she was feeling toward her mother was being ratcheted higher.

When Amy arrived at the corner where her mother's Land Rover was parked, Linda was leaning into the car, buckling Zack into his baby seat, her every movement smooth and serene. It made Amy want to scream. She grabbed her mother's arm and dragged her away from the car. As she did, she understood that she would lose control while Linda would remain cool and composed. But this was the dance she'd always done with her mother and she didn't know how to stop.

Her voice was high and tight. "What did you mean when you said there's no reason I have to stay here, Mother? You know Daddy asked me to help with the new house. What was I supposed to do? Come on, tell me! What choice did I have?"

"Amy, have I ever shown you my favorite cartoon?" Linda said. "Two ancient men in a jail cell, one saying to the other, 'I've got good news and bad news. The good news is, the door's open. The bad news is, it always has been.' " Linda took the blueprints and the toys out of Amy's hands. "The door's open, my darling. You can walk through it anytime you want."

"Just say 'No thanks'? To Daddy? Anytime I want? What a crock. When have you ever said no to him?"

"We're married. We have a contract; every married couple does. My arrangement with your father is my arrangement; it has nothing to do with you." Linda took Amy's face between her hands and said, "If you want to go home to your husband, pumpkin, go home."

"How can I? The new house is Daddy's present to us. You know what it's like when he thinks somebody's tossing one of his presents back at him. It hurts his feelings. It's like he's a big tender-hearted kid."

"Or maybe he's a bully who likes getting his own way." The comment was delivered blandly, without rancor or judgment.

"Is that what you believe about Daddy?" Amy was uncomfortable. She wanted to be able to love her father without question.

"It isn't important what I think, darling girl. I've struck my bargain with the devil. Now you need to strike yours."

"It's like you're trying to make this all Daddy's fault," Amy said. "We wouldn't even be having this conversation if Justin hadn't been such a prick about this trip."

"The prick is in the point of view, baby. Maybe Justin's a prick, or maybe he's a decent guy who wants to call his own shots. Bottom line? It doesn't matter. Your husband has run out of patience with your father, and you have to choose a side."

Linda put her arms around Amy and held her. "Sometimes, pumpkin," she said, "life's a bitch."

After that, Linda had returned to the car and driven away. And Amy had returned to the restaurant—not because she wanted to sit and dutifully wait for the arrival of Willow Chase and the fabric samples, but because she didn't know where else to go.

Several busboys were at the table where she'd been before; they were mopping up pools of soggy crackers and spilled Cheerios. So Amy went to a table near the bar—a place that was polished and spotless.

She was opening her purse, searching for her phone, when a drink was placed in front of her. The click of the martini glass coming to rest on the brushed steel of the tabletop caused Amy to look up. What she saw was impossibly glamorous. The glass was exuberantly oversized, frosted with a glitter of ice, and filled with what looked like liquid satin. Suspended in the satin—on a curved, thread-thin length of silver—were three tiny perfectly matched olives.

"Vodka martini. I took a guess." It was the man Amy had seen at the bar earlier, the one who had been watching her. He smiled. "You looked like you could use a drink."

It didn't occur to Amy to be offended, or frightened. He seemed so familiar. "You look like someone I used to know," she told him.

"If I'd ever met you before, trust me, I'd remember." He extended his hand. "I'm Lucas."

When Amy had seen him earlier, she'd thought he looked like Ryan, a boy she had deeply loved. But now that they were only a few feet apart, she could see that he was smaller than Ryan, and not quite as handsome. But the resemblance was there; it made her feel as if she were in the presence of an old friend.

He sat down and moved his chair closer to hers. "Okay. On our planet, this is how we do it. I tell you my name, Lucas, and then you tell me your name. Which is . . ."

"Amy."

They shook hands. His skin was warm. His touch had the feel of a tempting question. As Amy pulled her hand away, he grinned at her and said, "How's the martini?"

She wasn't used to drinking during the day, and when she did, it was rarely anything stronger than wine. She could already feel the vodka slipping through her, gliding and flowing, bringing with it a strange sort of giddy relaxation. As she was saying "The martini is absolutely wonderful," she couldn't be sure, but it sounded as if she was slurring the word *absolutely*. It worried her for a moment, but only for a moment, because a man who looked like someone she'd once loved was smiling at her, and she was smiling back.

After Linda's decorator had come and gone, Lucas ordered more martinis, and when they had finished the second round of drinks, he offered Amy a ride home. As they walked across the parking lot toward his van, he explained that he worked at an orchid ranch.

When Amy slipped into the passenger seat, it was as if she had been delivered into the heart of an exotic garden. The van's entire cargo area was filled to overflowing with masses of orchids as vibrant and sensual as a symphony.

Lucas drove along a road that ran inland, a short distance from the ocean, and Amy held her hand out of the van window and trailed her fingers in the breeze while she told him about Ryan, the person he so much resembled. When Lucas asked why she hadn't married Ryan, she surprised herself by saying: "My father. And his fucking money." The statement surprised her.

But once she had spoken the truth, it was easy to tell the story behind it. Ryan had wanted to earn his own way and had balked at her father's insistence on paying for graduate school and buying Amy and Ryan a house. Amy's father had called Ryan "an arrogant little bastard." Ryan had stormed out, and Amy's father had begged her not to marry someone cold enough to deny a father the simple joy of caring for his only daughter.

Lucas had turned the van off the road and was parking it in a lush grove of trees as Amy was saying: "Ryan wanted me to come with him, but I just stood there, letting my father hold on to me. That was a terrible mistake."

A misty Hawaiian rain had begun to fall, and Lucas was leaning toward her, one hand stroking the back of her neck, the other already slipping under the hem of her skirt and slowly sliding along her thigh. His sleepy almond-shaped eyes were fixed on hers, holding her still, telling her he knew about the tingle he was stirring in her, the one that would soon begin to make her shudder and shift against the seat.

Rain was falling in soft curtains around the van, watering the light, turning it pale and evanescent, cocooning Amy and Lucas in a private place, humid and luxuriant—a bed of orchids.

He moved his hand from the back of her neck and let it slip around and slide down the center of her, tantalizing, slow. The skin on his fingertips was slightly calloused. His hand came to rest on her breast, cupping and cradling it. The intimacy of his touch startled her, brought her back to reality. It made her know that the only man she desired was Justin.

In that instant, all Amy wanted was to get out of the van, to get away from this groping stranger. But he was already covering her mouth with his and filling it with the foreign, bitter taste of his tongue.

She tried to jerk her head away. He refused to let her. He jammed her back against the seat and the edges of his teeth cut into her lip. The raw sting of it was frightening, and her instinct was to scream, but his open, sliding mouth was suffocating her.

The hand he had on her thigh clamped down with painful intensity, while the other was raking at her breast.

Then she felt his upper lip slip between her teeth and she bit into it. The coppery taste of his blood was on her tongue and he was rearing back, shouting: "You fucking cunt!" Suddenly, he was across her, throwing the door open and shoving her out of the van.

She landed, crumpled, on a patch of grass at the base of a tree. As he sped away, he tossed her purse out of the passenger-side window. The van fishtailed onto the wet road. For a moment, the tires were screaming and the engine was gunned and roaring.

And then he was gone, and the only sound was the murmur of the rain.

A long time passed before Amy moved. She was so frightened, she couldn't stand; her legs wouldn't hold her. There was no option but to crawl through the marshy grass toward the spot where, when her purse had landed, it had broken open and scattered its contents.

Heavy veils of rain were misting around her and when she finally found her cell phone, she was chilled and aching. She instinctively pressed the first button she touched.

The number was automatically dialed and rang twice before the person at the other end said hello. It was then that Amy realized she'd reached a number she hadn't consciously intended to call. There was a pause. Then, in a rush, before the connection could be broken, she said the thing she had needed to say for weeks.

"Justin. I love you. I want to come home."

Caroline and Robert

*

Almost two months had passed since Justin's funeral and it was April. Glorious California springtime.

Robert could hear Julie and Lissa in the front yard, playing a rowdy game filled with bursts of laughter. Through the living room window, he could see that Caroline was on the porch. In a wicker rocking chair. Sitting expressionless and still. The youthfulness and openness that had always illuminated her before were gone. She was like a lovely room abruptly boarded up and closed off—an elegant, empty space to which Robert no longer had any access.

It had been weeks since the last of the winter logs had been burned. Robert was cleaning the fireplace, depositing the dead ash into an old bucket. Each small shovelful had a stale, cold smell to it.

The look of the ash, its odd feathery density, and the enigmatic sighing of it as it sifted down upon itself, was making him queasy. These were the same sights and sounds that had come to him on the day that he had last moved ashes. A day he had spent in a roadside cabin thousands of miles away from Lima Street. The day he had filled Justin's cremation urn.

The memory of what he had done on that day—and of his pitiful confession of it to Caroline—sent jolts of shame through Robert.

It had been his intention never to reveal, to anyone, the truth about the places he'd gone and the awful act he had committed in the hours before filling the urn.

But on the morning of Justin's funeral, Robert's resolve had been weakened by the overwhelming depth of Caroline's devastation. It had been staggering. He had called Dr. Johannsen and asked him to bring sedatives.

In spite of the medication, Caroline's anguish continued to rage unabated. She stopped speaking, stopped making any sound at all. She took scissors to her hair and chopped it ragged. Her movements were so freighted with the weight of heartbreak, so clumsy and slow, that she had been unable to dress herself. And her tears poured in continuous silent streams.

By the time they were leaving for the funeral, Robert was terrified. In eradicating Justin, he had wanted to punish Caroline, but he saw that what he had done had come close to killing her.

At the funeral Caroline seemed to be in a trance, and after they returned home, she went upstairs, alone, refusing any help or comfort from Robert.

He had remained in the kitchen with his parents.

And then the house began to fill with a sound so chilling that it could have been echoing from the gates of hell.

It was coming from the master bedroom, from Caroline. She was screaming like an animal. The noise had no sanity to it; it was pure deranged agony.

When he heard her screams, Robert knew Caroline would not

survive the full brunt of the vengeance he'd inflicted on her. He clearly understood that he would no longer be able to keep his secret. With the image of Justin's open, hastily dug grave still fresh in his mind, Robert had walked out of the kitchen.

As he climbed the stairs and entered the bedroom, he knew the only thing left to him—his only atonement—was to find a way to save Caroline, and to keep saving her, for the rest of her life.

He saw that she was still in her coat; one of the sleeves was soaked, so wet that it was dripping. She was crouched on the floor near the closet, clutching a toy—a white chenille-covered rabbit.

She slowly turned in Robert's direction and opened her mouth in readiness to scream, but before she could, he said: "I lied to you. Justin didn't die in Nevada. I never went to Nevada."

Caroline swayed backward, as if she had been punched. She again opened her mouth, but this time there was no scream; there was only the sound of her gasping for air, trying to ask a question she couldn't even form.

Robert knelt in front of her; he was wracked with guilt and anxiety. The voice that came out of him was so shattered, he didn't recognize it as his own.

He began by telling Caroline that Justin's ashes weren't in the urn they had buried at the funeral. Then he revealed the truth about the ashes, and about the urn.

Caroline fixed her eyes on him and never moved them.

As Robert told his story, the awfulness of what he had done took possession of him and it felt as if he wasn't simply recounting his actions; he was reliving them.

In saying the words, he was carried back into that moment when a large man in a black suit had been in the act of opening a double-doored mahogany cabinet and Robert had been stretching past him to grab a plain pewter cylinder from among several others that were on a top shelf. The man immediately stopped him.

"Those contain unclaimed remains, sir. Our available urns are here, on the lower shelves."

"Then that one." Robert pointed toward a small bronze-colored urn.

"Are you sure you don't want me to make the transfer for you, sir?"

"No. I'll do it myself. I want to bring my son's ashes back to my wife in something nicer than the cardboard box they gave me at the other funeral home, where he was cremated. But I didn't think of it until a few minutes ago, when I was on my way to the airport. I don't know why."

"People don't think straight when they're grieving." The man snipped the price tag from the urn. "Hard to be far from home and have your child up and die, the way you say yours did, in the time it takes for a sled to overturn. You said your boy died here, but you're from California?"

"Yes. I . . . uh . . . I'd brought him here to . . . to meet my relatives." Robert felt a twitch of anxiety. He was afraid he was bungling the lies he had been telling. "It's a long story. I really need to get going." Robert tossed several bills onto the counter; they added up to far more than the price of his purchase. He grabbed the urn and ran for the door.

Outside, the sky was low and gray, like a curving expanse of rolled steel. Frigid winter air was pushing through the layers of his clothing and chilling him to his core. His coat, the only one he had brought with him, was meant for February in California and he was the width of a continent away from there.

Robert was trying not to think about the terrible thing he'd done to Justin in this cold, alien place. He was turning his attention to something that, earlier in the day, he'd torn out of a phone book—an advertisement for roadside rental cabins.

An hour later, he was signing a motel guest register. The

woman behind the desk was glancing toward the rental car that was parked in the dusty driveway just outside the door. "By any chance . . . you hidin' a body in that car of yours?"

Robert's head jerked up. She had startled him. She was immensely fat and a deep chuckle rumbled out of her. "Honey, you look about ready to wet yourself." She tapped Robert's wedding ring. "Relax. You're not the first married man ever to slip in here in an 'empty' car askin' for privacy. Usually it means they've got a little somethin' crouched down in the backseat they don't want their wife and family to know about." She picked up the registration card and grinned. "Am I right, *Mr. Thomas,* or am I right?"

Robert's mouth had gone dry. It took him a moment before he could speak. "Yes. I guess you could say it's something like that."

Cabin number sixteen sat at the river's edge, dank and sagging, with a hazy grime on the windows and a burn mark where the triangular faceplate of a hot iron had scorched its imprint onto a faded throw rug. But Robert's attention went instantly and exclusively to the fireplace. It was the reason he had come.

There was no fireplace shovel but there was an empty soup can, abandoned on a shelf in the seedy kitchenette. Robert went immediately to work. It was cold in the cabin; there was no need to remove his coat. He opened the bronze urn and placed it on the floor beside him. Then he began using the soup can to ferry ash between the fireplace and the urn.

The ash had a stale, cold smell. The look of it, its odd feathery density, was making him queasy. It caused a shuddering moan to come out of him: wordless supplication, a primitive plea for forgiveness.

When he had completed filling the urn he fitted its cover into place and started toward the door of the cabin. But he stopped in mid-stride, suddenly unsure as to whether or not his work was finished. He moved the urn from his right hand to his left, testing the weight of it, trying to remember the feel of the cylinder he'd lifted from the shelf in the funeral home, the one that had contained actual cremation ashes. It seemed it had felt heavier than the one he was holding. His mind began to race: There were any number of variables to be accounted for, including the possibility that the cylinder had weighed more because it had contained the ashes of an adult, not the remains of a toddler. His instinct was to leave, to get back into the rental car and drive to the airport as quickly as possible. But he was being gripped by a fear that was edging into frenzy; he couldn't take the chance that the urn would give him away when he returned home.

As Robert put the urn on the floor, and grabbed the soup can, he was already running out of the cabin. Running toward a large tree near the riverbank—toward the wide circle of sandy soil at its base.

Later, when Robert drove past the motel office and pulled out onto the highway, he saw the fat woman at the desk switch on the VACANCY sign. He imagined her picking up a set of clean sheets and shambling down the dirt path toward cabin sixteen; and he knew what she'd discover when she arrived. In the middle of the floor, there was a chaotic spill of fireplace ash and riverbank sand riddled with the tracks of clawing fingertips. And near the door, there was a wash of fresh vomit.

After Robert had driven away from the cabins, he had gone to the airport and boarded a plane bound for California. During the flight, he had used the time to go over the story about the camping trip, and about Nevada being the site of Justin's death: the story he had told on the phone, at dawn yesterday, when he'd broken the news to Caroline—the same story he'd told his parents when he had called their home in Arizona.

After the flight landed, Robert had gone directly to Lima Street. He stood for a long time outside the front door of the house, holding his suitcase. Although its contents were minimal—some underwear, a shirt or two, a shaving kit, and the small ash-filled urn—the weight of it felt enormous.

Before he could gather the strength to reach for the latch, the door was swung open and a bolt of light shot across the porch. His mother was there, waiting for him. She and his father had driven all night; they had come to offer their consolation.

Almost simultaneously she was embracing and railing at him, sobbing and then screaming: "You have caused me to lose my grandson! I want an explanation!"

Robert had to edge past her to get into the house. "I already explained," he said. "It was an accident. Justin was bitten by a snake and I couldn't get him to a doctor in time." Then he quickly walked away from her and went into the kitchen.

When his mother followed him a moment later, her eyes immediately flickered over the scotch bottle that was in his hand. He tensed, waiting for a caustic comment. But she seemed preoccupied. She circled in front of him and said: "You're wearing slacks and a sports coat."

Her observation rocked him. For a panicked moment, he was certain he'd given himself away and that she knew there had been no camping trip.

"You look dressed up," his mother insisted. "Like you've been to a business meeting."

Robert's grip on the bottle tightened; he could feel the metal cap pressing hard against his palm. "I borrowed this stuff," he said. "I had to deal with the funeral home. The cremation. I didn't want to do it in camping clothes."

His mother seemed baffled. "Cremation! What cremation?"

"Justin's," Robert replied. "The snake venom, it's poison. The bruising and the disfiguration were awful. I didn't want Caroline to see him that way."

His mother sank into one of the wooden chairs at the kitchen table. "Oh God," she whispered.

She looked undone, and old. Seeing her that way devastated Robert. He sat on the floor in front of her, dropped his head into her lap, and began to cry. His mother made no move to comfort him. She pushed her way out of the chair and left him slumped against it, like a scorned penitent at a makeshift altar.

"I want a funeral," she said. "I want him buried."

Robert remained sitting on the floor, his hands covering his face. "I told you. He's been cremated."

With an iron-voiced determination, she said, "I don't care. I want a place on this earth for my grandson. You cannot erase that little boy, Robert. I will not allow it."

There was a silence, then the sound of shattering glass, and then another silence. Robert didn't have to look up to know what had happened. Before leaving the kitchen, his mother had smashed the scotch bottle into the sink.

Within hours, Robert had made hurried arrangements for a funeral.

Fred Bryant, the funeral director, considered him a friend; Robert had written the insurance policies on the mortuary for years. Fred's only thought was to make the situation as simple and easy as possible for Robert and Caroline.

The story of Justin's immediate cremation after dying from a snakebite was never questioned. The bronze urn that Robert had brought back as a prop to validate that story was never opened. It had gone from Robert's hands to Fred's, and then into a child-size silver coffin that had been swiftly sealed and blanketed with a spray of red carnations. No one, other than Robert, had known that the funeral was simply a palliative for a grieving mother and grandmother; an empty gesture for a little boy who had already been disposed of in a more careless, and much colder, way.

No one had known the truth about what Robert had done to Justin.

But now Caroline knew. Robert had just finished telling her the details of his crime. The knowledge that her little boy hadn't died in a desert, snakebitten and bruised, was the only comfort Robert could offer her.

For a long time Caroline continued to sit on the floor near the closet, saying nothing, running her fingers over the wet sleeve of her coat. When he could no longer stand the tension, Robert reached out and tried to hold her. She pushed him away and slowly struggled to her feet.

It was clear she was in shock, beyond rational thought. She started to leave the room, then stopped in the doorway. "When you did it, did he realize what was happening?" she asked. It was the first time she'd spoken since Robert had returned from taking Justin away. "Did he cry?"

"Yes, he cried." Robert's voice was quiet—so quiet that for a moment he thought Caroline hadn't heard him.

Then she said, "And you? Did you cry?"

"I cried afterward," Robert replied. He wanted to hold her. To tell her that what he had done had been done because he loved her, because he wanted her to belong solely to him, because without her he would not have a home, or his daughters. And without those things, he would be rudderless.

"It's cold back east this time of year," Caroline said. "Justin's alone. In the cold. He hated being cold. You should have taken his Winnie-the-Pooh blanket." She turned to Robert, drugged and unsteady. A wail came out of her as she said: "You bastard. You didn't take his blanket!"

"It doesn't make any difference." Robert said this as he was again reaching out for Caroline. "The blanket doesn't make any difference. He's all right now. I promise."

There had been tears in Robert's eyes as he was making that promise, tears that had felt hot and brackish and unclean.

And from that moment to this—from the day of Justin's funeral until now, for the past two months—Caroline had shunned Robert.

She had deliberately taken a part of her soul and locked it away. She had made herself—in some essential way—gone.

But in another, more pragmatic way, one that comforted Robert greatly, she had never left him at all. She had remained with him—silent and still—on Lima Street.

Robert set aside the bucket of ash. He looked toward the living room window and saw Caroline on the porch. She must have sensed him watching her. She glanced in his direction, then moved to a chair that was out of his line of sight.

He turned his attention back to the fireplace. He had scrubbed away every trace of ash and soot, every stain.

He picked up a copper vase that was new and flawless, filled with daffodils. He set it onto the bare, clean hearth, into the midst of a dazzling pool of sunlight.

Justin and Amy

*

He was home early. Amy was thrilled. But when she put her arms around him, she could feel the strange ambivalence that had taken root in Justin during their separation.

Every time they touched, she could feel him simultaneously yearning for her and guarding against her, as if her defection to Hawaii had cut into his soul and the wound was still dangerously raw.

"I have something to tell you," he said. He moved awkwardly out of Amy's embrace.

The look on his face sent chills through her. There was an unsettling expression in his eyes, as if he was seeing some dark thing recently emerged into light and uncomfortable with being there. It was so disturbing and so intense that Amy couldn't stay in the same room with it.

She went outside onto the patio and lit the logs in the fire pit. Then she sat on one of the chaise longues, braced herself, and waited for Justin to come out of the house.

She was steeling herself for the news that he'd been irreparably hurt by her time in Hawaii, and that he no longer wanted her. The thought was terrifying to Amy. To an equal extent, it was infuriating. She had given up something very precious in order to return to Justin, and now she was preparing for him to say he no longer loved her because she hadn't done it quickly enough.

She didn't want to be looking at him when he said it. When Justin walked out onto the patio, Amy turned away from the light of the fire pit and faced the darkness instead. She was expecting him to tell her things that would break her heart.

It was with startled, wide-eyed relief that she heard him say: "While you were gone, I spent a lot of time talking to Ari. I know some stuff about who TJ is, and about who the red-haired woman is. I need to tell you about it."

Amy immediately opened her arms to him and he lay down beside her. They gazed up at the night sky. It resembled the blank, silent landscape of a deep sleep. It was, Justin told her, much like the place in his mind from which the fragmented knowledge of TJ and the red-haired woman had emerged.

He said that the information was presenting itself to him in erratic bursts. In bits and pieces. Out of nowhere.

It was as if he were being granted skittish, fleeting access to the private lives of ghosts.

A room in a house. Shelves and shelves of books. The walls deep green and the crosspieces of the windows glistening white— like the snow falling outside. And Justin, little. Not yet school age. On a rag rug playing with a puppy. The fur black. The puppy's name Inky. And a toy train. Wooden. With a string to pull it by.

A book. Bright, extravagant pictures. The comforting cadence of nursery rhymes. And the red-haired woman's voice saying, "Come into my pahlah, said the spider to the fly."

The red-haired woman leaning over the edge of a deep, curving bathtub, reaching out to float a family of rubber ducklings through a sea of bubbles. The tops of her hands rounded, like pillows.

A quilt on a bed. Patterned in fields of blue-and-yellow pinwheels. The sensation of being tucked in, snug and safe. Above the bed, a slanted ceiling. Slatted wood. In the air between the bed and the ceiling—magic. The moon and stars. Silver. And dancing.

The red-haired woman. Her smell fresh, like new lilacs. The soft place at the base of her neck warm against Justin's cheek. The feeling of being curled in her lap and fitted against her. The creak of a rocking chair. And the sound of her voice. Hushed and vibrant: "Oh how I love my TJ. Oh how I love my baby." Serenity. Love. Perfect safety.

A table near a door. Dark wood. Curving legs and clawed feet. Always a canvas bag and a stack of books. The red-haired woman putting on her boots and scarf. The door opening, and a rush of cold. Her fiery red hair and pale skin. Her odd, clipped gait and sloping shoulders. Then the door closing again. And Justin asking where has Mommy gone, and a young female voice saying, "Where she always goes. To Wesley Anne."

"Those are the things I remember," Justin told Amy. "I know I lived in that house and she was my mother. She had the *ah* sound where the *r*'s should be when she said *parlor*. And my name was TJ and I loved her. And every day she left me to go to someone named Wesley Anne."

"Wesley Anne?" Amy shook her head, trying to make sense of it. "Are you sure? That's such a strange name."

"I know. But that's who she said she was going to see."

"The 'pahlah' thing," Amy said. "That sounds like maybe she was from Boston. And you said there was snow. Do you think that's maybe where you lived, Boston?"

"It's a possibility. But I don't know how to start figuring it out.

My name was TJ. My mother had red hair, and a friend named Wesley Anne. If that's all you have, where do you begin?"

"Are you sure her friend's name wasn't *Leslie* Anne?" Amy asked.

"No, I can hear it in my head, clear as a bell. It was *Wesley,* not Leslie. I'm positive."

Amy turned toward Justin. She wanted to see him. She wanted to be able to look into his eyes as she said: "I love you. I need you. And I never want to be without you."

She paused and looked away. She needed to find the words that would explain to Justin exactly what she had sacrificed for him. She wanted him to know that in coming home from Hawaii, she had defied her father; and in defying him, she'd been banished by him. As she had been leaving Maui, he'd told her: "Baby girl, you're gonna be sorry you did this." The statement had blended a father's unhappiness with a mobster's threat.

Later, as her mother had been gathering up Amy's luggage and preparing to carry Zack to the waiting taxi, Amy had been searching the villa for her father. When she went out onto one of the balconies, she saw that he was on the beach below. And when she called to him, he did something he had never done before: He turned his back on her. He turned his back and walked away.

As Amy had stood on that balcony in Hawaii, she'd felt heartbreak moving toward her with the same speed that her father was moving away.

Amy settled herself close against Justin and said: "I need you to be everything to me now. And I need me to be everything to you." Justin looked at her as if he wasn't sure he understood what she was trying to tell him. "I gave up my father for you," Amy said. When Justin still didn't seem to fully comprehend, she added, "You owe me for that. It's only fair."

Justin looked amazed, and immeasurably happy. "Ames, you

still want me? In spite of everything? In spite of all this craziness? You want me even though—"

Amy stopped him by putting her hand over his mouth. "Even though anything. I want you. All of you. Always," she said. "No matter what the craziness turns out to mean. No matter how weird or sick or scary it is. I don't care." She slid her hand away so she could kiss him. "I almost lost you. I was almost stupid enough to let my father come between us. But I didn't. And I don't want anything to ever come between us again."

She laid her head on Justin's chest, and after a while she fell asleep. But all through the night she was circling a dark border between dreams and nightmares.

*

"Every day? What kind of person would leave a baby alone every day to go hang out with some *friend*? That doesn't make any sense." Amy was saying this as she was stepping out of the shower.

Justin gave her a noncommittal shrug. He was shaving and she was hesitating at the shower door, waiting for him to stop, and to wrap her in a towel. It had been their rhythm for years. Whenever they were in the bathroom together and Amy stepped out of the shower, before she could reach for a towel, Justin would already have one in hand and be putting it around her. It had begun in the early days of their marriage and had, over time, grown to be an accustomed intimacy between them. To Amy, it was an affirmation of their closeness as a couple.

But Justin was preoccupied, almost oblivious to her, lost in the mystery of TJ and the red-haired woman. Amy leaned around him and took a towel from the rack. He rinsed his razor, then walked away.

When Amy came into the bedroom, Justin was already

dressed. She wanted desperately to connect with him, to engage him. "Are you sure that's what you remember her doing every day?" she said. "Leaving TJ to go hang out with some friend of hers?"

"Yeah." Justin was picking up his phone and wallet, slipping them into his pocket.

"And you're sure of the friend's name? You do know it's a really goofy name, don't you?"

"I know. But that's the name. Every day she took books and went out the door, and that's who she said she was going to see." Justin kissed Amy lightly on the cheek as he passed her. In the instant it took her to turn her head to kiss him back, he was gone.

The room was empty and at the same time ferociously occupied. The space around Amy had been emptied of Justin's presence, but it was full of the specters who had become his relentless companions—a lost boy named TJ, a red-haired woman, and a faceless entity called Wesley Anne.

Amy went to Justin's side of the bed. On the nightstand was an assortment of minor clutter—several discarded credit-card receipts, books on corporate management strategies, and a black leather-edged notepad. Justin had left his fountain pen lying across the top sheet of notepaper. Amy lifted the pen and studied what Justin had written. His handwriting was clean and bold, a confident flow of crisp block capitals. The notation contained only two words: "Wesley Anne," the odd, lunatic name that had been haunting Amy since Justin had first mentioned it to her last night.

She slipped into jeans and a sweater, and as she was leaving the bedroom she was murmuring to herself, "Wesley Anne. What kind of person is named Wesley Anne?"

Amy's arrival in the kitchen was greeted by a smile from Rosa and excited squeals from Zack. Rosa was wiping down the stove and Zack was near the breakfast bar, traveling around the base of one of the bar stools in slow, wobbling circles, cautiously propelling himself by hanging on to the legs of the stool as he took one tottering step after another.

Amy picked him up and covered his face with kisses. "Zack, you're amazing! You're an amazing boy."

As Rosa passed, she rubbed Zack's back. "You are going to be walking all by yourself any day now, aren't you *mijo?*"

The television was on. Rosa had been watching a morning talk show. But now it was gone, replaced by a newscast. Neither Amy nor Rosa enjoyed listening to the barrage of local and national mayhem. Rosa reached for the remote just as the aftermath of a fire at an East Coast strip mall was being reported. A middle-aged woman in a lumpy coat was on camera. "I can't believe it's gone," she was saying. "The whole mall. My beauty pahlah was in there. I been going to that place for twenty years."

Amy snatched the remote from Rosa, stopping her before she could change the channel. Amy's attention was fixed on the printed information at the bottom of the screen. It identified the fire's location as Portland, Connecticut.

"Connecticut!" Amy handed Zack to Rosa, grabbed the car keys, and ran for the back door. "Did you see that?" she was saying. "It's Connecticut!"

*

Less than half an hour later, Amy was in Justin's hotel, rushing toward his office.

She was short of breath as she burst through the door. "Wesley Anne," she said. "It isn't a person, it's a place."

Justin was signing letters. He stopped in mid-stroke.

"I figured it out." Amy was tingling with excitement. "Some

people in the central part of Connecticut have that same Bostony kind of sound when they say words like *parlor*. And you were a little kid when you heard the name Wesley Anne. Little kids misunderstand things they hear all the time. When I was little, I thought the Pledge of Allegiance was to the Republic of some guy named Richard Stanz . . . but what people were actually saying was 'to the Republic for which it stands.' "

"Okay. But what does that have to do with Connecticut and Wesley Anne?" Justin's smile made it clear he wasn't taking her seriously.

"Just listen," Amy insisted. "You said the red-haired woman had lots of books in the house, and that when she went to see Wesley Anne every day she always took books, right? Well, when most adults go somewhere every day like clockwork, they don't go to visit their friends. They go to their jobs."

Justin shrugged. "So maybe she worked for someone named Wesley Anne."

"No, I think she worked at some*place* named Wesley Anne." Amy's gaze was intense, and fixed on Justin. "After we graduated, my best friend in high school went to college in Connecticut. I went to see her all the time. Right in the center of Connecticut. A working-class place called Middletown. She went to Wesleyan University."

Justin's smile vanished. Amy had his full attention.

"Books all over the house," Amy said. "Books every day. Every day, Wesley Anne. I think the red-haired woman could have been a teacher, and she could have worked at Wesleyan. I think we've found the place where some of the answers might be hiding."

Caroline

*

The touching of Barton's lips to Caroline's cheek was as swift and light as the brush of an angel's wing. "Oh, Caro," he said. "I'm so sorry."

Barton had been walking across the park with Caroline, back toward the house on Lima Street. He had seen that her face was damp with tears and that she was unaware of it.

"This happens to me every once in a while." Caroline was embarrassed. "Tears just leak out of me without me knowing. Sometimes the girls have to tell me . . . 'You're leaking again, Mommy.' "

"I'm a priest. And I'm your friend. And I'm completely worthless to you." Barton walked a few steps away, let out a frustrated groan, and circled back. "I want to heal your hurt. And I don't know what to say to make it go away. What can I do, Caro? Please. Tell me how to help."

Barton's eyes were beautiful, changeable. Sometimes they appeared green, deeply flecked with golden brown. At other times the green receded and became burnished gold. In them now, Caroline was seeing the purity of Barton's love for her. Suddenly, she had the impulse to tell him the truth about Justin. The temptation to unburden herself and receive forgiveness was strong and sweet; and for a moment, it seemed possible. But even as Caroline was forming the words of her confession, she was seeing how innocent and how absolutely fine Barton was; she knew she didn't want to pollute his soul with knowledge of the perverse thing that contaminated her own.

In addition to protecting Barton, she also wanted to protect herself. Telling the truth would reveal that she hadn't been able to prevent the commission of an unforgivable crime against her own child. She couldn't stand the thought of Barton knowing that. She needed him to see her as he always had—as his "Caro"—someone sweet and good, and innocent.

So she explained her tears by saying: "My little boy was taken away from me three years ago, Barton. He's gone and I can't ever get him back. And I don't know how to breathe around the pain of it."

Julie and Lissa were on the gravel path ahead of Caroline, dashing toward the iron gate at the park entrance. They would soon be teenagers, and the roundness of childhood was beginning to smooth and lengthen into the beginnings of adolescence. But for the moment, they were still little girls with their hair flowing behind them like silken taffy as they ran toward home.

"Look," Caroline whispered. "Look at how strong and happy they are." In the presence of her children's joy, Caroline's grief dimmed. It folded inward, becoming quiet, allowing itself to be hidden.

But in hiding her grief, she hadn't erased it. She had only obscured it. There was still torment when she thought about the things she had done, and, most of all, the things she had been unable to do.

As she walked through the park beside Barton, Caroline

couldn't tell him that she was still haunted by what had happened to her in the days and weeks immediately following Justin's funeral, when she'd learned Justin hadn't died in Nevada but had been taken from her in the cold of New England.

Caroline had almost drowned in a swamp of sedatives and grief, unable to think logically or to act rationally.

She had rampaged through the house with the frenzy of a maniac, hunting for photograph albums and tearing out pictures of Justin. She'd run into the front yard with Justin's little stuffed rabbit and stood with it, defiant, in front of a Polaroid camera, documenting her anguish. She had grabbed a spiral notebook and frantically taped the torn-out photographs onto its pages and then slipped the Polaroid picture of herself, along with Justin's birth certificate, between the last page of the notebook and its back cover. And then she had cried. She had wept and howled.

Caroline had done these things in a desperate fight to reassemble Justin's life. It had been her mad, futile attempt to do the impossible—to touch Justin again, to somehow bring him back to her.

She wanted to tell Barton about what she'd done. She wanted to explain, to have him understand. But instead, Caroline took his hand as they were leaving the park and murmured: "Tell me about New York. Tell me about the other side of the world."

When Caroline and Barton and the girls walked into the kitchen, Barton's wife, Lily, was there. She was letting a stream of cool water wash through a colander piled with fresh-picked tomatoes. A shaft of late-afternoon light was slanting into the room. Lily was in a white cotton dress, bending over her work at the sink, her blond hair, cropped and curly, her skin honey-colored. She looked like a beautiful summer sprite.

Barton went to her and kissed her. Lily let her head drop back and gave a bright, silvery laugh. Caroline saw the potent intimacy in the look that passed between them, and it made her feel a grudging envy. She glanced away and wished that they hadn't come from New York for this visit.

But the kiss lasted only a split second before it was interrupted by excited questions from the girls.

"Aunt Lily, Uncle Barton said that your friend, the one you went to see today, lives all alone in a spooky cabin in the woods that looks like a witch's house." Julie cocked her head to one side, brimming with little-girl skepticism. "Is that really true?"

"He said the only thing she ever eats is nuts and berries, just like a squirrel," Lissa added.

Lily laughed. "Uncle Barton needs to get his facts straight. My friend is not a witch. She's a writer. And she lives in the mountains in a pretty little house that looks out on a lake. And she eats all sorts of different things, except for meat. She's a vegetarian."

"She's a very cranky vegetarian," Barton said.

Lily looked at him with a teasing grin. "Uncle Barton thinks she's cranky because she's a feminist."

"What's a feminist?" Julie asked.

"Someone who thinks women are fish," Barton replied. He was smiling at Lily. "And that men are bicycles, which makes us basically useless to anyone of the fish persuasion. But it does categorize us as creatures who exist solely for the purpose of being ridden."

"Women are fish? And men are bicycles? That's silly." Lissa looked at Julie, and both girls giggled.

"You are very wise children." Barton took a box of cookies from the counter. "Now who wants to come with me and watch TV and eat Oreos until we explode?" Barton sprinted out of the kitchen; the girls followed in hot pursuit.

"Cookies before dinner. No wonder my kids love him so much." Caroline lifted the colander out of the sink and began to dry the tomatoes.

"Barton's great with children . . . he'd be the perfect dad." There was an odd hesitancy in her tone. It caught Caroline's attention. And Lily explained: "We've really been trying, but so far no luck. Still no baby for us."

Caroline wanted to console Lily, but she didn't know what to say; she had always felt awkward around her. Lily seemed too rarefied a creature to ever be within Caroline's grasp.

"I'm doing 'Poor Me.' " Lily made a funny, wry face. "I hate people who do 'Poor Me.' The truth is, the doctors say Barton and I are healthy, and relatively young, and that all we need to do is keep working at it." Lily briefly rested her head on Caroline's shoulder, watching her dry the last of the tomatoes. "Is there anything in the world more delicious than ripe summer tomatoes?"

Lily's skin was cool against Caroline's, and her breath smelled fresh and sweet.

"I knew you'd love them," Lily was saying. "We're alike, you and I. We're both kitchen people, food people." As she moved away, Lily left a light kiss on the back of Caroline's neck. "We were destined to be girlfriends."

To Caroline, the feel of Lily's kiss and the sound of the word *girlfriend* had an intoxicating effervescence. They had been delivered casually. But they had been received as if they were magic.

In the rootlessness of her growing up, Caroline had never remained anywhere long enough to establish a place in the company of other girls. She had always been the new girl, the one who had arrived late in the school year, or had left early. There had been no access to best friends. And certainly no opportunity for a friendship with anyone as lovely and refined as Lily.

"There was this roadside farm stand on the way back from Lake Arrowhead . . . bushels of the most beautiful tomatoes. I couldn't resist," Lily told her. "But I think I bought way too many. I don't know what we're going to do with all of them."

Caroline was already gathering up the tomatoes. She was feeling wondrously happy as she said: "We're going to make spaghetti sauce."

Then Caroline and Lily opened a bottle of cold sparkling cider and they filled and refilled each other's glasses and told each other funny stories as they took the bounty of summer and created a feast for the people they loved.

The time she spent cooking with Lily had brought Caroline such pleasure, and taken her out of herself so completely, that she hadn't thought to put on an apron before beginning work in the kitchen. Now she was upstairs in her bedroom, shedding her sauce-splattered shirt and shorts and preparing to take a shower before dinner.

Through the open bedroom window, coming up from the lawn, Caroline could hear the sounds of a raucous game of tag— wild bursts of laughter from Lissa and Julie and cheerful hoots from Barton and Robert. Julie's voice was loud and triumphant: "You're out, Uncle Barton!" It was followed by a shout from Lissa: "Daddy's turn to be it. Daddy's turn! I want Daddy to chase us now."

Caroline went to the window. She saw the oak tree, and the lawn, and Robert darting across it—Julie and Lissa racing after him, Barton cheering them on. Robert was keeping his movements quick enough to make the girls' chase exciting, but never fast enough to carry him completely out of their reach. He was doing what he always did when he and the girls played together: He was seeing to it that they would win the game.

Barton caught sight of Caroline at the window. "Caro, come down here. Robert and I are getting slaughtered, we need backup."

Before Caroline could respond, she heard Julie call out: "Mommy never plays games anymore. Only Daddy does."

Caroline quickly moved away from the window. The lightness she'd felt in the kitchen with Lily disappeared and was replaced with the weight of all the things that were wrong on Lima Street. It made her feel singed and shredded. She went into Robert's newest addition to the house—the master bathroom that now adjoined the bedroom. She was looking for painkillers. But none were there. She had taken them all.

The pain Caroline was trying to kill was rooted in the heart-break of having come of age in a world where being pregnant and unmarried was a scandal. She now understood how that restricted world had consigned her to a powerless place in which she had received a wedding ring instead of a college degree; in which she had never once in her life held a job; in which, if she were to leave her husband and take her children, she was not equipped to provide a decent home for them. Caroline had no way to survive beyond the walls of Lima Street—walls that were both a fortress and a prison.

She returned to the bedroom and stood near the window. She watched Lissa temporarily abandon her pursuit of Robert and run across the lawn toward Barton. When Lissa came to a stop in front of him, Caroline heard her say: "It isn't always just Daddy we play with. Sometimes we have fun with Mommy, too . . . just never with Mommy and Daddy together." Lissa's expression was exquisite in its sweetness, and in its wistfulness.

Later, they all gathered around the table in the dining room. The girls ate mountains of spaghetti. Lily talked for a while about her life with Barton in New York, and Caroline said very little.

Barton and Robert discussed politics and got into a trivia contest over their knowledge of old war movies and Robert announced that he knew more about them than Barton could ever possibly know and Barton laughed and said he could bring Robert down in one move. Barton bet Robert the last meatball remaining on the spaghetti platter that Robert couldn't name the movie Barton was thinking of. And Barton said: "Here's your clue, name the movie . . . *Ping, ping, ping,"* and he reached his fork toward the last meatball and Robert grabbed the fork away from him and with a flourish speared the meatball from the platter and said: *"Run Silent Run Deep."* Then Robert jumped to his feet and waved the forked meatball in the air and proclaimed, "To the victor belong the meatballs!" The girls and Lily applauded and Barton held up one of the three empty wine bottles that were on the table and announced that the party was going downhill at an alarming rate—he was being deprived of both meatballs *and* wine. Robert went into the basement to bring up the only expensive bottle of wine in the house, one that a client had given him and that he had been saving for a special occasion. When Robert opened it, he asked Lily to take the first sip and she said the wine was superb.

Barton raised his glass. "To Robert. A terrific host. A fantastic human being, and a good friend." Lily, too, raised her glass. And Lissa and Julie chorused, "Yay for Daddy!"

Caroline, meanwhile, dabbed at a spot of spaghetti sauce that was on her dress. Then she sat up straight and finished off her fourth glass of wine.

Barton draped his arm across the back of Lily's chair. "I can't remember when I've had so much fun."

"Probably not since the last time we were all together," Robert said. "That's our magic, Barton. The three of us."

"The three of us, you, me, and Caro. We were always something special. The Three Musketeers."

Lily laughed. "Don't tell me you were corny enough to call yourselves the Three Musketeers."

"Be kind," Robert said. "We were young and stupid and from California. For us, that was being pretty damn erudite."

"Oooh," Julie crowed. "Daddy said 'damn.'"

"Daddy meant 'darn.'" Robert looked at Julie and feigned a scowl.

"Daddy, are you guys going to start talking about olden times again?" Julie's scowl was genuine.

"Oh, I hope so." Lily caught Caroline's eye and smiled. "I'd love to hear about what the three of you were like in your wild youth."

"Nothing to hear, really. It was a long time ago, Lily. And anyway, Barton must have told you all of it already." Caroline was tired and on the edge of being drunk, and in no mood to hear the old stories.

"He's shared a few tales with me," Lily said. "But I have the feeling he hasn't told me the truly interesting ones. I want to hear them all."

Julie began to recite in an apathetic monotone: "Daddy was a really good surfer and Mommy was really really pretty and all the boys liked her and Uncle Barton was Daddy's best friend and they all did a bunch of dumb stuff together. I want to be excused if that's what you guys are going to talk about. It's boring."

"Then you're excused," Robert said. The girls were already rushing past him.

Lily was refilling Barton's wineglass. "Wait a minute," she said. "How come it was the Three Musketeers? Weren't there four of you? It was you. Robert. Caroline. And Mitch. Right?"

"Mitch came later," Barton said. "Then we were the Four Musketeers. But Robert, Caro, and I were the founding members. The three of us met on the first day of Caro's freshman year, and—"

Lily interrupted him. "I know how the three of you got together. But what about Mitch? When did he come into the picture?"

Robert glanced at Caroline. "You should probably answer that, Caroline. You're the one who knows the most about when Mitch came and went."

"Shut up, Robert." Her words were thrown at him like a knife. The silence in the room was absolute. Then Caroline said, "You want to know who all of us used to be, Lily? Well, Robert was the simple, good-hearted surfer from a nice middle-class family. Barton was the sensitive intellectual, raised by a widowed father who taught English at a ritzy boarding school. And I was a nothing girl who pretty much raised myself. And as far as Mitch goes, he was a sexy bad boy whose parents were rich and serially divorced. I had crazy sex with Mitch and was hooked on him like a drug. But I thought I should love Robert because he was so wholesome and nice, the all-American boy."

"Caroline, that's enough!" It came out of Robert in a growl.

"Oh but we haven't told our story in such a long time, Robert. And there's so much more to it now." Caroline was full of wine. And she was angry.

She turned back to Lily. "I used to keep Barton up night after night whining about not being able to decide between Mitch and Robert. Then I got knocked up. By Robert." Caroline snapped her fingers. "And just like that, the decision was made. I got married. A quick trip to city hall and a basket of burgers on the way out of town. Why? Because I was pregnant and I didn't have any money and I didn't have a job and the only girl I ever knew who had an abortion ended up bleeding to death on the floor of a gas station bathroom on her way back home."

"Caro—" Barton's voice was full of concern for Caroline.

She continued, refusing to be interrupted. "I got married

because Robert said we should do it, and because I was too weak and scared to see that I had any other options."

"Caro," Barton said again. "Don't do this. It's ancient history. It's not important anymore."

"Since when isn't the truth important, Barton?"

"What's not important is how you and Robert began. All that matters is how far you've come, that you've made a good life together."

Caroline laughed. The sound was harsh and loud.

Robert threw down his napkin and walked out of the room.

Caroline's attention was on Barton. Her eyes were wide and fiercely bright. "You want to know how far Robert and I have come? Not very far. I'm still doing things because Robert says I should do them. But now instead of just doing mindless things, I've graduated to unforgivable things."

Robert reappeared in the dining room doorway, his attention fixed on Caroline.

"I've done the unforgivable because I'm weak and I'm stupid." Caroline's voice became louder, and then it became a shriek. "If I was stronger and smarter, Justin wouldn't be gone now. I would never have allowed Robert to take him away from me!"

The color drained from Robert's face.

Barton instinctively put a comforting hand on Caroline's shoulder. "Some events are beyond our control, Caro. We can't blame ourselves for the randomness of things that can happen to a child."

Caroline turned on him with furious hostility. "It's easy to feel blameless when you don't actually *have* any children to be responsible for, isn't it, Barton?"

"That's not fair!" Lily's response flew at Caroline like a bullet.

"You want fair?" Caroline shot back. "Go to Pomona."

Lily looked at Caroline, then at Barton, puzzled.

"It's the county fair," Caroline said. "Pomona's the only fair there is, Lily."

Robert watched as Caroline sat back in her chair and closed her eyes. She looked depleted and tired. He saw that the rage had gone out of her. And he left the room.

Barton was offering Caroline a glass of water. She pushed it aside. "Barton, don't even think about talking to me about God and his infinite love for me. The things that I've done are things that I'll never be forgiven for. Never."

"God's love for us is limitless, Caro. It's the reason he allowed Christ to die on the cross. To forgive us our sins."

"No, you're wrong." Caroline's voice was low and weary. "God put Christ on that cross to show us the truth about what we can expect from life. It's God's way of saying to us, 'If I'd do this to my own son . . . what do you think I'm going to do to you?'"

Caroline didn't wait for a reply. She shoved her chair away from the table and went upstairs.

As she lay down, she could feel something bunched beneath her. It was the half-finished costume she'd been constructing for Lissa—an outfit for a musical version of Goldilocks. As Caroline was dropping it onto the floor beside the bed, she heard the girls across the hall arguing. Then there was the sound of a door being slammed and a shout of "I hate you, you idiot! I'm going to tell!"

Caroline sat up, intending to go out into the hall and explain to her children that shouting and name-calling were ugly, uncivilized things to do. But she dropped back onto the bed, laughed at the irony of her message, and let the wine and her emotional exhaustion overtake her.

At some point, Caroline fell asleep and began to dream. She and Barton and Justin were on a stage, dressed as the Three Bears.

Their costumes were loose and fastened down the back with ties, like hospital gowns—everyone could see that they were naked inside of them. Barton's was billowed and balloonlike, and because of that, he floated above the stage—above Caroline and Justin, not seeing them, gazing heavenward and humming the song "Blue Skies." And in front of the stage, in the midst of the audience, Robert and Mitch were engaged in a brutal dance contest. The song was a cruelly sped-up version of "California Girls." Their feet were bleeding and the auditorium was filled with the sound of their bones snapping and shattering. A Judge was loudly banging a coffin-shaped gavel and shouting: "Justice. Justice." A bricked, ovenlike arch began to belch with flame and The Accused was being led toward it. Caroline struggled to see through the mask of her Bear costume, to see who it was that had been found guilty. But she could see nothing. She could only feel the heat of the flames.

And then she woke up. Someone was knocking on the bedroom door.

When Caroline opened the door, Barton was there, holding a bowl of ice cream. "All of us were worried about you," he said. "I've been sent up with a peace offering." Caroline took the ice cream and went back to the bed. Barton came and sat beside her. "I'm not exactly certain how we got so off track at dinner, Caro."

"My fault. I had too much to drink. Drinking and grieving don't mix." Caroline tried to smooth the skirt of her dress; it was covered in a confusion of wrinkles. The fabric looked bunched and dull, so different from what it had been when she'd put it on before dinner—when she had wanted to look as fresh and pretty in lemon yellow as Lily did in summer white.

"What's the story with you and Robert and Mitch? Why was there such tension when his name came up?" Barton's question took Caroline by surprise.

He plowed ahead without waiting for an answer. "I know there's a problem, but when I asked Robert all he would say is that you aren't in contact with Mitch, that neither one of you has seen him in almost ten years."

"We drifted apart, that's all." Caroline went into the bathroom and filled the air with deliberate clatter, rooting through drawers, rattling hairbrushes and lipsticks. It didn't deter Barton. He simply raised his voice and said: "When was the last time you saw him?"

"Years ago," Caroline answered. "That time when he was in town just before you left for New York. Remember? That day I came by the church. Your last day."

"That's not true." Barton's voice was louder than she had expected it to be. He was standing in the doorway of the bathroom. "I know that he was here, in this house, about a month after Justin's death."

Caroline felt as if she had been slapped. "How do you know that?"

"Mitch told me. I ran into him right after he'd gotten back from seeing you. His law firm has a branch office in Manhattan. We bump into each other every now and then. But the question is, Caro, why didn't you tell Robert?"

"This is none of your business."

"You and Robert and I have been friends for a long time. And you, Caro, you're part of me. That makes everything that happens to you my business."

Caroline studied Barton for a minute. She needed to know how much danger she was in; how much of the truth he suspected. She waited before she said: "Mitch did come here. But I sent him away. So, there wasn't anything to say to Robert."

"And that's it? That's all you're going to allow me to know?"

"It's all you need to know. Because even if I am part of you, Barton, I'm only a part, only Caroline. I'm not Lily. Lily would owe you more. I don't."

It wasn't clear to Caroline whether it was irritation or hurt in his voice as he said: "Come downstairs soon. Robert and the girls are waiting to have ice cream with you."

When Barton had gone, Caroline closed the door of the room she shared with Robert, and she thought about the last time she'd seen Mitch.

It had been on a day in late winter, shortly before noon, and Caroline had answered the door wearing a lavender-colored nightgown that had floated around her ankles like a cloud. Her hair was pulled back and tied at the nape of her neck with a lavender ribbon. The nightgowns and the tying back of her hair with matching ribbons had become a sort of uniform for her.

Justin had been gone for almost a month. Since returning from his funeral Caroline had not once left the house. She was pale, and her expression was dreamy and unfocused. She moved as if she were floating in fog. When she saw that it was Mitch who was at the door, it took her a long time to comprehend the reality of his being there.

"I didn't know what to bring." As Mitch said this, he was giving her a mass of hothouse violets, glittering with dew and resplendent in a cone of glossy white lace-edged paper.

The flowers were cold and heavy in her hand, like a fistful of jewels. She gazed at them and said, "Justin's gone."

"I know. That's why I came."

"To see Justin?" She looked around the room, perplexed.

"Caroline, what's wrong with you? Are you here by yourself? Where's Rob? Where are your girls?"

"In school, but they'll be back later." The violets slipped from her hand. She watched them fall. "I'm a little not myself right now. I take pills sometimes. But I try not to when the girls are here."

Mitch cupped her chin and gently forced her to look at him. "Somebody should be here to help you. Jesus God, Caroline, is there somebody I can call? . . . something I can do?"

"It's not your fault, Mitch. You're not the one . . ." She returned to gazing at the violets. When he had touched her face, she had felt the familiar shape of his hands; somewhere far off inside her, something had stirred, and then gone quiet again.

"Why did I have to hear it from Barton about your little boy dying? Why didn't you let me know? Why didn't Rob?"

"Because of what I did, Robert doesn't like you anymore. He'll never like you again." She said it without emotion. "And he won't ever like me again, either. He just doesn't know it yet." Then she leaned forward and collapsed into his arms—slowly, like a kite spiraling into soft green grass.

Mitch had carried her into her bedroom and stayed beside her as she slept. He had sat smoking cigarettes, looking toward the window and the oak tree in the backyard. Caroline had awakened just before the girls were due home from school, and she had said: "You have to go now, Mitch. You have to promise, please, never to come back. Because if you do, Robert will take this house down from around me and my girls. We'll be alone. And we have no way to survive."

Mitch had kept the promise she had asked of him. He had never come back to her. Caroline had taken root in the house on Lima Street. And life had gone on.

Now she was picking up the bowl of ice cream that Barton had brought and she was going downstairs—because her girls were there, waiting for her.

Twilight had deepened into darkness and coolness had finally found its way into the summer air. The house had its windows flung wide and its doors standing open. Lamps were lit in every room. The feeling was expansive and joyous. Caroline's outburst at dinner had been attributed to too much wine and too little sleep, and had been put aside.

Everyone was gathered in the living room. Julie and Lissa were holding candlesticks, and Robert a rolled-up newspaper. The Motown song "My Girl" was playing on the stereo. Robert and the girls were singing along to it, using the candlesticks and newspaper as their "microphones." The three of them were serenading Caroline.

And Caroline was remembering other summer nights, when she'd lived the kind of hungry life she had never wanted her children to experience. A life in which she had haunted the sidewalks of neighborhoods that weren't her own; where there were places that looked the way the house on Lima Street looked tonight, big and festive and full of light. Caroline had hidden under the bright, open windows of those houses and listened to the music emanating from them.

And in their melodies, she had heard the promise of safety and the sound of surety. It was what she was hoping, in this moment, each one of her children was hearing—the music of home.

ESSEX, CONNECTICUT, AUGUST 1977

*

"Is this my baby?" Margaret had barely been able to speak. He was the most beautiful child she'd ever seen. She had carefully taken him as he was being lowered into her arms, and the feeling had been delicious. She'd waited for him for a very long time. He hadn't come to her until the day before her forty-fifth birthday.

When she brought her child home, it was through a snowfall as crisp and white as freshly ironed lace. It was February and she was thinking that she should have gotten the Christmas decorations from the attic and put them back up in honor of his arrival. Her son was a miracle; he should be coming into a house dressed for the season of miracles.

As she carried him, bundled in a blanket, toward her front door, she wondered what she looked like to people passing on the street. What would they think of this middle-aged woman with her unruly red hair, sloping shoulders, and limping gait, running toward a modest New England clapboard house as if she were running toward heaven? Would they know that she was not what she appeared to be; that she had been transformed; that this house was now a home, a place where a mother was being born and a son would grow?

Before Margaret could reach the door, it was thrown open by Kati. Huge bouquets of helium balloons were tied to the legs of the dark wood table just inside the doorway, and Kati was singing: loudly and off-key, "Happy baby to you! Happy baby to you! Happy baby, dear Maggie. Happy baby to you!"

Kati was nineteen—adorably pretty, free-spirited and spontaneous. She was the daughter of an old friend. Margaret had hired her a year ago as a temporary assistant to run errands and type lecture notes until someone (someone whom Margaret assumed would be more serious-minded and scholarly) could be found. But Kati had proved to be a conscientious, enthusiastic, and completely competent employee. Within weeks, her status had become permanent.

"I tried to sing quiet," Kati said. "I didn't wake him up, did I?"

"No," Margaret told her. "You sang very quietly. He's still fast asleep."

Kati lifted the edge of the blanket away from the child's face. His skin was creamy white and his hair was the color of chocolate. She gave a quick, soft gasp—as if she had encountered an exquisite work of art. He stirred. For a moment, his eyes opened. They were green, with eyelashes that were dark and extravagantly long. He sleepily closed his eyes again. A tear that had been caught in his lashes slid free and Margaret gently wiped it away. "He was crying a little in the car," she explained. "It's hard to be so new in a whole new world."

Margaret went to a chair near the fire and carefully lowered herself into it, never taking her eyes off her sleeping child. Kati followed and sat on the floor beside her. "What are you going to name him?" Kati asked.

"His name is Thomas Justin. I'm going to call him TJ."

Kati leaned close and whispered, "Hi there, TJ. I'm Kati. I'm gonna be your baby-sitter while your mama's off at work. I am gonna take such good care of you." She looked up at Margaret. "Oh Maggie, I can't wait to hold him."

"Maybe later. Maybe in a little while." Margaret's smile was tremulous. "I can't let go of him yet."

*

After almost three months, Margaret was settling into the routine of motherhood and TJ was beginning to sleep through the night.

When he had first come into the house, he had wept daily. There was nothing that would comfort or distract him—not the toys that filled his nursery, or the funny faces that Kati made, or the songs that Margaret sang to him as she slowly danced him through the book-lined rooms of the house. His tears had ceased only when he had become too exhausted to shed them. Each night his wailing had filled the dark and he had refused to be consoled.

On the first night, at the first fretful sounds of his unhappiness, Margaret had entered his room and taken him out of his bed, out from under his blue-and-yellow quilt, and he had instinctively curled against her. And as she'd felt him trembling like a newborn kitten, she had whispered: "Everything's going to be all right, little one. Your mommy is here."

In the instant that she had said *mommy,* he had lifted his head and held his hand out in a sudden desperate gesture, as if he had been groping for a miracle. He had looked around the room, continuing to hold his hand out, frantic to see and touch the thing he'd lost. And when he understood that it was not there, he threw himself against Margaret and wailed. Every night, for months, he had continued to wail.

And in each of those nights, Margaret had held him and promised that she would find a means by which to take his tears away.

On the day in May when she had run into the house and knelt in front of him, when she had opened her light spring coat and shown him what was huddled beneath it—a tiny black cocker spaniel puppy with a sky blue ribbon around its neck—Margaret had, at last, been able to fulfill her promise. The puppy went directly to TJ and settled into his lap. The little boy lowered his head, rested it against the puppy's silky fur, and made a sound that was small and indistinct. Later, when Margaret had tried to describe it to Kati, she couldn't define it. All she could say was that it had not been the sound of weeping.

With the arrival of the puppy—whom Kati christened Inky—TJ began to change. He began to smile, and to play with his toys, and to cautiously reach out to Margaret.

His weeping had stopped. It was then that Margaret first heard the plaintive sound of his singing. It had begun in the early hours of a Sunday evening, a short time after she had put TJ to bed. She was downstairs in her study. It was raining and the house was filled with the sound of water slipping under the eaves and tapping across the windowpanes. But then there was a momentary lull, a cessation in the noise coming from outside the house, and Margaret heard the strange sorrow-stricken sound that was coming from the room above—from TJ's room.

It was a song, almost whispered and unbearably sad, going in circles, without beginning or end. It was the sound of a mantra, an opiate for a hurt lodged in a place and a time that were refusing to be forgotten.

Margaret went to the door of her study and listened. She heard the sound of TJ's voice. It was eerily high, reedy and fragile. "Do I know my name?"

He was singing in the lisping, uneven cadences of a three-year-old. "Yes I do. Yes, I do. My name is Justin. And my name is Fisher, too. Do I know my home? Yes I do. Yes I do." There was fleeting hesitation. And then: "I live on Lima Street. Right at 822. Do I know my town? Yes I do. Yes I do. My town's Sierra Madre, and it's California, too. Do I know my parents?" Another hesitation. And then: "Yes I do. Yes, I do. One's named Caroline. And one's named Robert, too. Do I know my sisters? Yes, I do. Yes I do. I have a sister Julie. And a sister Lissa, too."

For a moment there was silence. Then the song began again. Margaret realized she was listening to the memories of a little boy who no longer existed. And for the first time, she comprehended the depth of the void into which her son had been thrown.

*

"You've taken to this like a duck to water," Andy said. "Your mothering is as natural and pretty as flowers in springtime." Andy was sitting in a wing chair near Margaret's front window. He was a massively big man. He made both the chair in which he sat and the teacup he was holding look small enough to be toys.

Margaret laughed. "You missed your calling. You should've been a poet. Or a Baptist preacher." She turned her attention away from Andy, concentrating on keeping Inky at bay so that she could deal with the stuck zipper on TJ's jacket.

"I'm happy being what I am, your simple servant at the bar." Andy winked at Margaret and grinned.

Margaret nervously redoubled her efforts to open TJ's jacket. She was uneasy with compliments and, to some extent, with men. When she'd been young, still in elementary school, she'd been keenly aware that her height, her wild red hair and round, pale face, and her serious nature were not qualities most boys found attractive. She'd been able to tolerate their distinterest because there were other things that interested her—her family and her circle of girlfriends.

Then, in high school, there'd been a shy, awkward boy who had found her lovely and had read poetry to her; and for a while, Margaret saw herself through his eyes. Her hair was Titian, her skin was alabaster, and she walked with the height and grace of a goddess.

After the accident, the boy had gone away. And Margaret became herself again, but more so. The accident had left her with a slight limp, with an odd, clipped gait. The fall from the top tier of the bleachers at the side of the empty football field had carried Margaret down through a maze of iron struts and supports; by the time she hit the ground, one of her legs had been mangled, and the boy—his face still pink with the frost of Margaret's lipstick—was frantically buttoning his jeans and scurrying home. The custodian who heard the noise of Margaret's crashing descent had called an ambulance. The following day was graduation and the bleachers were filled with caps and gowns and cheerful speeches. Margaret was already in the process of being forgotten.

The boy and the accident saddened Margaret for a time, but they didn't hobble her in any essential way. She'd never been a girl who was passionate about boys, or overly sensitive to her appearance. Her passions had always been books and words and the idea of motherhood.

When her mother had bought a hope chest for Margaret's sixteenth birthday—and, over the years, filled it with embroidered linens and filmy lingerie—Margaret later emptied it to make room for things that she herself had collected. Things that were more appropriate to her own dream: exquisite books of English nursery rhymes, a hand-carved wooden train from Germany with a red silk cord to pull it by, a little yellow-and-blue quilt made on a Pennsylvania farm, a silver crescent moon as big as a dinner plate and a constellation of shimmering stars, all fabricated from some gleaming pliant metal, hammered tissue-thin, by an artist in SoHo. These were things that Margaret wanted to give to her child when, someday, she became a mother.

"I mean it, Margaret," Andy was saying. "You look right at home with that puppy and that little boy." He set aside his tea and opened his briefcase. "It's a joy to see how well this has all turned out."

Margaret had managed to get TJ out of the jacket and she was holding him in her arms. The feel of his cheek against hers was as fresh and firm as a winter apple. "Say hello to Mr. Abbott," she told TJ. "He's the wonderful man who gave us to each other." TJ hid his face in the soft place at the base of Margaret's neck, and she kissed him and allowed him to scamper out of the living room with his puppy close at his heels.

Margaret's expression was eager as she sat in the chair across from Andy's. "You've brought the final papers?"

"Yup, I've got all your legal stuff." Andy waited for a moment. "And there's something extra." He was holding a flat rectangular package the shape and size of a wall calendar. Its covering seemed to have been cut from a brown paper grocery bag. And it looked as if it had been wrapped hurriedly; the corners were uneven and the bits of tape holding them closed were at odd angles and chaotically spaced. As he handed the package to Margaret he said: "It arrived in the mail a few days after TJ had been brought to my office."

Margaret was immediately apprehensive. "Why didn't you tell me about it before?"

"I haven't been keeping anything from you. My secretary was out on maternity leave. The girl who was filling in for her left it in a pile of mail on her desk. The box this packet was in didn't get opened until a few days ago."

"Who sent it?"

Andy shrugged. "Don't know. There was no return address."

Margaret took a slow, nervous breath. Andy held up his hand, stopping her before she could speak. "There's nothing to worry about," he told her. "Yours is a legal, sealed, private adoption. No one, and I mean no one, not even the birth parents know, or ever can know, who you are or where to find you. You are that little boy's mother. Just as if you'd given birth to him."

Margaret glanced down at the package in her lap. "How do you know this was meant for me?"

"When I opened the box, the only items inside were that thing and a sheet of paper with the name Justin Fisher on it. He's your son now. So that makes it your property."

Margaret moved to open the package, then pulled back. She was suddenly ambivalent about encountering whatever it was that lay beneath its crazily taped cover.

"Don't worry," Andy told her. "You don't have to open that thing. I can simply dispose of it for you."

"No. Wait. Let me think about this." Margaret put the package on the table beside her chair. The uncertainty of what it might contain was making her apprehensive. But for some reason, she wasn't comfortable with the idea of relinquishing it.

"There's going to be difficult moments like this for a while, Margaret. Putting together a family this way is complicated," Andy said. "Just take things slowly, you'll be fine."

"You've worked a miracle for me, Andy. I can't tell you how grateful I am."

"I don't know that I deserve credit for a miracle. This one was just plain coincidence."

Margaret suddenly sat up very straight, as if she needed to bring her full force to what she was telling him. "No, I don't believe that." She wanted Andy to feel as awed by her situation as she did. "Think of all the years that, for one reason or another, I couldn't ever succeed at finding a child to adopt, and yet this child came to me so easily. It was no coincidence. It was meant to be. Someone or something was looking down and orchestrating all of it."

Andy's smile was indulgent. "Margaret, most of the time, a cigar is just a cigar. And this one's just a cigar. Trust me. All that happened was I answered my own phone because my secretary's fill-in was late coming back from lunch . . . and TJ's father was on the other end of the line. That's all there is to it."

"But how did he know to call you? How did he know about you?"

"He didn't. He was taking shots in the dark," Andy said. "If I hadn't answered, he'd have gone on to the next person on his list. Apparently he'd called the state bar and asked for the names of attorneys who handle private adoptions. I got alphabetically lucky. Andrew Abbott. I was probably the first name that came up."

"Why was he looking for an attorney here? You said he was from California." Margaret's voice was faint. She was preoccupied, realizing now that she had been so euphoric about the miracle of having a child, she hadn't thought about the details of how her miracle had come to be.

"He told me he had chosen the East Coast because it was as far from California as possible, because he wanted complete anonymity in the transaction." There was disgust in Andy's voice. "That's what he called it, 'the transaction.' "

"Why did he choose Connecticut?"

"He's an insurance agent, and apparently one of the companies he does business with is Hartford Insurance." Andy shook his head, as if the story was still unbelievable to him. "From talking to this guy, I got the feeling he had no idea which East Coast state he was going to select. He probably walked into his office one morning, looked down at his desk and saw a ballpoint pen or maybe a pile of paperwork from Hartford Insurance, Hartford Connecticut, and that was that. In a way, he threw a dart at a board and hit Connecticut."

"And me, what about me? Why was he willing to let his child go to a middle-aged woman with no husband?"

Andy thought for a moment; then he said: "Because I don't think he cared where his son went. He just wanted rid of him."

"Why?" Margaret could barely speak. She couldn't comprehend how any parent could have so grotesque an impulse.

"All he said was he and his wife had agreed that it was best for the boy to be raised by someone else." Andy's tone was contemptuous. "I believe he didn't care one way or another who that 'someone' was."

"And his wife felt the same way?" Margaret asked.

"Apparently so. Her signature was scrawled on the paperwork, like she did it drunk or half-asleep. I don't think the woman gives a damn. Anyway, according to what the father told me, they figure the child is still young enough that he won't remember any of this, so in the long term it won't do him any harm. Win-win. They get rid of the little boy and he gets a nice home where he's wanted and loved." Andy finished the last of his tea and put the cup aside. "The guy was so relieved to hear I had a client willing to take a three-year-old, after we hung up, he flew out here on the next plane."

Andy took Margaret's hand. "And that, Margaret, is the story of how your child came to you. What do you say now? A sorry mess made by a couple of staggeringly selfish people? Or a sweet miracle sent from God?"

Margaret knew that at its heart it was indeed a mess. But she needed to believe that her part of it—the part in which she and TJ had found each other—was a miracle. "His name is Thomas Justin Fisher," Margaret said. "And my name is Margaret Fischer. He was meant to be mine all along. There was simply a little spelling glitch that delayed him in getting to me."

There was something pitying in Andy's gaze, as if he was sorry for her naïveté. It embarrassed Margaret; she looked away. Then she reached for the package he'd given her earlier. "Are you sure you want to deal with whatever's in there?" he asked. "My offer's still good. I can dispose of it and we can leave it at that."

"No," Margaret said. "I want to open it. I want to know everything there is for me to know." She carefully tore open the brown paper and found a slim spiral notebook. An array of photographs had been hastily pasted onto its lined pages. The photographs were of TJ, of a tree-shaded house surrounded by a deep, wide porch, and of two beautiful little girls. Margaret realized she knew who they were. "These are his sisters," she said.

She held the notebook so that Andy could see the photographs. "Their names are Julie and Lissa. And this house, it's in a place called Sierra Madre, California, on Lima Street."

"How could you know any of that? How could he have told you about it?" Andy was genuinely surprised. "I've never heard TJ speak. Have you found a way to get him to talk to you?"

"No, not yet." Margaret looked down at the photographs again. Encountering the reality of these girls, and of this house, was overwhelming. "There's this little singsong that TJ does," Margaret murmured. "The sound of it is so sad."

Until this moment, Margaret had recognized only one truth:

that her prayers had been answered. And because TJ was an answer to prayer, Margaret had believed having him was unequivocally right. But now as she touched her hand to these photographs that had clearly been assembled with such desperation, she realized her truth was only one of many. She was being told that her joy had its roots in someone else's sorrow and that she was not as immaculate and righteous as she had believed herself to be. These photographs and their passionate, hectic arrangement were showing her that the account Andy had been given of TJ's situation was only a small part of some darker, more complicated story.

Margaret instinctively knew who had assembled the contents of this notebook, and she knew why. She understood that when TJ had left the house on Lima Street, only one of his parents had been truly happy to see him go.

As she turned over the last page of photographs, Margaret discovered—tucked against the back cover of the notebook—a single Polaroid snapshot. It had been taken at a peculiar angle, as if the camera had been balanced on a chair seat or at the top of a set of porch steps. It was of a young woman standing on a patch of dormant winter grass. Her hair was the color of chocolate and her expression was utterly still. She was looking straight into the lens. Her gaze was so direct that it seemed she was wanting the camera to see into her soul and to record what was written there. She was holding a toy rabbit. Beneath the Polaroid, folded into a small square no larger than a credit card, was a copy of a birth certificate bearing the name of Thomas Justin Fisher.

Margaret picked up the Polaroid and looked closely at the expression in the young woman's eyes. The ferocity, and the raw pleading that was there, made Margaret recoil as if she had touched lightning. In that instant, Margaret knew that she and the woman in the photograph were both complicit in the commission of a crime—a crime in which the identities of perpetrator and victim were frighteningly unclear.

*

"Swing set!" TJ's eyes were bright. "A swing set and roller skates."

"You're sure?" Margaret said. "That's all?" She pulled her raincoat on and began gathering her books.

A single cornflake was caught in the red cotton of his Mickey Mouse sweater. The twill of his pants was scuffed lighter at the knees from climbing trees in the yard and sliding down the stair banister and crayoning dinosaurs onto large sheets of art paper scattered across the living room floor. TJ's hands went into his pockets; he lowered his gaze and swayed gently from side to side. His brow furrowed. He deliberated. And then he said, "Maybe one more thing. A piano."

This unexpected and slightly outrageous announcement caught Margaret off guard. It made her laugh. "A piano? But we already have a piano."

"It's not in my size." TJ scrambled up onto the bench of the baby grand that was in the corner of the living room and spread his arms over the keyboard. "See, Mommy? Too big. It's not in my size."

Seeing TJ there, talkative and happy, almost brought Margaret to tears. For more than a year after he'd come to her, TJ had not spoken. But almost from the beginning, he had been drawn to the piano. Every night after dinner, he had allowed himself to be seated in Margaret's lap and to be comforted by the steady beating of her heart at his back as he listened to the music she played for him, the music of Beethoven and Bach and Chopin.

And then one night, a few months ago, when Margaret had pulled away from the keyboard and stopped playing, TJ had put

161

his hand on hers and guided it back to the piano and said: "Make more music." They were the first words she'd ever heard him speak. And behind them came a torrent of others. It was as if Margaret and TJ's time together, lost in music, had unbound whatever had become paralyzed in him when he had been taken from the house on Lima Street.

Now TJ was asking for a piano of his own.

"Oh how I love my TJ. Oh how I love my baby!" Margaret scooped him up and whirled him around the room—around her simple Yankee living room with its white walls and rag rugs and dark furniture and gleaming brass.

"For this moment in time," she said, "in this room, holding this child, I, Margaret Marie Fischer, am experiencing perfect happiness!"

"It's my birthday today so I'm five now, Mommy," Justin reminded her. "My size is five, when you get my piano, don't forget."

"I won't forget. Now go find Mommy's bag so she can pack up her books and hit the road, so she can do her summer-session teaching, and her piano buying, and then get back home in time for your birthday party."

TJ went to the table near the front door to retrieve Margaret's canvas book bag. Just as he did, the door opened and Kati came rushing in. "Sorry to be late, Maggie. But I had to run a very important errand involving gift wrap and a stop at the bakery."

"I have a similar errand to run myself," Margaret said. "Mine's going to involve the acquisition of a miniature Steinway."

"Really?" Kati shrugged off her yellow rain slicker. "I didn't know anything like that was on the list."

"It was a last-minute addition." Margaret was smiling as she tucked her stack of books into the canvas bag and buckled it closed.

When she kissed him and left, TJ ran to the window and watched her car pull out of the driveway. "Where's Mommy going?" he asked. It was the same question he asked every day. It was a game that he and Kati played.

"You know where she's going," Kati told him. "Where she always goes. To Wesleyan."

*

Margaret rushed through the morning English lit class and canceled her afternoon graduate seminar. She couldn't keep her mind on her lectures. All she could think about was finding a piano— one that would be perfect for someone whose size was five.

To find such a thing, she knew she'd have to search outside of Middletown, the community where Wesleyan was so incongruously located. Middletown was blue-collar, a factory town that banged out rubberized work boots and auto parts and smelled of sulfur and hot metal and was home, mainly, to the children and grandchildren of Italian and Polish immigrants. It was where Margaret had grown up in the company of a mother and father who doted on her. Margaret's father had been the librarian at Wesleyan—a poetic, scholarly man with eyesight so fragile that it did not allow him to drive. This was the reason he had settled in Middletown, to be near his work. But Margaret and Middletown had never quite fit together; she was always too bookish and (like her mother) too Irish for the place. Margaret had made her first and final exit from it when she had gone north to attend the University of Connecticut. Through her undergraduate years, and through her time in graduate school, and in the summers after she began teaching, she used travel to distance herself from Middletown. She wandered—across Europe and Asia and every state in the United States. Years later, when she'd come back to Connecticut to accept a faculty position at Wesleyan, she chose to settle in Essex, a quintessential New England village that was twenty miles, and a world away, from the location in which she had spent her girlhood.

Middletown was not the kind of place in which a tiny, perfect grand piano was waiting to be discovered, and as Margaret got into her car to go in search of TJ's present, she knew she would not rest until the piano was found. She wanted him to have his heart's desire, to be blissfully happy. Happiness was something Margaret instinctively possessed, and delighted in sharing.

Once when she had been traveling in Italy, she had gone to see a fortune-teller—a woman with skin the color of ripe peaches, who had received her into a cool stone house that was airy and open and looked out from a terraced mountainside toward an expanse of glittering ocean. There had been fragrant almond-flavored tea and a glazed platter filled with tiny buttery cookies. The fortune-teller had told Margaret that God was pleased with her, that she had lived many lives before and had lived them well, and that now, in this life, it was Margaret's destiny to be happy and to be filled with enjoyment, and to share that happiness with others. And Margaret had gone away feeling the fortune-teller had told her things that she had, in her heart, already known.

Margaret drove half the length of Connecticut in search of TJ's piano. When, at last she found it, it was waiting for her in a tiny jewel box of an antiques store—in serene and affluent Westport. The owner was as elegant as her showroom, her only accessory a bracelet—a single thick braid of brushed silver. Her white hair was gathered in a neat coil at the back of her head, and her simple black dress and flat shoes had the feel of Paris about them.

Margaret stood beside her looking frowsy and windblown and feeling elated, because, as the woman was leading Margaret toward the back of the store, she was saying: "I have exactly what you're looking for. I'm not certain of how it came to be . . . It might have originally been intended as a window display, or it could possibly have been a custom-made toy." The woman stopped near a marble pedestal, stepping aside to let Margaret see the item and judge for herself. "Either way," the woman said, "I suspect you're going to like it."

The store was softly lit with small silk-shaded lamps. The light coming through the front window was watery and dim. It had been raining all day and the rain was beginning to come down harder now. But even in the muted half gloom, Margaret could clearly see that what the woman had led her to was a treasure—an exact replica of a grand piano, scaled to miniature, to child size. The black lacquer of its finish was so smooth that it had a kind of liquid depth to it. The fittings and hinges were polished brass. The keys had yellowed with age but were free of even the slightest imperfection. Their sound was rippling and light—the music of fairies, or fireflies, or snow melting in mountain streams.

"It's a bit pricey." The woman looked at Margaret and tilted her head slightly—a gesture of genteel inquiry. Margaret answered the unspoken question by opening her checkbook and uncapping her pen. There was no price she would not pay for her son's happiness.

*

The search for the piano had taken longer than she'd expected, and Margaret arrived home much later than she usually did. It was already dark. The rain had become a storm and was falling in heavy wind-driven sheets.

When Margaret walked through the front door, instead of finding TJ and Kati running toward her in their party hats, eager to begin the birthday celebration, she found an empty room where crepe-paper streamers were hanging, limp, from the curtain rods and a cluster of helium balloons was floating in a corner like a gathering of blank-faced ghosts.

From near the door came quick movement and sudden sound—a streamer slipped to the floor; a balloon bumped against the ceiling with a single hollow thud. Then the house went quiet again. Margaret quickly put TJ's tiny piano on the closed lid of her own larger one. She called out to Kati and TJ. There was no answer. She called out again. And still there was no answer.

Margaret took the stairs at a run. As she arrived at the top, she saw Kati standing in the doorway of TJ's room, pale and tense. "He's doing it again, Maggie," Kati whispered. "He keeps doing it, over and over. I'm scared. I can't get him to stop."

TJ was in the farthest, smallest corner of the room, where the slatted wood ceiling sloped low above a dormer window. His knees were drawn up against his body, his arms wrapped tightly around them. His little dog, Inky, was circling him, anxious and whimpering.

A muted light was coming into the room from the gate lamp at the end of the driveway, but TJ's face was in shadow. He was look-ing toward the window, staring at the pounding rain. In an eerie haunting singsong he was repeating: "Do I know my home? . . . Yes, I do. Yes I do . . . I live on Lima Street. Right at 822."

Margaret knew that it could be hours before he came back to her, back to his life and his happiness. She knew this because, although they were less frequent now, these episodes were a fact of TJ's existence. They were, for him, a hiding place, a walled dark-ness into which he fled when he was frightened. They were the hypnotic remnants of his past, fragments from which he had fash-ioned an ephemeral, self-made sanctuary.

"What happened, Kati?" Margaret kept her voice low. She knelt beside TJ and cautiously put her arms around him, wanting him to feel the safety of her embrace but not wanting to startle him. His body was rigid and his breathing was rapid and shallow. His gaze remained fixed on the rain. "Do I know my parents? Yes, I do. Yes I do. One's named Caroline. And one's named Robert, too . . ."

"He was having this great time, helping me get the decorations up for the party," Kati was saying. "Then when you didn't come home at your usual time, he started getting antsy. He went all hyper and started asking me every two minutes, 'Where's Mommy? Where's Mommy?' "

Kati came and sat close to Margaret. "And then when it started to rain really hard and get dark, he just took off; he was up the stairs and in his room so fast that I couldn't even stop him. Then it started to happen . . . y'know, like he always does when he's scared . . . that creepy song, over and over. I kept begging him to look at me and stay here with me and not go to that weird place he goes." Kati's eyes filled with tears. "But I couldn't help him. Why can't we stop him from going away like that, Maggie?"

Margaret kept one arm around TJ and reached for Kati with the other. "Oh Kati-bug, we do it every day. We've been doing it all along," she whispered. "Remember how, at first, it used to happen all the time? Now things are so much better. This hasn't happened for months and months."

TJ's breathing began to slow and his body became more pliant. Margaret lifted him into her lap and he rested his head in the curve at the base of her neck. "We're going to keep this little boy so safe," Margaret said. "And we are going to love him so much."

Kati smoothed TJ's hair, letting it fall across her fingertips as she finished Margaret's thought: ". . . so much that, someday, he won't need to run away and hide in a place that's not there. A place where nobody wants him."

Margaret carried TJ toward the door. It was time to go downstairs. There were birthday wishes to be made, and candles to be lit, and a piano, whose size was five, to be played.

Ultimately, the birthday party had been a great success. TJ had opened to it in stages, like a flower to the morning sun. And, at the unveiling of his piano, he was overjoyed. He ran toward it, shouting: "Look, Mommy! Look! It's just my size!"

When he positioned himself on the floor with his legs splayed on either side of the piano and danced his fingers across the keys, filling the house with swirling, disjointed music, Margaret slipped her arm around Kati's waist and asked: "So what do you think, Kati-bug? Are we looking at a budding Beethoven?"

"I don't know . . . I think maybe he looks more like that little guy in *Peanuts*. Charlie Brown's pal, Schroeder."

Margaret's laugh was spontaneous and loud enough to catch TJ's attention. He looked up from the piano, curious. "Why are you laughing so loud?"

"Because I'm very, very happy," Margaret said.

TJ held her gaze. His eyes were lit with joy. "Me, too, Mommy. I'm very, very happy, too."

Later, after Margaret had put TJ to bed, she stood for a while in the doorway of his room. There was a tightening in her throat as she saw, curled at the foot of the bed, the dog, keeping watch over her little boy, and, shimmering above them in midair, suspended from the ceiling on satin ribbons, a crescent moon and constellation of silver stars.

Margaret arrived downstairs to discover Kati gathering up crepe paper and balloons. Kati was apologetic: "Maggie, I don't want you to think I forgot to get TJ a gift. It's just that next to that incredibly cool piano, my present might have been a little bit of a comedown. So I left it in the kitchen. Do you think you could give it to him for me, tomorrow, when you give him the roller skates?"

"Oh no, the skates! I forgot them at school. They're still in my office." Margaret was already crossing the room, preparing to take her purse and raincoat from the chair near the door. "Can you stay awhile longer, Kati? Just till I get back?"

"Maggie, I don't think this is a good idea." Kati followed Margaret to the door. "Listen to that rain, Maggie. It's really coming down out there."

"I'm just going to Middletown and back." Margaret was rummaging in her purse for her keys. "I'll creep along, I swear. But I have to go get his skates. I promised him we'd have pancakes tomorrow and then go to the rink so he can try roller-skating for the very first time, on his brand-new birthday skates."

Kati saw that the car keys were dangling from an outside pocket on Margaret's purse; she took them and held on to them. "So do it on some other day. What's the big deal about tomorrow?"

"Don't you know that you can't break a promise to a little boy on his birthday? It's against the law." Margaret put her hand out for the keys.

Kati ignored her and continued to hold on to them. "What law?"

"The law that says the number of promises kept to us when we're children is directly proportionate to the number of promises we keep as adults," Margaret said. "And, someday, I want my son to hold the world record for promises kept." Margaret took the keys from Kati and headed out the door. "I'll be right back. I promise."

Kati went to the door and called, "Maggie!"

All Kati could see of Margaret was a blur as she was running toward the car through the downpour. The drumming of the rain was making it sound as if Margaret were already far away.

"Yes, Kati?"

"Did your parents keep all their promises to you?"

The rain was thundering now, falling between them like a curtain. Margaret's voice floated back to Kati out of the darkness. "Every last one of them, Kati-bug. They kept every last one of them."

*

Margaret had made it to her office without incident. She had quickly retrieved TJ's skates and then gotten back on the road. But now the storm was swiftly building in intensity and she was having difficulty seeing the lines on the highway and the signs at the side of it. The rain was sheeting, and the wind was hammering at the car like a battering ram. The noise was wild and fierce, and Margaret was worrying about TJ. She was praying that he wouldn't awaken in this terrible storm and find his mother gone. What had seemed like a lighthearted impulse—the dash through the night for roller skates—was now beginning to feel like a dangerous miscalculation.

The light from her headlights was penetrating only a few feet into the downpour before being swallowed by it. Margaret was in virtual darkness. The car felt as if it were hurtling through space like a rocket. She started to put her hand on the radio, then put it back on the steering wheel. There was no need to listen to the weather report. She was a native New Englander. She knew what was happening.

The storm that had been building for days was unfurling into something much more—a lashing Atlantic gale, bringing down torrential rain.

Margaret was tensed over the steering wheel, trying to catch glimpses of the road through the waves of water rushing across the windshield. Suddenly, the dim uncertain light cast by the car's headlights flicked across something massive that was blocking the road ahead. Margaret slammed her foot onto the brake; as she did, she felt the brakes lock. The car began a slow, whirling skid. She knew she was going to die.

She hadn't seen the jackknifed truck in time. And in the split second that was left to her before her death, a rushing kaleidoscope of images came, blossoming and clicking and shifting . . .

Her Irish mother, young and so very pretty, leading Margaret through the spring wildflowers blooming in the vacant lot behind their house on Grand Street.

The voluptuous feel of the Italian sun and a tiny handmade leather sketchbook, its pages thick and ivory-colored, its binding as sensuous and soft as the parted lips of a sleeping lover.

A sea of young faces looking up at her, listening to her, admiring her.

The scent of a fresh lime and the sound of Beethoven.

A hand slipping under her sweater and along the curve of her breast and the boy, to whom the hand belongs, gasping with pleasure.

Roller skates.

Lightning above the Arizona desert opening up a blazing fissure in the night sky.

The fetid smell of her grandfather's breath.

Astronauts and a circus elephant and Shakespeare and the feel of uncooked pie dough and Richard Nixon and spiders.

The sound of the rain. And screaming brakes.

And TJ's face. And TJ's face. And TJ's face.

At the moment of impact, Margaret saw the image of a young

woman standing on a patch of dormant winter grass. Her hair was the color of chocolate. She was utterly still. Her gaze was so direct that it seemed it was demanding that Margaret look into the core of her, recognize what had been stolen from her.

Margaret screamed. But her screams were consumed by the shrieks of tearing metal and shattering glass. The roadway went bright for a moment with an explosion of white-hot sparks.

Then the rain and the darkness rushed in as a soul rushed away. And it was finished.

Justin and Amy

*

Cool morning fog was drifting in from the ocean. A solitary runner was crossing the pale sand at the water's edge, leaving a trail of evenly spaced footprints, uniform and perfect, like a line of stitches on buff-colored suede. The sight of the woman's silent passage momentarily calmed Amy. Then she heard her mother's voice come at her again: "We're all guilty of something, pumpkin."

Amy quickly left the balcony and hurried to close the bedroom door. She didn't want Rosa or Zack to overhear this irritating, wrangling phone call.

"Mother," she said. "I am not going to apologize for coming home to take care of my husband instead of hanging around in Hawaii. This is crazy." She could hear that her mother was opening and closing cabinets, probably preparing breakfast. "Mother, are you even paying attention to what we're talking about?"

"Darling, I am the one who called you. Of course I'm paying attention."

"Then explain something. If Daddy loves me as much as he says he does, why can't he act like a normal father? Why can't he just let the whole Hawaii thing slide?"

"And why can't you get eggs at the dry cleaner's?"

"What?"

"Eggs can be what you want, and what you need, Amy. And you can go to the dry cleaner every day for the rest of your life expecting to find them, but all you're going to get is dry cleaning. It doesn't make the dry cleaner a bad guy . . . You're asking him to give you something he doesn't have. If you want eggs, pumpkin, go to the grocery store. Then grow up and stop whining about your dry cleaner . . . start appreciating how well-pressed your clothes are."

"I don't need this from you, Mother."

"Oh, I think you do." Her mother's tone was icy. "Don't forget who's buttered a lot of your bread, Amy. Start with that house you're living in and go all the way back to your first pair of custom-made baby shoes."

"Daddy's the one who's wrong, not me," Amy insisted.

"Someday," her mother said, "your son will be grown and it will be clear that although you gave it your best shot, you failed to be the perfect parent. And you'll need Zack to absolve you of that by loving you and being kind to you in spite of it. And if he refuses you that absolution, he'll have turned out to be a shallow, selfish waste of time."

"It's more complicated than that," Amy said.

"No, it's not complicated. All I'm asking you to do is something nice for someone you love. Amy, give your father a gift that will mean the world to him, and won't cost you a damn thing."

She knew her mother was right; she needed to say only two words—*I'm sorry*—and her father would go back to the way things had always been. But she also knew there was nothing that would ever make Justin go back. And the truth was, she didn't want him to. She had no desire for a husband docile enough to spend his life as part of another man's entourage. Amy had always been attracted to tough guys—men who, not unlike her father, had a taste for combat.

"Mother," she said, "I have to go now." Then she hung up. She had no more time to deal with her mother, or her father. She needed to be in Ari's office, with Justin.

*

Justin and Ari had been waiting for over half an hour. Both of them were on edge.

Justin was at the table near the window, where Ari's assistant had set out coffee and muffins. Like everything else in the room, there was a geometric precision to the arrangement: the muffin basket, a triangle of webbed chrome; the plates and cups, square-shaped and made of thin jade-green glass.

"Do you think he's found anything?" Justin asked.

Ari was leafing through a travel magazine. "There's no use speculating. It's best to just wait and hear what he has to say when he gets here."

"I feel like I've spent my life waiting for this to happen. You're my shrink, and that's the best you can come up with? Just *wait*?"

Ari got up and handed Justin a muffin. "Okay. Then how about this? Sit down. Eat some breakfast."

Justin dropped the muffin back onto the table and walked away. "I don't want any breakfast." He glanced at his watch. "And where the hell is Amy?"

There was a noise on the other side of the office door. Justin looked up, alert and anxious.

But it wasn't the person he was hoping for; it was Ari's assistant, Emily. She flashed him a sympathetic smile and quickly slipped a folder onto Ari's desk.

Just as Emily was leaving, Amy rushed in, flushed and frantic. "I'm late. I'm so sorry. Traffic was . . ." She glanced from Justin to Ari. "Oh God, I didn't miss it, did I? He hasn't been here and left already, has he?"

"Relax, Ames," Justin told her. "We haven't seen him yet."

"Don't worry. Everything's fine." Ari gave Amy a reassuring nod. "He called a little while ago and—"

There was a brisk knock on the door. At the sound of it, Justin looked startled, as if he'd been surprised by the very thing he'd been waiting for all morning. The door was being opened by a man in his late twenties—Latino, and tall, at least six inches over six feet. He was wearing a black designer workout suit and immaculate white sneakers. In one hand he carried a phone, in the other an expensive titanium attaché case. "Apologies for the delay," he said. "Something on another case popped. I had to jump on it right away."

He crossed the room in two swift strides and shook hands with Ari. "Good to see you again, Doc." He chuckled. "Glad there's no dismemberment and decapitation involved in this one." He turned to Justin and Amy and explained: "The doc and I worked for the same defense attorney on a big nasty-ass murder case a couple of years ago." He smiled and his teeth were dazzlingly bright against the creamy brown of his skin. "I'm Gabriel Gonzales, your private investigator." He glanced at Amy. "You're staring," he told her. "Don't worry about it. Everybody always expects I'm going to be older, shorter, and a lot less Mexican." Then his easy grin vanished as he looked at Justin. "So, are you ready?"

"Yeah. Let's do it." As he said this, Justin felt as if he were balancing on the edge of a knife blade—one that was cutting between fear and hope.

Gabriel Gonzales sat down, pulled a sleek laptop out of his

attaché case, and flipped it open. "Okay. I'll start with the chart topper. I found the red-haired woman."

Justin's legs went weak. Something cold and dark was coursing through him—the same nameless fear he'd experienced in the parking lot of the convalescent hospital when he had been struggling to comprehend that his father was dead, when he'd had the first inkling that there was some terrible secret hidden in the house on Lima Street.

He fumbled his way to a chair and sat. A growing sense of dread was overwhelming him.

"I've gotta tell you," Gabriel was saying, "a red-haired woman with a limp, who might've had a kid named TJ and might've taught at Wesleyan, in Middletown—it wasn't exactly a bonanza of background information. But after digging through the archives at Wesleyan, going through every picture and article about the faculty members from thirty-some years ago, I found your girl."

Gabriel swiveled the laptop so Justin could see the screen, and her face was there—in a photograph in a campus newspaper article.

Justin felt his guts jump and tumble.

Below the picture was a name: Margaret Marie Fischer. The red-haired woman was Margaret Marie Fischer. Justin had not imagined her; she was real. He was vindicated, and intensely sad. He had remembered her scent and the feel of that soft place at the base of her neck. But he hadn't remembered her name. Margaret Marie Fischer.

"And what about TJ?" Justin's mouth was dry and burning hot, as if he were tasting the distilled essence of fear.

"Once I'd gotten Margaret's name and address it wasn't hard to unearth the rest of it. You go through enough public records and you talk to enough people, you can find out almost anything," Gabriel said. "In this case I got lucky. Even though Margaret had been an only child and didn't have any surviving family, I did find an old man living on Margaret's street who knew her back in the day. He turned me onto the fact that she did, for a couple of years, have a kid named TJ and that she also had a local girl who baby-sat him, Kati Sloane. I tracked her down. She still lives in the area, a food-service worker in a school cafeteria. She told me that Margaret Fischer had adopted a little boy when the kid was maybe two or three years old. A private adoption. Apparently Kati had been pretty tight with Margaret, and Margaret told her all the details."

Justin's voice was shaking. "Where did the boy come from?"

Gabriel tapped the keyboard of the laptop and information flashed onto the screen. "According to his birth certificate, he was born in Sierra Madre, California."

"What was the home address?" Justin whispered.

"It was 822 Lima Street."

Justin could feel Amy's hand on his shoulder. He wanted to reach up and hold it, and keep holding it for a long time, but the name *Lima Street* had immobilized him.

"I have the birth certificate info," Gabriel was explaining, "because the kid ended up in the foster-care system, a ward of the state."

Amy looked toward the computer screen. "But you said Margaret Fischer adopted him."

"She did. But a couple of years later, she died in a car accident, and that's when the foster care started. He was in two different foster homes."

"Why was he adopted in the first place?" Amy asked. "Where were his parents? What happened?"

"According to Kati Sloane, his parents were around," Gabriel said. "They just decided to 'unload' him for some reason—that's her word, not mine. They had two other kids, two girls. As far as Kati and Margaret knew, the parents kept the girls and that little family unit stayed intact."

Hearing this made Justin feel lost and sick. His parents had disposed of him as if he'd been garbage.

*

After yesterday's meeting, Justin had gone home and pored over each item of information Gabriel Gonzales had provided. Then he had replayed the audiotapes of his sessions with Ari—every word they had exchanged since Justin's collapse on the beach. It should have been over; all the questions should have been answered.

But the more Justin thought about the things he'd discussed with Ari, and the information he'd gotten from Gonzales, the more certain he was that his puzzle was still missing one crucial piece.

That missing piece was the reason he was in Ari's office now.

Ari was settling into his usual chair and saying, "You look tense, buddy."

"Given what's going on with me at the moment," Justin replied, "how should I look?"

"If you're asking me as your friend," Ari said, "the answer is 'As tense as hell.' If you're asking me as your psychiatrist, the answer is 'Relieved.' You've blown away a lot of cobwebs. True, you've found out some disturbing things, but you've also turned up some comforting ones."

Justin gave a sardonic laugh. " 'Comforting'? You've got to be kidding."

"You found out that, in spite of having information on a grave-stone to the contrary, you haven't been dead for the last thirty years. And you found out that you're not crazy. Considering the alternatives, I'd call that comforting."

"Yeah. Well, right now I'm not feeling anything even close to comfortable." Justin wasn't in the mood to be mollified.

"I want you to be clear on where we are here," Ari said. "What happened was that you were faced with a series of overwhelmingly negative events at a very young age, and you needed a way to process that."

Justin was impatient to get to the reason for his visit. He cut Ari off. "I know the rap," he said. "You've explained it to me. I get it. Dissociative identity disorder, which means at some point I sealed off TJ from Justin and kept them in two different places in my head." The statement mortified him; it made him sound pathetic and broken.

He began to pace the room. "I don't care how much you tell me that what I did was a form of self-preservation. It still feels like a made-for-TV freak show. What I did was find a way to lie to myself on such a monumental level that I was able to block out— what, ten, twelve years of my childhood? I just erased being adopted and living in foster homes, painted over it with my imaginary life on Lima Street. Call it survival all you want. But from in here, it feels like I'm a friggin' maniac."

Ari's tone was calmly professional. "You were barely a toddler when you were thrown into a psychological hell. By your fifth birthday, you'd already been ripped away from two different mothers. And after that, you were in an astoundingly bad foster-care situation. That's a history of extreme psychological abuse. And, yes, at the point when you left Middletown and went to college, for some reason, in order to deal with whatever was going on, you detached TJ from Justin. You were a kid in a world of absolute chaos. You came up with a way to survive. You should be proud of how well you coped."

Justin's voice had a bitter edge to it. "Finding out that I've been 'psychiatrically challenged' for most of my life makes me feel a lot of things, but proud isn't one of them."

"That's too bad," Ari said. "Because the truth is, given the same kind of beginning that you had—no opportunity to form even one secure emotional bond in early childhood, no chance to establish any trust with the people who were supposed to be taking care of you—most of us wouldn't have turned out half as healthy as you did."

"Being thirty-three years old and thinking I was someone I wasn't," Justin said, "that's your idea of healthy?"

"Actually you *were* that person, there was just more to the story," Ari said. "But that's beside the point. What I'm trying to explain is that given your history, it would be expected for you to be seriously dysfunctional. At *best* a dropout or a felon."

"But I turned out to be a lying fruitcake instead." Justin shot Ari an exasperated glance.

"Look, it's very common for kids who are under no psychological strain at all to think they remember things they couldn't possibly remember, things that may have happened before they were born. But they *believe* they remember because they've heard the stories a million times from their parents and grandparents. The only difference is, you told the story to yourself. That little song had everything in it that you needed for the building of an emotional fortress."

"Ari," Justin said, "do you want to know what the fortress looked like from in here?" He tapped his forehead. "Like rotting, black . . . Swiss cheese."

"I'm going to need you to explain that one to me," Ari said.

"Imagine watching a movie through a sheet of tar paper with holes punched in it. That's how it was for me. I could only see pieces of the picture," Justin said. "In college, when I tried to think about my life, to remember specifics . . . I couldn't do it. It was totally weird. I knew I'd been a kid. I could remember what my room looked like, but the only house I could get a picture of in my mind was the one on Lima Street. And I knew I had gone to school . . . but I could only remember general things . . . like that the name of my high school was Wilson, but I didn't remember the teachers' names or what the kids in my class looked like. I couldn't even remember what I looked like." Justin stopped and gave a wry laugh. "Want to know something? I've never seen a photograph of myself as a kid. Only as a toddler, and then in college. Nothing in between." There was wistfulness as he added: "I have absolutely no idea what I looked like while I was growing up."

Ari leaned forward, his elbows on his knees. He was studying Justin intently as he said, "All those years, between college and when you came back here from London . . . you had absolutely no memory of having lived in either of the foster homes you were in?"

"It was crazy," Justin replied. "I could feel that there were these dark places in my head, stuff I couldn't get at, and it scared the shit out of me. But all I knew for sure was the Justin Fisher from Lima Street thing. The rest of it was a jumble."

"You did four years of college and you were in London for ten years afterward," Ari said. "That's a long time to live with something like that. Why didn't you ever try to figure it out? Why didn't you try to contact your family? Or talk to a shrink about it?"

Justin went to the window and gazed out. He waited for a while and then said, "The truth is, I knew there was part of me that was seriously fucked-up."

"So why didn't you do anything about it?"

"Because it was way too scary. Every time I tried to figure out what was hiding in those blank spaces in my memory, I'd get hit with this horrible feeing that if I didn't back away from it, I was going to die."

"What about friends and people you worked with—what did you tell them?" Ari asked.

"Not much," Justin said. Then he smiled. "Most people are a lot more interested in their own lives than anybody else's." As he glanced at Ari, his tone was full of irony. "Everybody thought I was the soul of empathy and charm. You know why? Because in being scared shitless of ever having to talk about me and my story, I learned to make it all about the other guy."

Justin let out an exhausted sigh. "And then I came home, and the Justin Fisher Who Never Was went to Lima Street. And the crazy came spilling out."

Ari fixed his gaze on Justin. "You used Justin Fisher from Lima Street to save yourself," he said. "There was nothing crazy about that. TJ's life was too hard. If you couldn't have gotten away from it, it would've killed you."

When Justin heard the word *killed,* he flinched.

His heart was beating with the force of a sledgehammer as he said: "Ari, there's something I need to tell you. I don't know if it's true or not, but if it is, it's big. Bigger than any of the other stuff we've found out about TJ . . ."

There was a long silence before Justin finished his thought. "It's bigger. And it's much worse."

MIDDLETOWN, CONNECTICUT, JUNE 1990

*

It was after midnight. The sidewalks on Main Street were empty. She was making a left turn—not far from the Greyhound bus station—coming home from her cousin's bachelorette party. That was when she saw him running across the street with a duffel bag in his hand.

The minute she saw him, she knew him. Over the years, from time to time, she'd stood at the edges of the playgrounds at his elementary school and his middle school, and she had watched him. And she'd wanted to call to him and say that she loved him. But she felt her declarations of love would have been valueless because, when he'd needed her most, she had failed him.

He was almost eighteen, tall and muscular now, but there was something about the way he moved that was unmistakably TJ. He was alone on the street, passing within inches of her. She was exhilarated and excited from the party, and before she realized she'd done it, she had called out to him and said: "TJ! It's Kati."

His stride faltered and he slowed. For a fraction of an instant, their eyes met. "It's me. Kati, your old baby-sitter," she said. "How are you?"

There was a flicker of hesitation, as if he was on the verge of stopping and saying something to her. But he turned and sprinted away, quickly crossing the street and disappearing around a corner.

Kati's initial instinct was to follow him, but the moment had passed and the things she had wanted to say suddenly seemed pitifully insufficient.

As she drove away, she thought about the last time they had been together—the terrible night in which she'd failed him, and lost him, by not finding a way to keep him safe.

After Margaret had left the house to go back to Middletown and retrieve TJ's roller skates, the sound of the wind and the rain, growing progressively stronger, kept Kati on edge. She was worried that the storm's increasing noise would wake TJ. She knew if he woke up and discovered his mother was not in the house, he would be terrified.

At some point, Kati began calling Margaret's office at Wesleyan, hoping against hope that she would suddenly be there, safe and well—with the explanation that she'd had car trouble, or gone for a snack, or fallen asleep at her desk. And then, when Margaret's phone continued to go unanswered, Kati stopped calling and began circling through the house, terrified, frantic to see a break in the storm, to hear the sound of a key in the lock, to understand what it was that should be done now that she and TJ had been set adrift, in this empty house, on this furious night.

Just before one in the morning, the doorbell rang. The abrupt ring of the chime, echoing in the stillness of the living room, sounded thunderously loud. But it was Kati's scream that had awakened TJ. It had happened when Kati saw the state trooper standing in the doorway, his rain-soaked hat in his hand. The look on his face told her Margaret was dead.

Upstairs, TJ, still half-asleep, had shouted: "Mommy!" And

the night split apart. Everything changed. And by the time morning had come, TJ was gone.

The trooper had placed a series of phone calls as soon as he'd discovered there was a young child in the house who was now motherless and, in the purest sense, an orphan. The house had quickly filled with people—additional troopers, neighbors, and local police. Within hours, arrangements were being made to put TJ into foster care.

Kati pleaded with the troopers. "Please," she said. "Couldn't you just let him stay with me until, until . . ." But even as she was saying it, she knew she had no way to take care of TJ. Her parents had recently moved to Florida, she lived in a tiny apartment with three other girls, and every cent she had was in her purse—less than fifty dollars.

In the midst of the confusion, a social worker had arrived. She was young and pretty, and TJ's was the last case she was ever going to handle; in a week, she was getting married and moving away. She was scattered and distracted, descending on Kati like a whirlwind: wanting Kati to make TJ stop crying, wanting Kati to admire her engagement ring, wanting Kati to show her where the phone was so she could call her fiancé, and wanting Kati to quickly pack for TJ—whatever Kati could fit into a single suitcase.

The final thing the social worker wanted was for Kati to give her access to Margaret's files; she needed to locate TJ's birth certificate.

Kati, numbed by the shock of Margaret's death and the sadness of TJ's plight, stuffed TJ's clothes into an old blue suitcase and handed over a large envelope that had been at the bottom of one of Margaret's desk drawers.

Across the front of the envelope, in Margaret's elegant handwriting, was the inscription "For TJ." Inside the envelope were two items: a birth certificate (folded into a small square, no bigger than a credit card) and a spiral notebook full of snapshots. Neither Kati nor the social worker examined them closely. The social worker was in a hurry to be on her way. Kati was in a daze of grief.

The last Kati saw of TJ was as the social worker was carrying him away from the house. He was holding his hand out to Kati in a frantic, anxious gesture—as if he were groping for a miracle. And he was asking the question—"Mommy?"—over and over and over again.

Kati closed the door of Margaret's house, leaned against it, and looked around the living room. It was then that she saw TJ's piano.

In the driveway outside, the social worker had buckled TJ into the backseat of her sedan. She had opened the envelope and removed the contents—the birth certificate and the spiral notebook. The birth certificate was not the updated document issued when TJ's adoption had been finalized; it was the one that had come to Margaret tucked inside the notebook. It identified TJ as Thomas Justin Fisher, a boy who lived on Lima Street.

The certificate was put into a file folder—a folder that would, from this point forward, hold the official documentation of TJ's life and identity.

As the social worker was in the process of tossing the spiral notebook into TJ's blue suitcase, she looked up and saw that Kati was at the rear door of the car, sliding a child-size grand piano onto the backseat.

The social worker was about to tell her to stop, to take the piano away. But she was looking into Kati's eyes. The determination that was there was forbidding her to utter a single word.

*

TJ's new home was a ramshackle dwelling in Middletown, its paint faded to the colors of ash and rusted things, the colors of neglect. The house belonged to Kevin Loudon and his wife, Angela.

The Loudons' desire to be foster parents had been motivated by their misguided belief that the venture would be lucrative. The child-welfare system's desire to have them as foster parents had been motivated by necessity. There were more children than places to put them.

The Loudons were gift horses into whose mouths the bureaucracy chose not to look too closely. They were sloppy, aggravated people who wore their disappointments like clumsily concealed war paint. Their failures had stayed stuck to them like gum to the bottom of a shoe. There was a row of aluminum lawn chairs and a pair of young boxer dogs, in a crate, on their sagging front porch. And in the yard at the back, there was an old Pontiac without an engine, and a brand-new cherry red motorcycle.

The interior of the house was surprisingly bright and clean. The walls were painted in pastels and the windows were hung with spotless curtains. The matched maple furniture, bought on credit from Sears, was dust-free and polished. Angela took pride in the rooms she inhabited, the same pride she had once taken in herself, in the days before she had become a Loudon—in the time when she had been Angela DiMarco.

Angela had been born in Middletown and had once been so beautiful that she'd made an altar boy's knees buckle just by winking at him while she was kneeling at the communion rail of St. Sebastian's Church.

And then she had married Kevin.

Kevin came from a large brawling family of swamp Yankees—an uneducated, prejudiced clan whose meager allotment of pride came solely from the fact that they were born and bred New Englanders. He was thin and wiry, and violent when he drank. He worked in a supermarket warehouse, forklifting canned soup and breakfast cereal and pinto beans, because the auto repair shop he'd started with his brother, and his time as an Amway agent, and the job selling swimming pools over the phone hadn't made him rich, even though he'd been certain that they would.

Angela was now thirty-five and pregnant with a child she hadn't planned, disappointed that she could no longer make men's knees buckle with a wink, and unhappy that the man she'd married had taken her no farther than a dilapidated house with an engineless car in the yard.

Kevin and Angela had two preadolescent children—a daughter, Angie, and a son, Kevin Junior, who was deaf. And when, on an August afternoon, TJ came to them, they had their first foster child.

In the beginning, they'd been on their best behavior. It was as if they had been blessed with a paying guest who took up very little space, rarely spoke, and spent most of his time either silently looking at a set of photographs pasted into a spiral notebook or sitting in front of a miniature piano, teaching himself to play and producing disjointed, melancholy music. But it wasn't long before the Loudons became accustomed to TJ's presence and their old grievances and failures dragged them back to being themselves. By Christmastime, Kevin had begun drinking again, Angela was into the seventh month of her pregnancy, and they were arguing.

The argument was about money. It started at dinner and continued late into the night. When the muffled boom of their voices reached the room that TJ shared with Kevin Junior, TJ awoke. He sat up with a start and saw that Kevin Junior was asleep, cocooned in his deafness. TJ knew he was alone, and he began to shake.

Since he had been in the Loudons' house, he had become terrified by, and schooled in, the rhythms of its violence—violence that was like a cradle being pushed and shoved, first by Kevin, then by Angela, each of them moving deliberately faster, until they rocked the cradle to the point of madness, until it exploded. Then there would inevitably come the sounds of objects being smashed, and Angela screaming, and the dogs barking, and Angie waking up and running from room to room, crying and begging her daddy to stop.

In the darkness of his bedroom, TJ knew from the roar of the voices in the living room that the chaos had been let loose, and soon the house would be raucous with shattering glass and breaking furniture. He scrambled out of his bed like a small wounded animal trying to outrun wildfire. He ran to the closet and took the spiral notebook out of the blue suitcase and quickly crawled back into bed. He lay with his trembling arms crossed on his chest, the notebook held tightly beneath them. The shaking in his body began to subside as he turned his face to the wall and said: "Do I know my name? Yes, I do. Yes I do . . . my name is Justin. And my name is Fisher, too."

In the living room, the argument raged on. Kevin was shouting that the Christmas presents Angela had bought for Angie and Kevin Junior were crap. Angela was screaming that crap was all they could afford because he was a failure and she wished he was dead.

Kevin grabbed at Angela and ripped her nightgown in two. And Angela ran, unclothed, into Kevin Junior's room. She tried to lock the door behind her, but Kevin kicked it open and sent bits of the door frame splintering onto his son's bed. Kevin, his face red and the veins in his neck roped and bluish and his breath sour with the smell of whiskey, grabbed his naked, pregnant wife by her hair and threw her across the room.

In that moment, TJ turned his face away from the wall and saw Angela falling past him, toward the corner, toward his piano, a flow of red slipping between her legs, like a snake, winding down onto the uneven floor. A buckled floorboard was causing the trail of blood to coil back on itself, then slide away again.

Angela fell. The piano broke apart beneath her. TJ heard the sound of music being shattered. And Christmas Day had come to an end.

*

Six other Christmases arrived and departed—most of them listless and forgettable.

TJ remained with the Loudons, sharing Kevin Junior's room and coming, slowly, over time, to enjoy his company. Kevin Junior was in some ways as coarse and unpredictable as his parents, but he was essentially a kind child, and a bright one. He taught TJ how to communicate in sign language, and he and TJ spent much of their time together in silent, lively conversation about comic books and Darth Vader and what Disneyland, and traveling there in a jet plane, might really be like.

At night, after Kevin Junior was asleep, TJ would open the spiral notebook and give himself over to the photographs that were pasted onto its pages. One of them was the image of a little boy in a bathtub, surrounded by tiles patterned in fish shapes. And there was also a photograph of that same boy, barely more than a baby, standing triumphant on the closed lid of a toy chest, tightly gripping the edge of a window frame. Near the boy's hand was an indentation that looked like the face of a clown.

Each time TJ gazed at the photos of the two little girls, each time he saw the girl who was invariably smiling, he would hear himself whisper the name Lissa.

And there would be other flickers of memory. He remembered his mother and how sweet her smell was. And he remembered his father and how fast he moved. When he ran.

Night after night, as the sounds of muffled rage would come seeping through his bedroom wall, burning and electric, TJ would turn his face to the darkness, and say: "Do I know my home? Yes, I do. Yes, I do. I live on Lima Street . . . right at 822." He would whisper it until it sealed him off from the noise and made him safe. Until it erased TJ who lived with the Loudons, and erased their house, and the town in which it stood, and the world in which it existed.

The world of the Loudons was a jittery place; moods shifted without warning and happiness and unhappiness careened into each other like the cars of a runaway roller coaster. It was a world so disturbed that a thing as simple as looking directly into some-one's eyes could be a terrifying and wounding blunder.

TJ came to understand that if he (or Kevin Junior or Angie) made the mistake of catching Kevin's eye when Kevin, drunk and furious, was in the act of upending the dinner table, sending food and glass splattering and shattering across the walls, it could lead to being singled out and grabbed and screamed at.

To look at Angela could be just as dangerous. To come into her line of vision when she was in one of her moods—usually after she'd had an altercation with Kevin—was to become the object of a tirade, a mad harangue in which she would weep and shout: "I sacrificed my life. I could have left years ago. Men wanted me. They did! Ask anybody. But instead I gave up everything. And for what? For you, you ungrateful little shits! One of these days, I'm gonna go. I deserve better and I'm gonna go! I owe it to myself." Then she would rush through the house, running her hands over tabletops and chair backs, screaming that the place was a pigsty and pulling out a wash bucket and scrub brush and dropping to her knees and scouring at the floors and shouting that she was working herself to death and that no one cared.

Because Angie and Kevin Junior were bound to her by the

irrational, strangling cord of birth, they could not learn to look away. They couldn't escape their mother's face and the craziness that was in it. They were forced to ride the currents of her rants like a series of raging rapids. And when she would finish, they would huddle around her and they would promise to be better. They would take the scrub brush out of her hand and work with all their might to find a way to make clean, for her, a house that was already immaculate.

And because the same irrational strangling cord tied them to Kevin, they couldn't look away from him—even when they were dragged from their beds and derided for being lazy and told to polish his cracked work boots until the boots sparkled, even when they were belt-whipped because no sparkle could be made to appear on snow-ruined, salt-stained leather.

But TJ was no one's child. He could look away. And he did. Over the years, he developed the ability to look at faces without seeing them. He learned to keep his gaze vague and his thoughts in another place—the world that existed in the photographs in the spiral notebook, the safe haven that was the house on Lima Street.

Years passed. Social workers came and went and TJ was left adrift as a foster child in the Loudon household. The Loudons continued to cash the checks for his care, and to become a family that was older and angrier and less stable. And finally, when TJ was almost twelve, Kevin Loudon rode out of Middletown in a Chevy truck with a girl named Donna. She wore no underwear and looked like Angela had once looked, in a time long gone.

*

In the wake of Kevin's departure, Angela and her children took up residence in the back bedroom of Angela's parents' home on Francis Avenue in Middletown and TJ was moved into the care of Stan and Suzy Zelinski.

The Zelinski house was a modest place with a manicured square of lawn at its front; a place where storm windows went up each year before the arrival of the first winter snow and promptly came down with the departure of the last.

Stan Zelinski was heavyset and carried himself with military precision. His daily uniform was a fresh denim work shirt and a pair of khaki slacks with a knife-sharp crease. He owned the same hardware store in Middletown that his father and grandfather had owned, and he was involved in community activities, especially those having to do with young people.

Stan and Suzy had one son and, over the years, countless foster children—so many, in fact, that they had often been written up in the newspaper and people had given the nickname "Zelinski Kids" to the children who cycled through Suzy and Stan's care. The majority of the Zelinski Kids had been girls because, as Stan had explained early on, he and Suzy had been unable to have any more children after their son had been born, and Suzy wanted little girls to fuss over. Suzy was sweet and unaffected. Plump and still girlish at forty-two, she was a woman who, when filling out any paperwork requiring the listing of an occupation, proudly wrote *mom*.

At the Zelinskis', TJ had a room of his own. It was small and neat. On the wall above the bed there was a framed poster from an air show. Suzy had told TJ that her son, Ted, when he was about TJ's age, had liked looking at the poster and dreaming about flying. "I thought you might enjoy having it," Suzy had said. "But if you'd rather have something else to dream by, just let me know, okay?"

TJ had no interest in her offer. He was already in possession of the images that fuelled his dreams; they were in a worn spiral notebook at the bottom of his battered blue suitcase.

The time with Suzy and Stan proved to be a welcome relief from the volatility of TJ's years with the Loudons—life there had been a Molotov cocktail; life at the Zelinskis', in comparison, was a glass of warm milk.

Suzy baked cookies. She had a vegetable garden, and helped with homework. Stan was a scoutmaster, and coached Little League, and never missed one of the high school baseball games in which his son was the pitcher. Ted was a good-natured kid who handled a ball the way Howlin' Wolf played the blues; he was a natural. It was from watching Ted Zelinski play baseball that TJ would ultimately develop a lifelong love for the game.

TJ was twelve and Ted was sixteen when they met; their lives ran in companionable parallel, but in the eighteen months they shared before Ted left the Zelinski house to go to college, there was no deep connection formed between them; nor was any real connection ever established between TJ and Suzy, or TJ and Stan.

Stan's life was consumed with scouting, and Little League, and fund-raising for a new community center. Suzy's attention was given to the foster daughters who came and went from the Zelinski house on a regular basis. While each of the girls was with her, Suzy hovered over her and doted on her, and then when she left, Suzy cried for her.

When he first came to the Zelinskis', TJ kept to himself and to his ritual of the notebook and the song. But by the time he was in middle school, he no longer needed the notebook to see the pictures it contained. He had made them his reality and his history. The contents of the notebook and the information in the song had been forged into a body and soul for Justin Fisher: a boy who had always lived, and been loved, in the house on Lima Street.

Toward the end of his stay with the Zelinskis, TJ was escaping to Lima Street less often; his attention was shifting from the past and moving toward his future. He was occupied with sports and girls and the pursuit of a college scholarship that would propel him out of Middletown.

In his final six months in Stan and Suzy's care, his heart was captured by the newest of the Zelinski Kids, a shy doe-eyed girl with ebony skin.

She was a child who loved books and music, and who wrote poems on bits of pink paper and folded them into tiny squares and kept them under her pillow, hidden, like an accumulation of compressed, unspoken wishes. Her name was Cassie.

On her first day in the house, she appeared in the doorway of TJ's room wearing a faded long-sleeved pink dress and a pair of pink socks. Her first words to him were: "Are you real?"

TJ was at his desk, studying. At the sound of her voice he looked up, and was startled by her intense blackness, and her fragility, and her sweet, little-girl beauty. When she spoke again, her voice was soft and cautious, as if she'd learned long ago to stay small and to keep secrets. "Are you real? Or are you like me?" she asked.

And because TJ, too, was no one's child, he knew what she was saying. "I'm like you," he told her.

She smiled a smile that was slow and widening and ultimately radiant. It reminded TJ of an Easter-morning sunrise. "I'm glad," she said. " 'Cause I didn't want to be the only one."

The most recent pair of Zelinski foster daughters had left over a month ago. Cassie was the new replacement, and by saying she didn't want to be "the only one," she was explaining that she didn't want to be the only foster child in the house, the only unconnected, temporary interloper, the only Zelinski Kid.

She came and stood beside TJ's desk. "How old are you?" she asked.

TJ grinned. "How old are you?"

"Ten," she said. "Are you gonna be here for a long time or a little time?"

"Six months. I'm going to graduate from high school in June," he told her. "Then I'm going away."

Again the sunrise smile. "Six. That's a lot of months." She slipped her hand into the pocket of her dress and withdrew a small smooth stone—milky silver-green and rounded. She put it on TJ's desk. "It's a present," she explained. "I found it under the house in the other place I was at before this one, and I've been saving it because it was so nice." She put a slender finger on the stone and slid it toward him. "It's for you."

"Are you sure?" TJ asked.

"I'm sure," she said. "I've got two of them." She opened her hand and showed him a second silver-green stone. "I put both of them in my pocket when I was coming to ask you so that if you said you were like me, I could give one to you and we could have . . ." She hesitated. "So we could have . . ." She bit her lip and looked up at him from under lowered lashes, suddenly embarrassed and a little unsure. "I brought it so we could share."

"Sharing would make us kind of affiliated, huh?" TJ said. Cassie looked away, shifting her weight from one pink-socked foot to the other and saying nothing. TJ realized that she was not quite certain of the meaning of *affiliated*. "Sharing would make us kind of a team," he explained.

"Would that be okay?" She looked ready to take a step backward and move away. "My name's Cassie Jackson." She said it as if it was something TJ should know before making his decision.

He picked up the stone and held it. It felt warm and vaguely heart-shaped. "I think us being a team would be great," he said.

After that, daily, for six months, Cassie continued to bring TJ gifts: puppets made of Popsicle sticks, bouquets of flowers picked from Suzy's garden, bluebird feathers, twigs that were fragile, delicate, and elegant. In the afternoons while he did his homework, she perched on a chair beside his desk, reading fairy tales and stories of high adventure. And in the evenings, she sat beside TJ at the dinner table, whispering to him about her dreams and her poems and her mama being dead and her grandma being in jail and how someday she, Cassie, intended to have a pony and how, when she did have it, she would ride it to school.

Cassie trailed TJ like a timid, obsessive acolyte. She was free to do so because the profound blackness of her skin had produced an immediate and dulling effect on Suzy's interest in her.

TJ knew that if he'd not allowed Cassie to claim him as her friend, her stay in the Zelinski household would have been a comfortless one.

*

In the early evening of TJ's last day in the house, the day he had graduated from high school, Cassie came into his room as he was packing. A black duffel bag, his graduation gift from the Zelinskis, was open on his bed. Cassie crossed the room in silence and solemnly slipped a sheet of pink paper into one of the bag's side pockets. The paper was rolled into a scroll and tied with a shoelace. "It's a poem," she explained. "For your graduation."

Then she stepped up onto the bed and looked him in the eye and said, "You're the best friend I ever had in my whole life, TJ."

After she had stepped down off the bed, she added, "The social worker says my gramma's out of jail and she's coming to get me." Cassie briefly smiled her Easter-sunrise smile. "I'm gonna be real. In one more week." She gave him a nod and a tight brusque wave.

TJ understood what she was telling him: There had been too many departures, too many changes, too many losses. All the goodbyes had been used up.

After Cassie left, TJ picked up the duffel bag and walked out of the Zelinski house. He'd already said his farewells to Stan and Suzy. Now he was in a hurry. He needed to get to the bus station; there was a Greyhound leaving in half an hour that would ferry him out of Middletown and deliver him to his summer job and to college. It would take him to Boston, the place where he could be born again.

As the bus had pulled away from the station—shortly after he let himself sink back into his seat and draw a deep breath that was intoxicatingly sweet and free—TJ suddenly sat bolt upright. "No!" came out of him with such force that the bus driver glanced into the rearview mirror and gave him a wary look, and several passengers shot nervous glances in his direction.

An hour later, when the bus rolled out of Hartford, headed for Boston, TJ was no longer on it. He was at the side of the road, hitchhiking back to Middletown.

The spiral notebook was still in the old blue suitcase under his bed in the Zelinski house.

*

It had taken TJ a long time to find a ride. The garrulous old man who had eventually picked him up had driven at such an incredibly slow pace that now, as they were leaving the highway and entering Middletown, it was after eleven and TJ was in a panic. He was due to report to his summer job in Boston at six-thirty in the morning; he needed to retrieve the notebook and start on his return trip as soon as possible.

As the old man was making a glacially slow turn, TJ grabbed the black duffel bag and jumped from the car. He rolled onto the soft shoulder of the road and ran the few remaining blocks that lay between him and his destination.

Stan and Suzy often left the back door unlocked, so TJ sprinted past the front of the house and headed into the alley behind it. He was hoping the Zelinskis would be asleep and that he could get the notebook and be gone without having to cross paths with them. The Zelinskis had never seen the notebook, and TJ didn't want to share it with Stan and Suzy now that he no longer had any business with them.

When he entered the alley, he saw that lights were on in the kitchen. He assumed it was Stan who was still awake. Suzy was unfailingly in bed by ten, but it wasn't unusual for Stan to stay up late watching TV or puttering in the garage.

TJ moved quietly toward the breezeway that connected the area between the side wall of the garage and the back of the house. The garage side of the breezeway was paneled in clear-lacquered Peg-Board. Hanging from the Peg-Board were a variety of lawn tools—mostly rakes and hoes, all of them vintage, from Stan's father's time. They had thick wooden handles and iron blades and tines, all carefully cleaned and sharpened. Stan kept them displayed like rustic L-shaped museum pieces.

On an area of grass under one of the kitchen windows, a sprinkler was turning. Its spray was falling onto the concrete at the entrance to the breezeway, near the back door. To keep the black duffel bag dry, TJ put it on a wooden bench a short distance away from the pooling water. Then he moved cautiously toward the house.

He could hear the radio playing. An oldies station. The Beatles singing about Eleanor Rigby. But there were no sounds that indicated anyone was moving around inside the kitchen. TJ knew that Stan was probably in the living room, watching television. As he put his hand on the doorknob, his pulse quickened; the back door was unlocked.

He pushed the door open slowly. There was no one in the kitchen, but the air was full of the bitter-sharp smell of gun oil. On a towel on the Formica tabletop was one of Stan's rifles, freshly cleaned. Beside it were an open box of shells and three or four hunting magazines. The room was long and narrow. On the wall immediately to TJ's left, just beyond the table, was a doorway. It led to a hallway that ran parallel to the kitchen and accessed the bedrooms. At the far end of the kitchen was another door leading to the same hallway. That door was closer to the living room, where TJ assumed Stan was, but it was also directly across from TJ's old bedroom.

He exited through the far end of the kitchen. In four swift, light steps, he had crossed into his former bedroom and was out of sight. When he carefully closed the bedroom door, he could still hear the Beatles singing in the kitchen. The radio had been turned up loud enough to be audible in the bedrooms, and he was grateful; it would help mask any noise he might inadvertently make.

TJ pulled the suitcase from under the bed and removed the notebook, positioning it between the small of his back and his belt. Then he went to the bedroom door and began the process of easing it open. He was straining to hear any sound or movement that might be coming from the direction of the living room. As he stepped out into the hall, he heard the Beatles singing about Strawberry Fields.

And then he heard something else, just below the music. It was coming from the other end of the hallway. From Cassie's room. It was the sound of whimpering, high-pitched and fearful. He instinctively moved toward it. As he did, he bumped into a low bookcase that was against the wall. A porcelain figurine fell from the top shelf and broke, loudly, onto the floor.

Almost instantly, there was a sudden scuffling noise in Cassie's room. Her door opened, and TJ saw Stan hurrying out. Stan was rumpled and stumbling. He was hiking his pants and groping for his zipper as he was moving through the doorway at the far end of the hall and disappearing into the kitchen.

The sound of Cassie's plaintive whimper and the sight of Stan fumbling at the crotch of his khaki pants set off a violent hatred in TJ. It was so intense that, for an instant, his vision was obscured by a flash of red, as if some incendiary, bloody thing inside him had burst.

TJ swiftly crossed the hallway and went into the kitchen. He wanted to put his hands around Stan Zelinski's thick neck and break it. Stan was at the other end of the room, near the table, hunched over, stuffing the tails of his blue work shirt into the waistband of his pants. He was glancing over his shoulder toward the doorway through which he had just come, nervously looking in the direction of the bedroom he shared with his wife.

"You fucking freak," TJ said.

Stan whirled around, startled. When he saw TJ, he went white with shock. "How long have you been here?" His voice was a ragged mix of confusion and fear; he was struggling to keep it low, to keep it under the cover of the music coming from the radio— the Beatles singing about a yellow submarine.

"You fucking, fucking freak." The expression in TJ's eyes as he was walking toward Stan was murderous. His first blow slammed into Stan's face and broke his nose. It sent blood splattering across TJ's knuckles. The second blow plowed into the center of Stan's barrel chest. TJ knew that if he allowed himself to do what he wanted to do, he would pound Stan, and keep pounding him, until Stan was bloody pulp, until he was dead.

Stan staggered back against the kitchen table. TJ moved away from him and reached for the phone on the wall.

"What are you doing?" Stan's breathing was labored and wheezing.

"I'm calling the police." TJ lifted the receiver and began to dial. It was then that he heard a *click!* and felt a small perfect circle of cold pressing against his temple. He knew it was the barrel tip of a cocked rifle.

Stan had crossed the room and was now between TJ and the open back door.

The sound of his own pulse was so loud in TJ's ears that he could hear nothing else. For a moment, he had the sensation that he was going to lose control of his bowels.

Without thinking, TJ reacted. To save himself, he crouched and drove his head into Stan's midsection, sending Stan stumbling backward, out through the open door, with the rifle still in his hands.

Stan immediately lost his footing in the pool of sprinkler water on the breezeway floor. His legs skidded out from under him and he was slammed into a sitting position, slammed back, hard, against the Peg-Board wall where the garden tools were. His eyes went glassy and a dribble of blood-pinked saliva bubbled from the corner of his mouth.

"You're not gonna get away with this." Stan's voice was a wheezing rasp. "You little bastard cocksucker. You're not gonna get away with this."

Before Stan could raise the rifle again, TJ grabbed the duffel bag from the bench near the breezeway entrance and bolted into the darkness.

As he ran, the spiral notebook was pressing against his spine, and all he could think of was sanctuary—the images of a sister named Lissa and a park swing sailing away from the ground, toward the sky.

When he came into the downtown area, it was after midnight. The sidewalks were empty. He wasn't far from the Greyhound bus station.

And he was still running.

As he entered Main Street, a car suddenly made a left turn. He was caught in the sweep of its headlights and he heard a woman calling to him, sounding light and happy, like someone who had been at a party: "TJ! It's Kati." The voice was strangely familiar. He glanced toward the woman and their eyes met. "It's me. Kati, your old baby-sitter," she said. "How are you?"

He experienced a brief shudder of emotion, as if she was a person he knew. He had a momentary impulse to say something to her. But instead, he sprinted away because she had called him TJ and that wasn't his name.

His name was circling in his head like a song: "My name is Justin. I know my name. Yes, I do. Yes, I do."

It was no longer TJ who was racing through the midnight darkness with a duffel bag in his hand and the spiral notebook at his back—it was Justin.

The confusion and terror and loneliness that was TJ and the Loudens and the Zelinskis and Stan's blood in the breezeway had been sucked into a past that could no longer be seen.

Justin was running toward his future. And, as always, toward the house on Lima Street.

Caroline

*

"The sins of our youth and of our riper years. The sins of our souls and the sins of our bodies. Our spontaneous sins. Our sins of igno-rance. The sins we know and remember, and the sins we have for-gotten. Forgive them, O Lord. Forgive them all."

The minister allowed a moment of silence before he spoke again. "In the name of Jesus Christ, you are forgiven." And from the congregation, the response rang out: "Glory to God! Amen."

Caroline abruptly rose from a back pew and walked out. The minister's words had filled her with bitterness. The space in her soul that should have been available for repentance and forgive-ness was too crowded. It was too full of confusion.

She was bewildered by a myriad of things. Foremost among them was how quickly time had gone by—how swiftly the begin-ning had become the end, how abruptly youth had collided with age and swept so much beauty out of reach.

The little, exquisite things that had been lost were numberless. And as they had evaporated one by one from Caroline's reality, they had firmly fixed themselves in her memory. She could still hear the banging of the screen door and the tinny clatter of metal thermoses rolling against the sides of empty lunch boxes and high, excited voices calling: "Mommy, Mommy! We're home!" She could still smell the unique scent that was the Fourth of July: charcoal lighter fluid, grilled hot dogs, and backyard fireworks. She could still feel herself as she used to be—the weight of her hair hanging long and thick down her back, the texture of her skin as soft as cashmere, the shape of her body when it had been supple and desired. These were the memories of things she'd once possessed without any real understanding of how pleasurable they were, or how fleeting they would be.

Caroline was in her sixties now. Time had slowed her step and etched lines onto her beautiful face; time had moved her girls away from her and turned them into women, separate and apart, their attention and love given to boyfriends, and husbands, and children of their own.

On her walk from the church to the house on Lima Street, Caroline's impulse was to weep for the sins she'd committed in her youth and ignorance. But overriding that impulse was a desire to curse God. She wanted to curse him for having failed to protect her from those sins, for having allowed her to fall into motherhood, and womanhood, so profoundly defenseless and stupid and unprepared.

Above all, she had wanted to curse God for Justin's absence. But the curse always died before it could be uttered—killed by an inescapable truth. It was a truth that had bored into Caroline the minute she learned Robert had taken Justin and given him away. She had immediately seen the awful symmetry: Justin had been stolen from a mother who was, from the very moment of his conception, a thief.

Her first theft had been from her marriage; she had robbed it of honesty and fidelity. And after Justin's birth, the proportions of her thievery had become astounding. By wrapping her child in her own complicated secrets and hiding him away on Lima Street, she had stolen a son from his father.

The weight of her complicity in what had happened to Justin was suddenly hitting Caroline with aching force. She was approaching the corner, and the mailbox—the same mailbox into which, all those years ago, she had put the spiral notebook and the photographs: the evidence of the life from which Justin had been taken and the proof of her desperation to have him back.

Full of Valium and loss, she had staggered to that mailbox and pushed the clumsily wrapped package into it and prayed for the miracle of her child's return. But in a small part of her heart, she sensed that it was a prayer that should perhaps go unanswered. Justin deserved a sweeter life, something better than being raised by a divorced mother who could offer him only an unmoored, scrabbling, hand-to-mouth existence.

Those had been Caroline's thoughts when she first lost Justin, and they were still troubling her now. But as she rounded the corner onto Lima Street, her mood lifted. There was a large sport utility vehicle parked at the curb in front of the house. On the car's bumper was a sticker proclaiming FAMILY FIRST, and in the rear window was a decal depicting five smiling stick figures—a father, a mother, and three boys of descending height. Beneath the figures, there were names: Harrison, Lissa, Graham, Fletcher, and Ethan. Caroline's pace immediately quickened.

As she was walking up the front steps, she saw that it was Ethan who was running to greet her. "Gramma, where've you been?" He sounded joyful and breathless. "We were waiting and waiting."

"I've been to church," Caroline said. She picked him up and

carried him into the house. His skin smelled warm and dusty, the way a puppy smells when it's been out in the sunshine, rolling on the lawn.

"But church got out a long time ago. You should have been here already." His expression let her know that in his opinion, as a four-year-old who had just come from church himself, her story was not holding together well. Before Caroline could explain that she hadn't gone to the same church he had, Lissa came hurrying down the hallway from the kitchen. Newly blond and sylphlike, in tapered pants and a fitted jacket that were dove-colored and expensively cut.

She swept in on Caroline, taking Ethan out of her arms. "What are you doing, Ethan? You're too heavy for Gramma to be carrying around."

"He's fine," Caroline said. But Lissa was already settling Ethan onto her own slim hip, handling him as if he weighed no more than an empty laundry basket. Caroline wondered if Lissa knew how smug she looked and how patronized Caroline felt; how demeaning it was, this business of being arbitrarily relegated to the status of frail-boned and ancient.

Lissa was already heading back toward the kitchen, calling over her shoulder, "Where have you been? We were getting worried."

"I went to church," Caroline said. "A new one. The Methodists." She made no move to follow Lissa. She stood her ground, determined not to trail behind her daughter. She walked into the living room and sat, irked by the fact that all she ever seemed to see of Lissa were quick flashes of her moving away. Always in a rush, always overscheduled and busy.

The last time Caroline had been alone with Lissa or Julie for any length of time had been the night before Lissa's wedding, seventeen years ago, the three of them curled up together on Lissa's bed, the girls promising that the house on Lima Street was their home and they'd be coming back, often and always. But after the wedding, Julie had gone off to Chicago, to an internship at an advertising agency, and Lissa had sailed away on a honeymoon cruise to Greece. Then Lissa became busy—being a newlywed and the wife of an ambitious young surgeon; being pregnant with her first child, and then with her second and third; and then she was busy with soccer games, and charity balls, and European vacations.

Across the years Lissa's busyness had become the bullet in which she was encased as she flew past Caroline. It was the opening statement with which she answered call after call: "Hi, Mom. I have to run." "Hi, Mom. I'm right in the middle of something." "Hi, Mom. I can only talk for a minute." And somewhere in the jumbled passing of time, Caroline had stopped calling. There seemed to be no point to it.

Now, sitting in the living room, the Sunday bulletin from the Methodist church still in her hand, she was recognizing the ironic truth of her situation. Meeting the needs of her children had been the thing to which she had devoted her life, and now in the twilight of it, when she desperately needed them, her children had no need for her.

Lissa appeared in the living room doorway, looking at Caroline as if Caroline had lost her mind. "Mom . . . you went to a *Methodist* church?"

"I was in the mood for a change."

"A change from *our* church?"

Caroline fought the urge to tell Lissa to mind her own business, to point out to Lissa that she and her sister had been raised in the Episcopal Church only because of Caroline. Because she had chosen it. Because of Barton and his connection to it. She wanted to tell Lissa that if, over the past decade and a half, Lissa had spent even a little uninterrupted time with her, she might have come to know who her mother was. She might have come to understand why such a woman could be searching for something new—a fresh nourishment for her soul, something to soothe the burn of a lifetime's worth of regrets. But it was too late to explain any of those things.

Caroline simply said: "It's good to see you. Why didn't you call and let me know you were coming?"

"We wanted it to be a surprise. For Dad."

"For Dad? Why?" Caroline was momentarily confused. It was October. It wasn't Robert's birthday, or Father's Day.

"Dad's getting that award tomorrow, when you guys go to San Francisco for the insurance convention."

At the mention of her father, Lissa's eyes lit up. She looked like a little girl again. And she melted Caroline's heart.

"This is a big deal," Lissa said. "He's been chosen as Outstanding Independent Insurance Agent of the Year. Julie and I thought it would be fun to surprise him with a celebration before you guys took off for San Francisco." Lissa pulled Caroline to her feet and put an arm around Caroline's waist. "Mom, I think it's so great that you're taking this trip. The two of you never go anywhere together. You'll have such a blast."

The feel of Lissa's arm holding her close flooded Caroline with a sense of possibility, as if her girls were not as far away as she had thought. She felt light and bright. "I have an idea," she said. "What if you and Julie and I go somewhere together? For a weekend. Just the three of us. Maybe we could go to—"

A car horn sounded in the street, three quick staccato blasts. Lissa slipped from Caroline's grasp. Gone like quicksilver. Running toward the front door, saying: "Julie's here. Great! We can finally get Dad's party started."

It made Caroline want to shriek and pound the walls.

As Lissa was pulling the front door open, she was glancing back at Caroline and saying, "We kind of need to get things moving, Mom. My crew's a little crunched for time. Fletcher has a session with his math tutor and Graham's got soccer practice."

"Math tutors, soccer practice. Jesus God, Liss. You're such a suburban cliché." The statement was Julie's, made as she was striding into the house, her hair beautifully wild and colored blue-black, her arms full of gold-foiled take-out bags from a Beverly Hills restaurant. Julie handed several of the bags to Lissa and blew a kiss in Caroline's direction. "Hey, Mom, how's it going?"

Before Caroline could answer, she realized that Julie and Lissa had already moved past her. They were hurrying down the hall, laughing at a joke she hadn't heard.

*

The celebration the girls created for Robert was superb. The setting was the old trestle table under the oak tree in the backyard. Lissa wove wide swaths of yellow ribbon into the oak's branches and dressed the table with a set of navy blue linen napkins and a sunflower yellow tablecloth that she'd found two summers ago in Provence.

From Julie's gold foil shopping bags came lemon pasta and poached salmon and roasted cherry tomatoes and paper-thin slices of a fragrant toasted rye bread brushed with olive oil and crusted with a delicate aged cheese.

Cheers were going up from Lissa and her husband, Harrison, and their three boys. Julie had just raised a champagne glass and said: "To Dad! Our hero!"

Fletcher, Lissa's twelve-year-old son, quietly nudged Caroline. "Pick up your glass, Grandma. We're doing the toast." Fletcher was gentle and beautiful in the way that some boys at twelve can

211

be. His eyes were luminous. His skin was pale and clear, with tracings of a rose-colored flush across the curve of his cheeks. There was something about Fletcher that reminded Caroline very much of how Lissa had been at his age, and of how Justin might have been. The sight of him made Caroline ache for Justin and wonder what he had looked like at twelve, and at sixteen, and at twenty-one.

When Justin had first been taken from Caroline, the pain of his loss had been unbearable. She had been drowned in guilt and driven to the brink of suicide. As years passed, the pain and guilt never abated. But in slow increments they were forced into a less visible shape by the needs of her two remaining children, and by the momentum of daily life. By skinned knees and sleepovers and braces and first dates. By the death of her mother, and the birth of grandchildren. By a mammogram and a biopsy and the loss of part of what had always defined Caroline as a woman.

In the initial days and weeks after Justin was gone, the desire to have him back had consumed Caroline. Her constant thoughts were of the pictures and the birth certificate she'd mailed to the Connecticut law firm where Robert said he had left Justin; she had been convinced they would make it clear that her son had been stolen from her. She had hoped they would prompt his adoptive family to return him.

When there had been no response, Caroline placed frantic phone calls. It was then that she discovered that the law, and its record keepers, had sealed her son away from her forever. And so she began to mother him in the only way she could: by imagining the beauty and safety in which he was growing up each day; by believing that the level of passion with which he'd been banished from Lima Street was being met and surpassed by the passion with which he was being cherished somewhere in New England.

And now after almost thirty years of losses and births and deaths and imaginings, Caroline had tamed her sorrow just enough to keep it from annihilating her.

Another cheer went up from her girls and from her grandchildren, and she heard Robert calling out: "Caroline, this one's for you!" He was at the far end of the table, holding a champagne glass and rising from his chair. Caroline saw that he was slightly shorter than he had once been. It was as if, with the burden of the years they had spent together, his body had become compressed. He was thicker and slower now, more substantial, his movements slightly arthritic. He was a grandfather. His hair was white. And his face was deeply lined from endless days spent gazing toward the sunlit glitter of the sea. It was only his smile that remained unaltered. It was still one that would have fit well on a good-natured Santa Barbara fraternity boy who wore baggy surfer trunks and flip-flops.

"To you, my sweetheart," Robert was saying. "A great mother and the most beautiful grandmother I've ever seen. Without you, none of us would be here today." His voice was tender as he said, "We made it. In spite of everything. We built a life. We built this family. No matter what we may have done wrong, it came out all right. In the end, it came out good."

Caroline looked away from Robert, toward the house—toward the place Justin had once, so briefly, belonged—and she knew that what Robert was saying was the truth, and that it was a lie. They had done well by Julie and Lissa and had done the unspeakable to Justin. In the end, it hadn't come out all right. In the end, it was a pool of light surrounded by an ocean of darkness. And Caroline knew there was a debt still owed on that inequity, she sensed that somewhere there was a final punishment still waiting for her, and for Robert.

When she glanced back toward the party, she saw radiant sunlight sparkling on the leaves of the oak tree, and Robert playing horseshoes with Graham and Fletcher. Lissa had Ethan in her lap, their heads bowed over an open book. Julie was sitting on the grass, her long legs tucked under her, laughing at something Harrison had just said. There was a happiness there that was dazzling. The beauty of it momentarily took Caroline's breath away.

*

After Lissa and Harrison and the boys had left, Caroline and Robert remained under the oak tree, listening to Julie's news about her love life and her career. Then Robert went upstairs. And now Caroline and Julie were alone together in the kitchen, cleaning up the aftermath of the party.

What had begun as an amiable mother-daughter chat was rapidly becoming an argument. "Mom, please," Julie was saying, "I'm sick of talking about this."

Caroline threw a handful of silverware into a drawer and slammed the drawer shut. "Well, we are going to talk about it, because it's important." She sounded snappish and quarrelsome. "It's important to me."

"Mom, why the hell are you obsessing about what's going to happen to this house after you and Dad are dead? It's depressing and completely pointless." Julie grabbed the tea towel she'd been using as a makeshift apron and yanked it out of her waistband. She tossed it onto the kitchen table and scooped up her purse. "It's not like you're sick and going to die anytime soon, so what's—"

Caroline snatched Julie's purse away from her. "You don't know when it could happen!"

She banged the purse back onto the table. Then in a movement that was more restrained, she quietly repositioned it. She was thinking about the flight she and Robert would be taking to San

Francisco in the morning. The September 11 attacks were still vivid in her mind and all she could see was the image of airplanes exploding into the World Trade Center. Caroline was terribly afraid. She sat at the table and put her head in her hands. "No one knows when they're going to die," she said.

After a while, she sensed Julie's presence beside her and she heard her say: "Okay. You're right. But we still don't need to talk about you and Dad leaving the house to me. I couldn't care less. Honestly. I don't want it after you and Dad are gone."

Julie's voice was uncharacteristically soft. Caroline knew she was doing her best to be kind, but the words had cut through Caroline like the blades of a chain saw. She looked at Julie, bewildered. "How can you not care about this house? This is the place where you were born, where you grew up."

"And it was a nice place to grow up in. But that's the whole point of being a kid and then becoming an adult. You grow up. You move on."

Caroline still couldn't comprehend what Julie was saying. "Move on to what?" she asked. "You're almost forty. It's time to think about settling down."

Julie's reaction was explosive. "Give it a rest!" She saw the startled look in Caroline's eyes and lowered her voice. "Mom, I don't need a house. I've got a condo. I'm head of publicity for a major movie studio. I've got a kick-ass life that I love. I have no interest in getting married and settling down. I'm not you. I'm not Lissa. I'm not ever going to want a yard for the kids and lots of storage for their old worn-out teddy bears and finger paintings and notes from the tooth fairy. I'd go fucking nuts living like that." Before Caroline could say anything, Julie stopped her. "Sorry. I'd go frigging nuts, okay?"

"What about security?" Caroline asked. "If you're not going to get married, what about security? For later, for when you're older?"

"I can take care of myself. Hasn't that ever occurred to you?" Julie picked up her purse. It was clear that she was impatient; she wanted to leave. "Now, please, let's just table this whole discussion for a while. We don't have to decide about the house tonight."

"Yes, we do! We have to settle this now." Caroline's statement had an unstoppable determination to it. The house on Lima Street was the most valuable thing she had ever possessed. It was home: the place she had devoted her life to finding and keeping for her children. It was her triumph and her legacy. She had battled and sacrificed for it. And she was desperate to know that it would ultimately have meaning. "If you don't take this house," she said, "what will become of it?"

"I guess Lissa and I would sell it. After you and Dad are gone."

"But what about all the memories that are here?"

Julie shrugged. "We'll still have the memories."

The offhandedness of Julie's attitude left Caroline stunned.

She got up and went to the open kitchen door and gazed out at the darkened backyard. For several moments, she saw nothing. Then in the space of a heartbeat, she saw, glimmering in the shadows, the seasons of her life. She saw Robert, at twenty-two, on a summer day, at work on a newly cut surfboard. He was turning toward the house, toward her as she stood at the back door. He was glowing with happiness. She saw herself, years later, sitting alone in dew-wet grass on a moonlit October night, thinking about how perfect a cream-colored dress in the back of her closet might look if she were to walk into the lobby of an elegant hotel in it. She saw all three of her children, in springtime, running past the open back door, waving bubble wands and surrounded by clouds of drifting, rainbowed iridescence—Justin, a wobbly-legged toddler, trailing behind his sisters. She saw Barton, in a time after Justin was gone, playing a game of tag with Robert and the girls and she heard Julie saying: "Mommy never plays games anymore." She saw the backyard empty, as it must have looked to Mitch as he sat upstairs, beside her bed, waiting for her to wake up and to get on with her life. And again she saw Barton. In a time after the girls had grown. He was wearing the robes of a priest, marrying Lissa to Harrison. And Caroline was thanking him for having come all the way from New York to perform the ceremony, and he was saying to her, softly, "Caro, how could I not have come? I've always loved your children as if they were my own." And then she saw herself and Robert, surrounded by their daughters and their grandchildren. Robert, grown old and raising his glass to her, saying: ". . . it came out all right. In the end, it came out good."

As Robert's image faded and the backyard was reclaimed by darkness, Caroline closed the kitchen door. She turned and looked at Julie. And, finally, she saw her.

She saw her pinning up her blue-black hair into a loose crown of curls—causing two of the buttons on her silk shirt to come open, revealing the laced edge of an exquisite piece of parrot green lingerie. She watched as Julie slipped into the plum-colored stiletto-heeled Italian boots that she'd shed earlier in the day, before going outside for Robert's party. She noticed that one of Julie's ankles bore the tiny tattoo of a bumblebee and that the other was encircled by a thin gold chain flecked with diamonds.

Caroline saw how exotic Julie was, and how out of place she looked in this worn wood-floored kitchen into which Caroline had always fit so well. Caroline understood that the conversation between them was over. She gathered up Julie's purse and gave it to her. Then she took Julie's hands in hers and said: "Good-bye, sweetheart. Thank you for a lovely day." It was all she could manage. That place in her soul—the tight, confined space where pain is stored—was too full.

After Julie had gone, as Caroline left the kitchen, she checked the sliding bolt at the top of the basement door to be sure that it was locked. She climbed the stairs and passed the broad, flat-crowned newel post at the top of the landing. She went past the closed door of the upstairs room that still had Winnie-the-Pooh patterns on its walls. She moved toward the bedroom where Robert was asleep, turned on his side, one hand under his head and the other resting on her pillow—as if he were saving a place for her. As Caroline was traveling the length of the house on Lima Street, she was hearing Julie's voice: "I can take care of myself. Hasn't that ever occurred to you?"

Her bold, strong-willed daughter had instinctively known from childhood something that had never occurred to Caroline— that she could indeed take care of herself; that there were options in the world other than being weak and dependent and corralled by fear. Julie's words had shown that Caroline had spent a lifetime searching for something with which she'd already been cursed. Caroline had thought home was a thing that could be created, and shaped into happiness. But now she understood that home couldn't be invented or amended. It was a fact. Established and fixed for all time.

Home was the place in which you were rooted by your beginnings, into which you were locked by your earliest consciousness. It marked and branded you. And if it was a broken, desolate place—the sort of place in which Caroline had begun—it would leave you hungry and dangerous, and punished, for the rest of your life.

*

"Mitch? You saw Mitch? Here? In San Francisco?" Caroline was thunderstruck by what Robert had just said. She sat on the bench at the end of their hotel bed in a single rapid movement, as if the wind had been knocked out of her. "Where? Where did you see him?"

"At the airport, this morning, after we'd landed. When I was in the men's room." Robert splashed cologne into his palm, then brushed his hand across his face and neck.

"Did you talk to him?"

"Briefly." Robert picked up the cummerbund of his tuxedo and put it on.

"What did you say?" Caroline felt as if she was choking.

"Nothing that he didn't already know." Robert went into the bathroom.

Caroline followed him; a terrible anxiety was building in her. "Robert, I need to know what you said."

Robert was checking his cuff links now. He didn't look at Caroline when he replied, "Leave it alone, all right? It's not important."

"Then why did you tell me you saw him?" Caroline grabbed his arm. She needed him to pay attention. She needed to see if her secrets were still safe. "I want to know what you said."

In an old familiar gesture, Robert rested his hands on her shoulders. "Come on, Caroline, we've got better things to do than this. There're hundreds of people filling up a ballroom downstairs, all here for a big overcooked chicken dinner in honor of the Independent Insurance Agent of the Year." Robert ran his hands down the sleeves of Caroline's cream-colored lace dress. "And they're also waiting to get a look at the incredibly beautiful woman that the Agent of the Year is married to."

This was the moment in which Caroline could back away from the explosion that was waiting to happen. All she needed to do was to let this thing about Mitch go; let it find its way into the same stale silence where so much of her marriage had gone. But Caroline knew it had the potential to do too much damage.

She was already hammering another question at Robert. "If you seeing Mitch wasn't important, then why did you tell me about it? Just to upset me?" Robert's hand was once again on her shoulder; she brushed it away. She was deliberately ignoring his offer of a truce, and he reacted as she knew he would.

There was menace in his voice as he said: "What's for you to be upset about? I saw Mitch. In an airport restroom. For half a second. He's somebody I knew a lifetime ago and somebody I'll probably never see again. That's all there is to it."

Robert slammed out of the bathroom and Caroline ran after him. "Did you tell him I was here, too?"

Robert picked up his tuxedo jacket from the bed. "I didn't think it was necessary to inform the man who used to bugger my weak-willed wife that she was within easy reach."

Caroline flinched. Robert instantly dropped the jacket and tried to pull her toward him. "Caroline, I'm so sorry." She batted his hand away. He looked sick with regret. "I shouldn't have said that." He reached for her again. "Please. Let it go. Mitch is history. We survived him. And we survived everything that he caused. We got through it. There's no reason to dig it up again."

There was a part of Caroline that wanted to agree with him, that yearned to avoid opening their dog-eared catalog of recriminations. But unlike other times when they'd argued about Mitch, and about what had happened on that October day over thirty years ago, this time Mitch himself had taken part in a conversation. Caroline had to know what had been discussed. She needed to reassure herself that certain details of that day still remained obscure.

"Tell me what you said, Robert." Caroline's statement had the undercurrent of a threat.

Robert gave her a look that begged her to reconsider. "We've been together a long time," he told her. "We're in the homestretch now. We've already lived the biggest chunk of our lives, and whatever time we've got left, let's not waste it beating each other up for things that can't be changed. I'm sorry about that 'weak-willed wife' crack. I didn't mean it. Jesus, Caroline, you know I love you. I've always loved you. You and the girls, and now Lissa's kids. That's my world, that's my reason for getting up every day. And I know that you've loved me. You wouldn't still be here after all these years if you didn't."

"Robert, I need to know!" Caroline was screaming at him with such ferocity that the last of her words came out choked and rasping. "What did you say to Mitch? What did you tell him?"

"It's not important!" Now Robert, too, was shouting. He walked away from her and went to the window.

"It's important to me!" Caroline pushed between him and the window. They were less than an inch apart. She could see the pulsing of a vein on his neck; she could feel the heat of his breath on her face.

"Why? Why is it so important?" Robert was furious. "What did you *want* me to tell him? That I've spent my life obsessed with the two of you? Eating my guts out over what you did to me three decades ago? That I spent every night, all those years, lying beside you and yearning for you to screw me with even an ounce of the enthusiasm that you had when you screwed him?"

"Shut up, Robert!" Caroline's voice was wild and shrill, but her words were lost in Robert's roaring shout: "Because if that's what you were hoping for, Caroline, you didn't get it. I didn't paint you as the beach nymph still pining for her playboy lover. I told him the truth. That you were exactly like the rest of us, sweetheart. Old and ordinary. I said you were a middle-class matron happily married to an insurance salesman. I told him you were a grandmother. And that for thirty years, every single time I banged you, you came so hard, you passed out."

There was a bitter vindictiveness in Robert's voice that Caroline had never heard before. It startled her. "How can you be so hateful?"

"Because I'm sick of this," he said. "I'm sick of you dragging this crap around with you endlessly. Endlessly, endlessly!"

"What are you talking about?" She was crying now. Because she was hurt. And because she was ragingly angry.

"I'm talking about you," Robert told her. "I'm talking about how you've turned your life into a soap opera, about how you've spent thirty years moping and mooning around and making me pay for a crime you committed."

"I hope I have made you pay. I hope I've made your life a living hell. And I hope I keep on making you pay until the day you die. Because you're the one who's guilty, Robert. I made a mistake, I slept with someone who wasn't my husband. But what you did to Justin, that was the crime."

"I did the kid a favor. At least he probably landed in a home with a functioning mother in it."

Caroline's rage flared and she threw herself at Robert, ready to hit him. "How dare you even think of accusing me of being a bad mother?"

Robert calmly pushed her away. "I'm not accusing you of anything. I'm stating a fact. You *were* a bad mother. I was there, I saw it all."

"That's not true." She was screaming again. "I stayed with you, all those years, even after you stole my son from me, so that Lissa and Julie would have a home, and a father. Everything I did was because I was trying to do the best I could for my children . . . so they would have safe places to grow up. I was a *good* mother."

"Good mothers don't screw around and get knocked up and try to pass their bastard kid off to their husband as one of the family."

"I made a mistake. One stupid mistake. And you didn't just punish me for it, you abused me, in the most evil way you could think of. And I hope you burn in hell because of it." Caroline was crying uncontrollably. Her belief that she'd been a good and sacrificing mother had always been the one shred of righteousness she was able to claim for herself, and now Robert was threatening to take it away.

"You weren't just a bad mother, Caroline," he was saying. "You were a rotten one."

"You're a liar! You're a *liar*, Robert!" Caroline was on the verge of hysteria. "I sacrificed everything for my children. My God, Robert, I stayed with you . . . after everything you did to me, and I only stayed for one reason, to do for my girls what nobody ever did for me. To give them a good home with two parents in it. They couldn't have asked for a mother who would have loved them more."

Robert's reply was swift and wicked. "But they could've asked for a mother who didn't lie around bombed on tranquilizers for over a year, couldn't they?"

"That wasn't my fault!" Caroline's screaming shout was laced with tears.

"Those pills didn't fly down your throat on their own," Robert bellowed. "You took them. By the fistful."

"I had lost a child!"

"Oh, here we go with the soap opera again." His voice was lower now and had a mocking quality to it. "Poor Caroline lost her bastard baby. Tragic, tragic story. And, man, did you know how to milk it. How many years was it that you spent what you used to call 'leaking'? Wandering around. Crying at nothing."

"I detest you." Her voice was hoarse. She was drawing ragged, gulping breaths.

"You know what?" Now, Robert was seething. "I don't care. This feels good, to finally tell you the truth. You were a lousy parent, Caroline. Your daughters spent the better part of a decade with a mother who was either stoned out of her skull or crying or staring out a window. They were in high school before you even *tried* to snap out of it."

"How was I supposed to 'snap out' of having a child torn away from me?" she asked. "He was stolen from me and given to people on the other side of the country. People I'd never even seen. You're not being fair, Robert." Her voice was filled with anguish.

"Don't talk to me about what's unfair, Caroline. Unfair was what landed me in Sierra Madre selling insurance. And it started with you. With us getting married way before we should have. And it just kept coming, with my father's heart attack, and my brother arranging a life sentence on Lima Street for me so that he could stay put in Hawaii and nail college girls. And then, of course, there was you again . . . spreading your legs for somebody else and bringing the little bundle home to me. You want to know about injustice? I'm the guy to ask. I've spent my life being rolled in other people's shit."

Caroline's fury at Robert was now complete. And it had taken on a killing coldness. "No, Robert," she said calmly. "You've been rolling in your own shit. It's been pouring out of you since the day you were born. Because you've always been timid and scared. Too scared to do anything but stay stuck in your pathetic, second-rate, hand-me-down life."

She walked over to Robert and backhanded him. The edge of her wedding ring opened a gash on the side of his neck.

When he spoke, his voice was so quiet that she could clearly hear the threat of violence it. "You'd better leave now, Caroline. Before I hit you back."

Moments later, Caroline stumbled out into the frigid air of the San Francisco night. She had left the room upstairs without a coat, wearing only the sheer cream-colored lace dress. She noticed that people walking past her were glancing at her. As she stepped onto the sidewalk, she understood why—she wasn't wearing shoes.

Grit from the sidewalk was pressing against the soles of her feet as she walked away from the hotel and down the steep, hilly street that was in front of it. She was shivering with cold. Among the crowds of people who were moving up the hill toward her was a group of men in Halloween costumes. Most of them were dressed in fantastic and outrageous drag, but one was outfitted as a vampire. And seeing him made Caroline remember another Halloween, thirty-plus years ago. When someone dressed as a vampire had blocked her way when she was trying to go home. At the end of that strange, enchanted afternoon in which she'd been in the company of two men whom she had cared about deeply.

A sense of desperation rose in Caroline. She was realizing that she had unwittingly written her life into a language of secrets, into an indecipherable code riddled with questions.

There were so many things she wanted to know, and that she would never know. She wanted to know if her life had accomplished any good: if she'd been a hero for her children, or if she had been a villain. She wanted to know how time had escaped from her so quickly; how she had, in the blink of an eye, gone from the pretty girl at the center of all the photographs to the older woman at their edges, wedged in behind children and grandchildren.

She thought about a photograph she'd tossed into a kitchen drawer in the house on Lima Street when she and Robert had first moved in. She'd always intended to take it out and to frame it, but now she realized it must still be in that same drawer, buried under a lifetime's accumulation of discarded rubber bands and unsharpened pencils. In the photograph, she was on the beach in Santa Barbara, flanked by Barton and Robert, and glancing down at Mitch. He was lying at her feet, looking up at her and laughing.

In thinking of Mitch, she realized she'd always wanted to know why he had kept his word: why he'd never contacted her after he'd come to the house on Lima Street to console her when Justin had been lost. She wondered if Mitch had stayed away out of a sense of chivalry or if he had simply forgotten her because, after a while, she hadn't been important enough to remember.

But there was a new, much more pressing issue with Mitch now. It was the issue of what had been said between him and Robert at the airport. Had Robert told Mitch about Justin's having been conceived in that single indiscretion on that long-ago Halloween? And had he told him the truth about what had happened to Justin?

She went to the curb and steadied herself against a parking meter. Her mind was racing with questions. If Robert had told Mitch the date of Justin's conception and the truth about what had become of him, then there was a chance that Justin's parentage had been exposed. A chance that the man who was Justin's father might discover Caroline had borne him a son and let that son become lost from him forever.

The thought of Justin's father knowing these things made Caroline frantic. It made her turn and begin to run, blindly and without direction. It sent her rushing toward the street.

Then there was the sudden clanging of a cable car's bell. And shouts from people on the sidewalk.

The moment Caroline stepped off the curb, she had seen that the cable car was rushing down the hill toward her. She knew that what she needed to do was to lift her foot and take a few steps back. But she also knew she was tired. Tired of asking questions that had no answers and tired of waiting for miracles that had refused to come. She knew that when Justin went away, she had sent pictures in a notebook and Justin's birth certificate, hoping they would someday bring him back to Lima Street. She knew she had waited for almost thirty years; and he had never come. She had stopped believing he ever would. And it had made her tired.

And now it was Halloween again, and Caroline was in a cream-colored dress again. She had been a young woman and an older woman. She had passionately loved and ultimately lost each of her daughters, and had married one man, and desired another, and adored a third. She had cooked ten thousand meals, and grown one perfect rose, and had drunk good wine with good friends. She had betrayed her son and the man who had given him to her. And now she was tired. Far too tired to lift her dirty bare foot. To step back onto the curb, and into her life.

When the cable car hit, Caroline felt the pain. It seemed to last only as long as it had taken her to go from her beginnings in Santa Barbara to this street in San Francisco. Only a moment.

Justin

*

The door was opened by a woman wearing red sandals and a girlish full-skirted summer dress. She was short and plump. Her hair was a drab ash blond. Her face was weathered, her eyes sparkling blue. Justin recognized her immediately. It was Suzy Zelinski.

She seemed confused for a moment. Then her face lit up and she said, "Well, I'll be . . . After you left for Boston, we never heard another word . . . It was like you'd dropped off the face of the earth. I always wondered what had become of you, TJ."

At the sound of the name, Justin felt a twinge of discomfort, as if it was an alias belonging to someone who had once befriended him. Someone he guiltily wished he'd never known.

"Come have some lunch with us." Suzy was ushering him into the house, and he was surprised by how modest and cluttered and low-ceilinged it was. When he had been brought here as a little boy, as TJ, it had seemed magnificent.

As Justin moved across the living room, toward the hallway and the entrance to the kitchen, he was checking to see if

Stan's recliner was still in place. And when he saw that it was facing the TV, exactly where it had always been, he experienced a sensation of lightness, as if he'd received a hoped-for but unexpected gift.

It was information about Stan Zelinski that had compelled Justin to make this trip.

When he had told Ari that he intended to come here, Ari had done his best to talk him out of it. He had tried to convince him to let Gabriel Gonzales handle this final detail. But Justin needed to discover for himself what had happened to Stan—after TJ had left him in the dark in the breezeway of this house, slammed against the iron tines of a garden rake.

Justin needed to know if, at the age of seventeen, TJ had killed someone.

When he had told Amy that he was planning to return to the Zelinski house, she had been frightened, and then she had been exasperated. It terrified her that Justin's connection to TJ might be a connection to murder. And the idea of Justin voluntarily making himself vulnerable to criminal charges, and possible jail time, infuriated her.

In the minutes just before they had talked about it, they were contented and sleepy, in the mist of lovemaking that had been as languorous and sweet as a river of slowly melting ice cream.

Then, abruptly, Amy was sitting up, glancing at the caller ID on the ringing phone, and saying: "It's Daddy."

The minute she said it, the mood in the room was infused with an anxious sense of waiting. Justin lay perfectly still. Amy held on to the phone as it continued to ring.

Finally, she tossed it aside. "Hey, that's why God made voice mail, right?"

She snuggled against Justin and whispered, "Anyway, I know

why he's calling. I talked to my mother. Big news. Daddy's decided he's speaking to me again. He wants us to come for dinner next week."

"No," Justin said. "Not next week."

"Not a problem. Under the 'new rules,' Daddy's agreed to work around our schedule, so maybe—"

"Not next week, because I'm going to be out of town." Justin was deliberately interrupting her. This was the time to tell Amy about the outrageous thing he planned to do; otherwise, he might lose the courage to go through with it. "I'm going to Connecticut," he said. "To Middletown."

"Why?" Amy's gaze was full of apprehension.

"I need to find out if Stan Zelinski is dead, because if he is, when I was TJ, I might have killed him."

Amy's eyes went wide.

"I caught him molesting a little girl." Justin was having difficulty getting the words out. "I hit him. He ended up slammed against a wall. I don't know what happened after that. I ran away."

Amy sat up in bed and looked around the room as if she was searching for something that would help make sense of what Justin was saying. "But if it was a fight, it would've been an accident, right? Why go back? Why dig it up after all these years?"

Justin moved to Amy's side of the bed. He put his arms around her and said, "Because I need to know if I'm responsible for killing a man. Even if I didn't mean to kill him. I need to know that I have the balls to tell the truth and take the consequences."

Amy shoved him away. "How can you even talk about going off and doing something like this, Justin? What about me? What about the stuff that I'm having a hard time with? I blew up my relationship with my father for you. I'll never have him back, close, the way I used to. I did that for you. And I want the same. I want you focused here. On me. And on Zack."

Before Justin could interrupt, Amy cut him off. "Justin, listen to me," she insisted. "You caught this guy molesting a little girl and you're saying *you're* the one who has consequences to pay? What is going on with you?"

"Zack's what's going on with me," Justin said. "Amy, if Stan did die after I ran off that night, I can't look the other way and keep quiet about it. I can't show Zack what a man's supposed to be if I'm a coward who cuts and runs and doesn't take responsibility for the fact that I may have caused somebody to die."

The look Amy gave Justin was cold and determined. "All you have to do is leave it alone," she said. "If you do that, then there'll never be any reason for Zack to know about it."

Justin was fighting tears. "I can't," he said. "I can't live with any more secrets. I've spent my life buried in them."

He rested his head on Amy's shoulder. "If Stan's dead, Ames, there's no way to know what'll happen . . . Maybe me doing some jail time, I don't know. But I want my life to be a clean slate. And I need to know I was the one who had the courage to clean it off."

Amy got out of bed and walked away. "This is insane."

"No, it isn't." Justin was calm and resolute. "It's the right thing to do. For Zack."

He raised his voice a little. He needed her to hear, and to understand, every word he was saying. "I want to be *the* guy for Zack, the father I never had. And I can't do that unless I'm whole. No blank spaces, no riddles. I want to be solid when I put him on my shoulders and let him ride around up there. I never knew the feeling of that . . . riding on my dad's shoulders . . . seeing the world from where he saw it. From up in the air. Like a king, or a giant." Justin stopped for a moment.

Amy's face was expressionless as Justin said: "I want to be a good man, Ames. I want my head clear, free of all the dark stuff. I want to think about things like teaching my son how to play baseball. And telling him everything I know about cars. I want to give him everything that's in me. I want him to know things like how much a guy can love his wife. How he can think about having sex with every good-looking woman he sees but still only want to make love to one, the one who really sees him." Justin paused. He was waiting for Amy to say something. "Ames, please," he said. "Please understand."

Amy got back into bed. As she lay down and pulled the sheet around her, she said, "I do understand. But what you want isn't possible. Nobody has a clean slate, Justin. Everybody's got secrets and whatever damage your parents did to you because of theirs is done." She flipped the sheet back on Justin's side, opening a space for him, waiting for him.

"Amy," he said, "can't you see why I have to go to Connecticut?"

"No, I can't. But go . . . if that's what you feel you have to do. Find out what happened. Then lay it, and TJ, to rest." Her words were clipped, and final. "This weirdness started a year ago, when we went to Lima Street, and I refuse to let you squander one more day of our lives on it. You need to close the door on that place. You need to decide to come home, Justin. Otherwise, this is where it ends."

Amy had switched off the light, and the next morning—this morning—Justin had gone to the airport and flown to Connecticut. Now he was walking into the hallway of the Zelinski house, following Suzy toward the kitchen as she was saying: "If I remember right, TJ, you were a big fan of my peach pies. And I made one this morning. I must've known that you were coming."

Justin glanced toward an open bedroom door midway down the hall. "Do you know what happened to Cassie Jackson?" he asked.

Suzy laughed and said, "Little black Cassie? Funny you should mention her. She was in the paper a few months ago, big write-up about how she bounced around, lived with her grandmother for a time, then lived on the streets but still found a way to keep going to school. She got herself through college, and got a law degree, on scholarships. Apparently, she's going to work for the government and they gave her a big send-off at one of the Negro churches. They even gave her a brand-new car to drive down to D.C. in."

"Was it a Mustang?"

"Why in the world would you ask that?"

"Don't you remember?" Justin said. "One of her biggest dreams was to have her own pony."

"Truth is, Stan and I never really got to know her. We didn't have a lot in common with her. She was in and out of here so quick." Suzy gave Justin an apologetic shrug, and as she was walking away, she was calling to someone: "Honey, you're going to fall right out of your chair when you see who's here to see us."

She was going into the kitchen; into the room where TJ had last seen Stan, rumpled and sweating and fumbling with his zipper; the place where Stan had put a cocked rifle to TJ's head. And now Justin was walking through the door of that kitchen, ready to grab Stan and beat him until he was reduced to nothing more than brain matter and bone fragments.

But the man in the kitchen wasn't Stan Zelinski; it was Ted.

Justin's hostility was replaced by surprise as Ted was shaking his hand and saying: "Good to see you, buddy. It's been a lot of years."

There were lines around Ted's eyes and gray at his temples, and it dawned on Justin that Stan, Ted's father, would be a senior citizen now. Justin wondered if that should make a difference, if it should diminish his desire to punish Stan. But what "should be" had nothing to do with what was; his hatred for the man was boundless.

Suzy was at the back door, calling out toward the breezeway: "Stan honey, come in here. We're gonna have peach pie."

At the mention of Stan's name, Justin's stomach clenched. But as Suzy stepped aside, it was a little boy who galloped into the room. A kid with short blond hair and Stan Zelinski's stockiness.

"TJ, this is Ted's boy." Suzy was beaming with pride. "He's named after my Stan. He's the image of his grandpa, isn't he?"

"Did you used to know my grandpa?" the boy asked Justin.

"Yeah," Justin told him. "A long time ago."

The boy's eyes lit up. "Wanna see Grandpa's hero stuff?" Before Justin could answer, the boy was already running out of the kitchen, saying: "I'll get it and show you."

Suzy hurried out after him. "Honey, let Grandma find the album for you. I don't want you climbing up on those bookshelves again."

Ted laughed. "They could be gone for hours. Mom never remembers from one minute to the next where that album is."

"Is Stan around?" Justin's question was abrupt. He couldn't wait any longer. He needed to know.

Ted's answer was an unhappy sigh. "Dad's dead, TJ."

It was as if a bomb had gone off. "When?" Justin asked. "When did he die?"

"The night you left for Boston. After you'd gone. Probably around midnight. That's what the cops told Mom." Ted looked toward the hall. "I don't want Mom and Stan to hear us. Stan doesn't know the whole story. And Mom, well, you know how much Mom loved Dad. It's still hard for her to talk about it." He turned back to Justin. "Mom was the one that found the body, the next morning. Dad died during the night, out in the breezeway. He bled to death out there."

Justin was holding on to the back of a kitchen chair. His knuckles had gone white.

"He was against the wall," Ted was saying. "One of the old iron rakes was embedded in his back." Ted stopped for a moment, then added, "He was holding a rifle. I don't know, there were some funny things about it. He had injuries to his face and a bruise on his chest. But the cops finally decided it was just a freak accident, that he'd been coming into the house and probably slipped in some water that was on the ground and fell backwards."

Ted looked at Justin. "I don't know if I believe that, though. Hell, I don't know what to believe. I guess the cops were probably right." Ted stood at the door, looking out toward the breezeway. "The truth is, a man like my father, he was so good and so kind. He didn't have any enemies. Nobody would've wanted to kill him." Ted's gaze was open and guileless. "Dad was my hero, TJ. I miss him."

Justin wanted to tell Ted Zelinski the truth about Stan's perversion, and about the circumstances under which he had died. But in the face of Ted's intense sadness, it felt heartless. Justin hesitated, and in that moment, Suzy came back into the kitchen.

She was holding a large scrapbook. "This is all of Stan's honors, the newspaper clippings and such," she said. "From way back when he was a Little League coach and up through all the years, the awards for his foster parenting. And of course everything about the Stan Zelinski Youth Center. He never got to see it completed but there's this wonderful plaque beside the front door. You should go see it, TJ. It's got Stan's face on it. And a really beautiful tribute to him."

"Open it up and look," Ted's little boy said to Justin. "Open the book and see. My grandpa was a hero. And his name was Stan. Just like mine."

Within minutes Justin had said his good-byes, and he was gone from the Zelinski house.

He had not done what he'd come to do. He had left Stan's secret, and his own, undisturbed. The truth was that Stan Zelinski had been a child molester, and that Justin Fisher, when he was TJ, had had a part in Stan's death and had gotten away with it. But to reveal this would be to deal a wounding blow to Suzy, and Ted, and to Ted's little boy. It would irreparably wound Amy and Zack if Justin were to be sent to prison, even for a short time. And it would steal something shining and bright from the Little League teams and the Youth Center volunteers who believed in Stan's legend.

Justin was beginning to see that the truth he'd traveled to Connecticut to unearth was obscured by a constellation of other, more ambiguous truths. Ones that were fractured and wickedly complex.

After leaving the Zelinski house, it took him several hours before he could call Amy.

All she said was: "Well . . . ?"

"I'm not ready to talk yet," he told her. "I need time to figure some things out."

There was steel in Amy's voice. "How much time?"

"A couple of days. I'm going to rent a car, and drive back." Justin didn't have the strength, or the will, to say anything more. He was exhausted.

He was in the process of hanging up when he heard Amy say: "At the house in Hawaii, my mother discovered somebody had driven a huge nail into one of the trees. She was frantic to pull it out, but the gardener said the damage was done, the nail had been put there a long time ago and pulling it out now would only make things worse. The trunk had grown around it and made it part of the tree. You could see where it had gone in, where the scar in the wood was, but the gardener said the tree was coping and if we left it alone, it would survive. Still be strong. Even with a spike through its heart. Justin, sometimes the right thing to do is to prevail. To let the wound heal over, and to keep on living."

After a while Justin said: "I'll call you in a few days. By the time I get back to California, I'll have made my decision."

"Justin." There was a brief pause. When Amy spoke again, it was with immeasurable tenderness. "Please be careful."

Justin was having trouble keeping his voice steady as he said, "I'm going to hang up now." And just before he did, he told her: "I love you, Amy."

Robert

*

Robert felt eager, aroused, like a teenager. It was surprising him. He wondered if he was about to make a fool of himself.

He had the sudden impulse to change his mind and put the meeting off until another time, but the female voice at the other end of the phone was saying: "I'd like to do a lotta very interesting things to you. And I'd like to do them tonight."

There was something in the way the statements had been delivered, something so blatantly suggestive, that it shot a rush of sexual excitement through Robert. It had been years since he'd experienced such a feeling.

"I gotta go take care of some business right now," the woman was saying. "Gimme a half hour. I'll call you back and let you know where to meet me." There was a quick beep and silence.

This was the first time they'd communicated other than on the Internet, and Robert was surprised by the woman's voice. It had an unexpected roughness, and youthfulness. The minute he heard it, he had been titillated by it.

Now, it was causing him concern. He was nervous about how

his body would look to the eyes of a stranger—worried that it would be too old, too lined and slack, to be a source of arousal to someone who sounded so knowing and so young.

Robert went to the other side of the bedroom, determined to find something appropriate to wear. He didn't want to arrive at his destination tonight looking like the grandfather and the widower he was. On several Internet dating sites he'd used the tag line "Mature & Up for Adventure." He wanted to deliver what he'd been advertising.

His clothes were in the same location they had occupied since he and Caroline had first come to the house on Lima Street decades ago. Robert's things were tightly packed into a few feet of space in the far right-hand corner of the closet. The remainder of the space, the area that had always held Caroline's things, had been empty for months. The vacancy and the bareness made Robert's heart ache. He quickly grabbed a shirt and a pair of pants and shut the door.

As he went to toss the clothes onto the bed, he caught sight of the group of framed photos on the nightstand: photos of himself and Caroline, of Julie, and of Lissa and Harrison and the boys. Seeing them embarrassed Robert.

He had an impulse to call the woman back and cancel their appointment. But in his earlier excitement, he hadn't thought to ask for her telephone number. There was nothing he could do; he could neither cancel the date nor quell his desire to keep it.

It had been a very long time since he'd had sex.

After Robert had told Caroline the truth about what he'd done to Justin, intimacy between them—with the exception of a few disconsolate encounters—had come to a halt. During their life together, Robert had never taken a single lover. It hadn't been as difficult as he would've expected. In those years, love was what he had been possessed by, not lust. And his love had been given to his daughters and then to his grandchildren, and, on those occasions when she would allow it, to Caroline. For the most part, Robert's life had been happy and full.

But since Caroline's death, his capacity for happiness had been permanently altered. For more than forty years, the love and anger Robert had for Caroline were the things that had directed and driven his life. When Caroline had been taken from him, he'd been left adrift and unbearably lonely.

He lifted her picture from the night table and rested it on his chest as he stretched out on the bed. When his head touched the pillow, he imagined he caught a faint waft of fragrance—Caroline's scent: perfumed sugar.

The pain of her loss swept through him. He said her name and the word *why*. Then he did what he always did when he was grieving for Caroline: He went back to that last day in San Francisco, and to the argument they'd had just before she died.

He thought about what had started the argument. He thought about Mitch.

Mitch had been in the airport men's room when Robert had entered. But Robert had been unaware of it. There had been a line of urinals along one wall, and Robert stepped into the first available open space.

The man to Robert's left was old and stooped, wearing a cardigan sweater that was emitting the smell of mothballs. The man to Robert's right was in a dark suit and had a sleek chrome-colored loop coiled around his ear. He was in the midst of a phone call. He was telling someone that he'd had the jury eating out of his hand from "minute one"; his clients were so happy, they were planning to buy him a Lamborghini as a thank-you.

The man moved away from the urinals a second or two before

Robert, and they ended up at the washroom sinks, not far from each other. Robert could hear the man's continuing conversation: "My plane's taking off for Kennedy in a few minutes. I've got meetings in the New York offices tomorrow. How about I come straight to your place from the airport tonight? Good. Keep it warm for me, Sweet P."

The nickname "Sweet P" had been said with a lazy, arrogant rhythm—Mitch's rhythm. The same salacious way that the name "Sweet C" had always been said when Mitch used it to refer to Caroline.

Mitch was turned away from Robert. He'd opened the door and was about to walk through it, when Robert grabbed him by the scruff of the neck and pulled him back into the restroom. Several other men, who were on their way out, shot questioning glances in Robert's direction.

Mitch had his briefcase in one hand. For an instant, it looked as if he was going to drop it and throw a punch. Then he suddenly recognized Robert. And he laughed. "Rob," he said. "What the hell do you think you're doing?"

"I'm thinking about smashing your face in."

Mitch laughed again. He shook his head as if he was both amused and confused by Robert. "I haven't seen you in what, maybe thirty-five years? And the first thing you do is try to start a fight? What in the world is your problem?"

"You slept with my wife. That's my problem."

"You're a sad piece of work, you know that, Robby-boy? What are you now? sixty-something? And you're still the same clueless doofus you were when we were kids."

Robert hit Mitch with a shove that bounced him off the tiled wall of the restroom. As Mitch was coming back at Robert, an airport security officer stepped between them. The officer rested his hand on his equipment belt, in the space between a thick baton and a pair of handcuffs. "What's going on, gentlemen?"

"Nothing," Robert said. "It's over."

Mitch casually smoothed his tie. Robert moved past him on his way out of the men's room. Mitch's voice was mellow and so low that no one, other than Robert, heard him say: "I fucked your girlfriend, Robby. But I never slept with your wife."

"You're a goddamned liar." Robert walked out and let the door slam behind him. If the security officer hadn't been there, Robert would have gone back and pounded the smirk from Mitch's self-satisfied face.

The memory of that confrontation still had the power to enrage Robert. He got up from the bed, trying to catch his breath. He suffered from hypertension and he'd forgotten to take his medication. A violent pain was blossoming in his head. His heart was racing; blood was pounding through his body. When his Internet date had called earlier, he had been in the shower, and now he was still in the same condition as when he'd rushed to the phone: He was naked.

As he was halfway out of the bedroom, he thought about grabbing some clothes, but it didn't seem important. He needed to get downstairs.

In the kitchen, Robert searched through the unopened mail and the clutter on the countertops. Finally, he found the medicine in a pile of things that included his wallet and his reading glasses.

The phone was ringing. He picked up the receiver and heard: "Hey baby. Ready to party?"

Just as it had done earlier, the woman's husky voice sent an involuntary thrill through Robert. "Yes, I'm ready."

"Lemme give you the address."

"Just a minute. I need to find something to write with." Robert opened a kitchen drawer, rummaged through an accumulation of discarded rubber bands and unsharpened pencils, and found a stub of green crayon. As he was taking it out of the drawer, he thought he heard a key turning in the lock at the front door.

He was humiliated at the possibility of someone coming in and finding him naked in his kitchen, arranging for a date he hoped would lead to sex. "Give me your number," he said. "I'm going to have to call you back." He grabbed what he thought was a scrap of paper from the tangle of things in the drawer. It was an old photo of himself, Barton, Mitch, and Caroline—on a beach. He flipped the snapshot facedown, and with the crayon stub, he scribbled the information that the woman was giving him. He hung up quickly and saw he'd omitted a digit, had written 768884, an incomplete telephone number.

Now he could hear footsteps coming down the hallway. Julie's voice was calling: "Dad, where are you?"

Robert jammed the photo into his wallet, threw it back into the clutter on the counter, and started toward the laundry area near the back door, intending to find something to cover himself with.

But before he could cross the kitchen, the headache that had come on him upstairs erupted like lightning, blistering hot. A profound weakness was clenching his body, laying claim to his left side, numbing his arm and leg.

Robert tried to take a step forward, to reach the privacy of the laundry room. But his movements were beyond his control—loose and stumbling. They pitched him sideways, leaving him tipped against the kitchen counter. With the one hand he could still control, he gripped the counter's edge, willing himself to stay standing.

Suddenly Julie was in the room, shouting, "Oh my God! Dad! What's wrong?"

Robert was struggling to say the words *call* and *ambulance,* but the weakness along his left side was hardening into paralysis and his speech was thick and slurred. He was falling away from the counter's edge toward the kitchen floor.

*

A faded watercolor of the house on Lima Street was the only thing remaining in the living room. It had been hanging there since the house had first begun. Lissa took it down. And then all that was left was a shadow of the painting's shape: a ghost mark on the wall.

A month ago, her father had suffered a stroke—one that would require him to remain in a nursing home for the rest of his life.

A Realtor was descending the stairs, running her hand along the smooth wood of the banister. "This place will sell in a snap," she was saying. "People are going to feel like they're in an old-fashioned summer house. Somewhere back east. At the seaside." As she came off the last stair, she turned in a slow, admiring circle. "How long did you say this treasure has been in your family?"

"It was built as a wedding present for my great-grandmother." Lissa was kneeling on the floor of the entryway, putting the watercolor beside a cardboard box filled with odds and ends she'd found while cleaning out the house.

"It must have been wonderful to grow up in a home like this." The Realtor was inspecting the intricate grillwork on one of the heating vents.

Lissa's only response was an enigmatic smile. The Realtor walked past her and gazed into the living room. "I can't believe that you don't want to keep this place in your family."

"Well, there's not much family left," Lissa said. "Just our grandparents. And an uncle."

"The grandparents are very busy playing bingo in Arizona." Julie was coming down the hall from the kitchen. "And as for our uncle, he's busy right now, too. Getting married to his pregnant forty-year-old girlfriend. In Hawaii. So my sister and I kind of need to get this place listed and sold, okay?" Julie gave the Realtor a look that told the woman her visit to the house was at an end.

She shot Julie a withering glance. "I'll take care of the paper-work, and we'll schedule an open house for next Saturday."

"Great. Thanks for coming." Julie went to the front door and held it open.

After the Realtor had left, Julie glanced down at the box near the door. In it were a few books, some old jigsaw puzzles, a skein of knitting yarn, a set of candlesticks, and a small stuffed bunny covered in white chenille that had gone gray with dust and age. "What's all this junk, Liss?"

"Bits and pieces I found scattered around, you know, in the backs of closets and things. Just trash."

Julie picked up the watercolor, preparing to put it into the box with the other castoffs. Lissa pulled it away from her. "I'm going to keep this."

"A picture of this place? Why?"

"Because it wasn't all bad, Jules."

There was a sort of wry acceptance in Julie's voice as she said, "You're right. We learned a lot of very important things here." She propped the watercolor against the wall. As she moved past Lissa, Julie took her hand and they began to walk through the empty house.

After they'd made a slow, silent circuit that carried them through the echoes and dust that were taking possession of the living room and the dining room and the kitchen, Julie and Lissa climbed the stairs.

As they moved toward the open doors of the bedrooms, Julie said: "Want to know a sorry truth, Liss? It was life in this place that scared me shitless on the idea of marriage." She laughed. And in the sound she made, there was sadness and mocking. "Dear old Mom and Dad. What a miserable deal they had . . . Dad turning himself inside out trying to make everybody happy all the time and Mom moping around, always seeming like her heart was about to break."

Julie paused in the doorway of the master bedroom. "They were probably in love at some point but look what happened to them. I mean, I think about all those stories about how they were when they were in college. And I remember how they used to be sometimes when Uncle Barton and Lily would come for visits. They were like different people. Laughing and dancing around the living room. And talking about the old days and all the fun they had when they were kids." Julie's laugh came again—the mocking gone, only sadness remaining. "But whatever it was they started out with, what they ended up with made it look like they were serving a jail sentence."

"I don't think it was like that for them all the time," Lissa said.

"It sure seemed like it was. For Mom, at least. She turned being married into a kind of living death, and you know it."

"Yeah. Maybe." Lissa's tone was wistful. "On my wedding night, just before I fell asleep, I promised myself I'd be a better wife and mother than Mom had been. And I decided I was going to do it by being everything she wasn't." Lissa glanced at Julie, one shoulder slightly raised, hands clasped, like a guilty child. "I've never cried in front of my boys. Never. Because of Mom, I've made a point of that. I used to get so tired of the crying."

"What about Harrison?" Julie asked. "Have you devoted your-self to making his life completely awful? For absolutely no reason?

Have you made a career out of being Our Lady of the Perpetual Funk?"

Lissa laughed. "God, I hope not." Then she looked around the empty master bedroom and said, "Dad got a really bad deal, didn't he, Jules?"

"Yup. Right to the very end."

Julie went to each of the windows in her parents' bedroom and closed the curtains. Then she walked out into the hall and entered the room that had once, briefly, belonged to her brother.

After a few moments, Lissa followed her. Julie was again going from window to window, closing curtains. Lissa went to the one window where the curtains remained open. She stood there for a long time, gazing out. She put her hand on the sill and absent-mindedly traced the outline of the circular indentation that was there. "Do you ever think about Justin?" she asked.

"No. Not really," Julie said.

"I used to think about him. All the time. He was my little buddy. I missed him so much."

"Maybe he was lucky, Liss. Maybe by getting out early, he got to skip a lot of heartache. Think about it. He's been an angel for almost thirty years now. Up there. Kicking back. Loving every minute of it." Julie shook her head and chuckled. "Not growing up in this house isn't the worst thing I can think of."

Lissa was lost in thought. "Remember when you and I were in middle school? And it felt like Mom hadn't looked at us in years . . . probably not since Justin died. And all that time Dad was trying so hard to please her. I remember thinking maybe they should get a divorce, that maybe it would make things better. I wouldn't have cared if they did. I just wanted for them to be happy. For us to be happy."

Julie came and stood beside Lissa and wrapped her arms

around her. "We were a sad family, Liss. I don't think I ever realized it before, but most of the time, we were. Each of us. In our own way. We were sad."

"Yeah. Sometimes we were. But a lot of the time it was so great. Remember the s'mores? And playing Barbies on the porch? And those incredible birthday cakes Mom used to make? And how crazy Dad was about all his old records? The Beach Boys? And the Motown music? And remember how all of us would sing into candlesticks and dance around the living room? I used to love that."

"Me, too." Julie's voice had the sound of tears in it. "Even though I hated so much of it, sometimes I wish we could go back. Sometimes I wish we could be back there, Liss. In the good parts. And do something to have it come out different . . . better. For everybody."

Evening shadows were slipping into the park across the street, circling at the bottom of the fences and the bases of the trees. When they had filled the park, they flowed across the street. Into the house, and into the room where Justin's sisters were.

As darkness was claiming it, Julie and Lissa walked out of the space that had once belonged to their lost brother. They went downstairs and they gathered up the faded watercolor and the box with the candlesticks and the puzzles in it.

And they left the house on Lima Street.

Justin

*

The resort was a monochrome of sand and buff carved directly into the face of a mountain. Dotting the landscape, white-hot in the burning morning sun, were several large metal sculptures: a herd of slit-eyed bighorn sheep.

In contrast to the hotel's rugged facade was the cool decadence of its lobby—expanses of pale green marble and oversize sofas roped in gold braid.

A startlingly handsome dwarf in dark sunglasses was escorting a willowy blonde into one elevator while a pair of beefy freckled women in matching bathing suits was stepping out of another. At the front desk, a concierge with a French accent was conversing in rapid, passionate Spanish with a Guatemalan valet.

In the hotel restaurant, Justin was alone, holding his cell phone to his ear, listening intently to what the person at the other end of the line was saying. He was sitting beside a wall of glass. On the other side of the glass was the infinite sprawl of the desert. In the distance, a mountain peak was still capped with a dusting of winter snow.

It had taken him almost a week to travel back to California—following the path of Route 66 as he meandered across the country through the iron gray crush of Chicago and the green hills of East Texas and the scream and glitter of Las Vegas.

As he watched these landscapes slipping past his car windows, Justin had been thinking about the last session he'd had in Ari's office: the conversation in which he had announced his intention to return to Middletown, in which he had explained about TJ's final night in the Zelinski house and what had happened with Stan in the breezeway.

With each mile that Justin had driven between Connecticut and California, he had continued to go over and over that conversation with Ari, searching for answers.

He still wasn't sure what the truth was about the time he had spent as TJ. Had he honestly, completely blocked all those years out of his consciousness? Or had he, in some twisted way, been lying to himself and everyone around him about what he did and didn't remember?

And there was the issue of Stan Zelinski's death. Was Justin's part in it somehow absolved by Stan's presence in Cassie Jackson's bedroom? Did that fact truly negate any obligation Justin might have to tell the truth about what happened between him and Stan just before Stan impaled himself on that garden rake?

After his encounter with Ted and Suzy in Middletown, Justin had called Gabriel Gonzales. Prior to becoming a private investigator, Gonzales had spent years as a detective with the Los Angeles Police Department. When he had heard all the specifics, he assured Justin that Stan's death wasn't a homicide—TJ had acted in self-defense. Stan had put a loaded rifle to TJ's head. It was an accident that Stan stumbled through the open doorway, slipped in a pool of water, and fell back against the iron rake. From a legal standpoint, Gonzales said, there was no eminently prosecutable crime. But, he'd explained, if the details of Stan's death were made public, there would be no guarantee that the Zelinski family wouldn't file a civil suit against Justin.

"If I was still a cop and you came to me with this," Gonzales said, "I'd tell you there's nothing here that needs the attention of the cops, or the courts. I'd tell you to go home and close the book on the whole thing."

But Justin wasn't sure that he agreed with Gonzales. He knew that telling the truth could land him in court and hold him up to public scrutiny as a killer—things that could hurt Amy and Zack. But he also knew how much he wanted the freedom that would come with being able to clear away the last of his secrets.

This was what Justin had been talking about on the phone with Ari for the last thirty minutes, it was what they were still talking about now.

Ari's tone was neutral as he was saying: "So we know the possible fallout from digging up Zelinski's dirty laundry and airing it. But what happens if you let it go? If you say nothing?"

"Then I'm a guy who got away with something," Justin replied. "For the rest of my life I'd know that part of me, right at my core, is a little bit of a coward."

Ari seemed to deliberate for a moment before he said: "You do know there are some questions that don't have one uniquely right answer, don't you?"

"Then how the hell are you supposed to be able to find the truth?" Justin asked.

"You find it in bits and pieces," Ari replied. "You sort through the possible answers and somewhere in each of them is a little bit of the truth, a shard of what's right."

"What if they all seem equally right, Ari? What then? What do you pick? Which 'truth' do you go with?"

Ari's answer was matter-of-fact: "Go with the one that does the least harm to the most people."

Justin snapped the phone shut. He was lost in thought, seeing Amy's face and Zack's, and Cassie Jackson's, and Ted Zelinski's, and that of Ted's young son, Stan.

A clatter of dishes—a busboy clearing the table—was what brought Justin back to the moment. He was in Palm Springs. Breakfast was over. It was time to finish his journey.

*

When Justin had left Amy to go to Connecticut, she had told him: "The only way I want you is if you're here completely. I want to know you'll never let anything be more important than what we need from you . . . Zack and me." There was a brutal honesty in the way she'd said it. And it had reminded Justin of fragments from a conversation he'd had with her father last year, shortly after that first trip to Lima Street.

"The only thing any man has to be ashamed of," Don had said, "is not doing what it takes to keep his family safe and happy. That's what's righteous. Everything else gets in line behind that."

What Don had been saying then was what Amy had been asking for when Justin left for Middletown. His only reply had been to kiss her. And he'd walked out of the house with the taste of her tears on his lips.

That taste had stayed with him the entire time he had been away. It was still with him now as he was on the road that was leading him out of Palm Springs.

The landscape on either side of the highway was extraordinary: expanses of blinding white sand studded with black boulders, and, rising out of the sand, forests of towering silver wind-mills, their slim blades a hundred feet in the air, turning in silent unison, moving on currents of hot desert wind.

Justin's drive lasted a little less than three hours. It carried him out of the Palm Springs desert and along a stretch of freeway that ran for miles beside railroad tracks jammed with open flatbed freight cars. The cars were stacked with massive shipping con-tainers that had bold clean names emblazoned on their sides: UNIGLORY and EVERGREEN.

His attention was caught by the poetry of those names and he wondered if they could be taken as omens, as heralds of the good he might eventually do. He had made his decision. But his cell phone remained closed on the seat beside him. He continued to wait, and to let the miles roll by. He still needed time to come to terms with what he was about to do.

When he felt it happen—when he perceived the shift, the full acceptance of the man he would be from this point on—he was just entering the cities and commotion of Los Angeles County.

He reached for his phone. Amy picked up almost instantly. "Before you say anything," she told him, "just listen, okay? I've been thinking about a lot of stuff." The sound of her voice made him suddenly feel as if he could breathe again.

"I know that this all has to do with your parents," Amy was saying. "It's about them throwing you away. And you think if you'd been able to grow up in a regular house, in a regular way, everything would've been better. But that's not necessarily true."

There was a pause. Amy seemed to be gathering her thoughts before she said, "I used to know this guy . . . a long time ago . . . He got a scholarship to Harvard, but he didn't take it, at the last minute he went to New York to be an actor instead. And he was always saying 'I should've gone to Harvard,' like that would've automatically made his life come out right. But there's no way of knowing. I mean, he could've gone to Harvard and been a bigtime corporate type and still could've married a bitchy wife, or got caught in some sleazy stock deal that wiped him out, or just ended up old and bored. There's no way to know." Amy paused. "Are you still there, Justin?"

"Yeah, I'm here."

"All I'm saying is, you turned out to be an incredibly good man. And maybe if you'd had a life different from the one you had, you wouldn't be you. Maybe we have to go through the craziness we go through so we can be who we are right at this moment. Maybe that's what destiny is. Maybe there's a plan to all of it and maybe all of it isn't about us. Maybe it's about other people and the things we do for them. Maybe it's something more amazing and more complicated than we can ever figure out."

"Amy, I . . ." Justin wanted to stop her, to tell her what he'd decided.

"No. Wait. Let me finish." Amy was quietly crying. "The other thing I wanted to say is that I really think there are times in life when a person can do the wrong thing for the right reasons. I think sometimes there can be a line between right and wrong that gets so fine that it disappears. We just have to trust it's still there, and then do the best we can. That's all any of us can do, Justin. The best we can."

"I know," Justin said. Then he told her: "Ames, I've made my decision."

There was a long silence. "Don't tell me now." Amy's voice was so soft it was almost disappearing. "Wait till you get here."

"Okay," he said. "I'll wait."

As Justin put the phone down, he was passing a cluster of freeway signs. He glanced at them and saw that the wait wouldn't be a long one. He was about forty miles from downtown Los Angeles, just going through Pomona. He was almost home.

But less than a half hour later, long before he reached Santa Monica, Justin left the freeway and drove north, toward the foothills, toward Sierra Madre, and Lima Street.

There was one last act he needed to perform before he could truly be finished with his past.

He drove along Sierra Madre Boulevard, toward its intersection with Lima Street, but once there, he didn't turn in the direction of the wide-porched house that had haunted his life; he turned instead into the parking lot of a hardware store.

The interior of the store was dim and cool. On a table just inside the front door there was an old-fashioned electric fan and a plastic tray stacked high with watermelon slices. An elderly woman was hovering behind the cash register of a small gift department where dishes and tea towels and knickknacks filled the shelves. A short distance away, in the center of the store, narrow aisles were crowded with tools and chains and bolts.

Justin was the only customer in sight. He moved slowly through the quiet and the clutter, choosing carefully, spending long minutes studying the shape and feel of each of the items he would need.

At one point, he went to a rack lined with work boots and methodically removed one of the rawhide bootlaces. Later, he searched out a pair of heavy scissors and a white canvas drop cloth and then used the scissors to cut a two-foot-by-two-foot square from the canvas.

When he'd found everything he needed, he took his purchases to the wooden counter near the store's rear entrance. He was waited on by a man wearing a plaid shirt, faded bib overalls, and a hand-carved name tag. According to the tag, the man's name was

Silas. He studied the assortment of things that Justin had placed before him. There was a total of seven items; included among them was the single rawhide bootlace, the square of snow-white canvas, and a small glass bowl as shallow and fragile as a child's cupped palm.

The man made no comment on the incongruity of Justin's selections. All he said was: "Can't buy the lace unless you buy the boots and you gotta pay for the whole drop cloth, not just that little-bitty piece of it."

Justin put his credit card down. The man glanced at it and said: "You gonna be needing anything else?"

There was a refrigerator case at the end of the counter. Justin opened its glass door and among the cans of soda and juices, he found a slender bottle of springwater. He placed it beside his credit card. "Just this," he said.

The trip from the hardware store to the cemetery took less than three minutes. Justin's walk across the uneven graveyard grass took less than two.

As he stood in front of the modest burial site, and its three headstones, he was in the center of a circle of oaks. Above him, a vaulted canopy of dark branches was swaying on a warm summer breeze. And surrounding him, floating down through pale green leaves, were a thousand dancing shafts of sunlight.

When he went to the weathered headstone that displayed his name, he knelt in front of it. A small bundle, wrapped in white canvas and tied with a rawhide bootlace, was cradled in his hands. He put the bundle on the ground and opened it.

On the smooth surface of the canvas, he quietly arranged the items that it contained: a bottle of springwater; a sea sponge roughly the shape and size of an apricot; an elegant paintbrush with China bristles as black and soft as fur; a mason's chisel, its blade sharp, its shaft cool and silver-colored; and a maul, a thick-handled hammer with two and a half pounds of forged steel in its blunt malletlike head. To these things, Justin added an item that he had placed in his pocket to protect it from breaking, the shallow glass bowl.

Into the bowl, he poured some of the springwater. Then he dipped the sea sponge into the water and began to carefully wash away the veil of dust that covered the words "Thomas Justin Fisher" and the inscription "August 5, 1972–February 20, 1976."

When the name and the dates were clean and clear, Justin took the chisel and fitted the slant of its blade against the carved edge of the number 6. And then he lifted the maul and began his work.

After he was finished, he reached for the elegant China-bristled paintbrush. He used it to sweep away the fine coating of stone dust that his labors had created—and to reveal what they had left behind: his name and his birth date.

"February 20, 1976" was gone.

His time on Lima Street had, at last, come to an end.

*

When Justin arrived home in Santa Monica, he got out of the car and walked toward the front door. He saw that it was open.

Zack was running across the wood floor toward him, on small bare feet.

Amy was there. Waiting.

Fog was rolling in from the ocean, filtering the light and making the interior of the house look both luminescent and obscure, like the essence of a delicate, beautiful memory.

*

It was Halloween. And the man who had arrived in Manhattan as a young priest thirty-five years ago was now the city's bishop. He was in bed, asleep, with his wife at his side.

The bishop was dreaming of a long-ago October, and of its last day.

He was dreaming of a girl he had loved. And of the only time he had ever made love to her. He was dreaming of an enchanted afternoon in St. Justin's Church.

In the dream, he was feeling as a newly crowned angel must feel when a rush of wind surrounds his wings and, for the first time, he is given the power of flight.

ACKNOWLEDGMENTS

*

Heartfelt gratitude to Alice Tasman and Phyllis Grann—two women who are, in the truest sense of the word, amazing.

Unending thanks to Todd Black. Without his advice and encouragement this book would never have found its way.

Deepest appreciation to Josh Schechter for his unwavering faith, and to Jackeline Montalvo for her patience and guidance.

Love and awe to the sisters of my soul—Sarah, Gail, Mary Lu, Jan, Sandy, Loraine, and Marice—for their clear insights, wise counsel, and precious friendship.

And the fullness of my heart to Hank and Denise, the perfect parents, and to my elegantly eclectic family: Elizabeth, Stephen, Chris, Jerry, Lauren, Amy, Aaron, Noah, Joshua, Carrie, Clara . . . and Steve (who, a very long time ago, believed that I would some-day be a writer).

The Language of Secrets by Dianne Dixon is a complex novel about family secrets and the many ways that love can cloud our judgment. The following questions are intended to enhance your reading experience and to generate lively discussions among the members of your book group.

*

QUESTIONS FOR DISCUSSION

1. *The Language of Secrets* opens with this quote from Thomas Moore: "The beast residing at the center of the labyrinth is also an angel." How does this quote set the stage for what transpires in the novel? Why do you think the author chose it for the opening page?

2. What were your first impressions of Justin? What did you think might have happened between him and his family? Initially, did it seem unusual that he held on to memories of his childhood home so tightly?

3. Discuss Caroline. Do you believe that in spite of the fact Caroline was born in the 1940s and came of age in a time long before the women's movement, she truly had no options, no way to escape the oppressive aspects of her life? Why was she unable to alter her situation?

4. Caroline's background and her passionate belief in the importance of a two-parent family were key parts of who she was. If she had at some point decided to get a divorce, what impact do you think it would have had on her as a woman and as a mother? Would she have been stronger? Or more damaged?

5. Along these lines, consider the theme of powerlessness: Which other characters believed that they were trapped by their circumstances? What do they do (or not do) to improve their respective lives?

6. Why do you think Robert could never truly love Justin? Do you think that, long before it was revealed, on some level Robert had known the truth about Justin?

7. Barton and Mitch were very different men, but Caroline had feelings for both of them and the feelings lasted for a lifetime. What were the qualities in each man that attracted her to him? Who do you think Caroline truly loved—Mitch, Barton, or Robert? Why?

8. Talk about the marriages in *The Language of Secrets*. Given the betrayal and tragedy that colored their union, was it surprising that Caroline and Robert remained married? Justin and Amy's relationship starts out strong but is battered by the mystery of Justin's boyhood and the interference of Amy's overbearing father, Don. In light of those things, did their marriage turn out the way you thought it would?

9. Consider how author Dianne Dixon constructed the narrative, by writing from the various characters' perspectives and by allowing plot points to develop in a nonlinear fashion. How would the novel have been different if only one character told the story from his or her point of view, or if the events unfolded in chronological order?

10. What do you think the book's title means, both literally and in the context of what happens in the novel? Was the Fisher family unique, or do all families have their own, individual, language of secrets?

11. Discuss Robert's bombshell revelation to Caroline about what really happened on the Nevada camping trip. What did you think about what Robert did to his son, and to his wife? Can his actions be explained or excused in any way?

12. Did you have empathy for Caroline or for Robert? Or do you feel each of them got what they deserved? Do you think that in any way (big or small) Caroline was responsible for what Robert did to Justin?

13. What are some examples of the line between right and wrong being crossed in *The Language of Secrets*? Can doing the wrong thing (even if it's for the right reasons) ever be justified?

14. After she sees the spiral-bound notebook that Caroline assembled, Margaret intuitively understands the truth—there was a monumental

difference in how each of Justin's parents felt about him. If you were in Margaret's shoes, once you discovered this important piece of information, what would you have done?

15. Even though he went to the Zelinski house intending to confess, why didn't Justin reveal the details of what happened on his final night in that house? Given Justin's quest to banish the secrets in his own life, what does it say about his character that he would voluntarily keep the secrets that existed in Stan's life?

16. When you look at it as a legal issue, what do you think Justin's culpability was in what happened in the breezeway of the Zelinski house? Is it different when you look at it as a moral issue?

17. When Julie and Lissa are leaving Lima Street for the last time, how do the impressions they have of their parents differ from the impressions you had of who Robert and Caroline were? Do you think it's ever possible for a child to have an accurate understanding of a parent? Did Julie and Lissa's conversation affect your perception of your own parents?

18. As Justin's story unfolds, how did you feel about Amy's attitude? Should she have been a more supportive and sympathetic wife? Or do you think she should have gone in the other direction and been more forceful in insisting that Justin let go of the past and focus on the family he has now?

19. Amy's mother, Linda, tells Amy to accept her father the way he is. Do you agree with that point of view? Or is Amy right in expecting her father to step up and start showing his love in the ways that she wants and needs him to?

20. Of all the twists and turns in Justin's story, which one surprised you the most?